Readers love the S
series by C.

The Mystery of Nevermore

"This book has an embarrassment of riches—an engaging plot that will hold your interest to the final page, two intriguing main characters with a sizzling sexual chemistry, a top-notch mystery with plenty of red herrings…"

—Gay Book Reviews

"The romance was sweet and hot, the mystery was well thought out and researched, and the ending was quite satisfying."

—Joyfully Jay

The Mystery of the Curiosities

"The attraction between Sebastian and Calvin sizzle off the pages. The author writes an interesting mystery and a wonderful love story… Pushes all my buttons…"

—Paranormal Romance Guild

"For mystery lovers, this is a must read full of action, suspense, danger, and a not-so-easy solving of the crimes. I'm really enjoying this series and my biggest curiosity is what historical subject matter C.S. Poe will come up with next."

—The Novel Approach

The Mystery of the Moving Image

"Amateur sleuth Sebastian Snow and his quirkiness is fast taking a place among my favorite sleuths!"

—Bookwinked

"The series on the whole has my recommendation, and one can only hope that Poe has many more stories like this one waiting for us in the future."

—Love Bytes

By C.S. Poe

Devil Take Me Anthology
Southernmost Murder

SNOW & WINTER
The Mystery of Nevermore
The Mystery of the Curiosities
The Mystery of the Moving Image
The Mystery of the Bones

Published by DSP Publications
www.dsppublications.com

THE MYSTERY OF THE BONES

C.S. POE

DSP PUBLICATIONS

Published by
DSP Publications

5032 Capital Circle SW, Suite 2, PMB# 279, Tallahassee, FL 32305-7886 USA
www.dsppublications.com

Trade Paperback ISBN: 978-1-64108-207-5
Digital ISBN: 978-1-64405-324-9
Library of Congress Control Number: 2019901907
Trade Paperback published September 2019
v. 1.0

Printed in the United States of America

This paper meets the requirements of
ANSI/NISO Z39.48-1992 (Permanence of Paper).

For Josh.
This series began with you.
I find it only fitting it concludes the same way.

THE MYSTERY OF THE BONES

C.S. POE

CHAPTER ONE

MY MORNINGS at the Emporium were dictated by a comfortable and quiet routine:

Nat King Cole on the speakers.

Tolerable coffee from the cheap maker in my office.

Coaxing the thermostat until the ancient radiators pinged and hissed with steam.

And when someone disrupted that sense of order, it had a tendency to irritate me.

A sudden bang on the front door caused me to lose track of the till I was counting. I leaned over the counter and squinted at the blurry shape on the other side of the glass.

Whoever it was knocked again and called in a muffled voice, "Courier!"

I grunted and handed my assistant, Max Ridley, the wad of small change. "Count that for me." I walked down the steps, made my way through the twists and turns of my cavernous store, then unlocked and opened the front door. A *whoosh* of bitterly cold, snowy wind entered. "We're not open yet."

The bike courier shrugged in her bulky winter attire. "Hey, man, not my problem," she countered, speaking through a face mask. She thrust a clipboard at me. "Sign the last line."

I brought the paperwork closer, but the details of the package's origin were beyond impossible to read in the chicken-scratch handwriting of the courier's office employee. "Hope you're getting paid extra to deliver before business hours," I said, signing my name on the form and handing it back.

The courier shoved the clipboard into her oversized bag, removed a square box, and all but threw it into my arms. "And many happy returns." She turned, stepped back into the cold morning, and unlocked her bike from the lamppost across from the shop.

"Yeah. Happy holidays," I muttered, closing the door. "What time is it?"

"Um… five 'til," Max said from the counter.

I left the door unlocked.

Max shut the brass register's drawer as I joined him once more. He picked up his mug and took a sip of coffee. "That's not the Depression glassware, is it?"

"I hope not," I replied, setting the box down. "Unless they sent the decanter in pieces."

Max visibly cringed at the notion.

Depression glass was too new to have any sort of permanent residency in my shop, but I'd agreed to taking on a rare seven-piece drinking set in what was promised to be a ruby red color, as a project for Max. He'd been more adamant of late about helping with research and amassing contacts of his own. And since the market was always alive and well for Depression glassware, I decided what the hell.

I used a pair of scissors to slice the tape down the middle of the box. I pulled the cardboard flaps back and removed a single sheet of folded paper from atop thick, opaque plastic. Scrawled in what appeared to be a modern rendition of Spencerian script was: *Mr. Sebastian Snow, Proprietor*.

"What's it say?" Max asked before I'd gotten any further than unfolding the note.

"It's not a winning lotto ticket," I remarked, glancing sideways at him. "So I'm already losing interest."

"Life isn't all about money, Seb."

"You can say that. You don't have a hospital bill the length of a CVS receipt."

I'd been shot in May. That batshit crazy Pete White had nearly taken me out with an antique revolver, and all I had to show for surviving was a nasty scar and enough debt to choke a horse. Unsurprisingly, upon learning the value of the Dickson drafts I'd saved, the surviving Robert family members wanted them back and had zero interest in letting me handle their affairs at auction.

As if my percentage would even make a dent in what I predicted their payment would be. Which—*fine*. Good luck to them trying to maneuver the world of high-end auctions without contacts. Meanwhile, I'd be over here dodging phone calls from the hospital's collection department. *No big deal*.

I pulled my magnifying glass from my back pocket and held it over the cursive that mimicked the aesthetic of business communications circa mid-nineteenth century.

An Intriguing Proposition for a Most Curious Man.

Who I am is of no great importance. What I am proposing is.

I, hereby known afterward as Party A, am looking to hire Sebastian Andrew Snow, hereby known as Party B, to recover a most unusual article lost to time and neglect.

I paused, touched the flap on the cardboard box, and tilted it to read, but the only address details were my own. Who the hell was this, and how'd they learn my middle name? I played Andrew pretty close to the chest. No offense to Pop, but I wasn't a fan.

"What's that smell?" Max asked suddenly.

I made a vague sound of acknowledgment before continuing to read.

Upon said article's salvage, Party A is prepared to reward Party B with a most substantial sum.

A Collector.

"Boss?"

"What?" I lowered the magnifying glass to the bottom of the page in order to inspect a disturbingly realistic hand-drawn eye. But that was it. No other details, no contact information, no nada.

"Did you shower this morning?"

At the second disruption to my thoughts, I set the paper down and turned to Max. "*Yes*."

"Then what smells like sour milk?" He raised his own arm before shaking his head and saying, "It's not me."

"What's it say about you that you needed to double-check first?" But then I got a whiff of the—*death*.

And as if Max and I came to the same conclusion at once, we both turned to stare at the steps on my left. Almost one year ago exactly, we'd found a rotting heart under the floorboards and my life forever changed when a redheaded detective came to the Emporium to investigate the mystery.

"'Villains!' I shrieked. 'Dissemble no more!'" I quoted under my breath.

"Don't." Max moved around me and tiptoed down the stairs.

"Don't what?"

He crouched and began to inspect the steps for loose boards that would allow one to successfully conceal a human body part. "Don't pull out your quotes. It makes everything go topsy-turvy real fast."

"It does not."

"It makes you obsessive."

"*Curious*," I corrected. "And it's human nature to be curious."

"Not you. And when you get obsessive, people try to kill you." He looked at me briefly with an expression that read sort of like *fight me*.

"You act like you're going to find me dead in a gutter on Staten Island by tomorrow. It *stinks* in here—I have a right to be curious."

Max shook his head and continued checking for a floorboard that'd give way to a macabre surprise. "Hello, 911? My boss thinks he's Columbo…."

"Keep it up and I'm going to trash your holiday bonus."

Max glanced up a second time, considered, but ultimately dropped the conversation. "The floor's fine." He stood, took a step, then frowned as his gaze lowered to the package on the counter.

I looked at it too. It was a very unassuming box. I leaned in and took a sniff. The rancid stench coming from within the plastic made me gag.

"Who'd you piss off now?" Max whispered, a wobble in his voice.

"No one."

We both studied the box again.

From the corner of my eye, I saw him raise his fist in the classic gesture of rock-paper-scissors. I followed, and on the silent count of three, threw scissors. Max knocked my hand with rock. I let out a breath, squared my shoulders, then grabbed the heavy plastic bag stuffed into the package.

I hoisted out a decapitated human head.

LUCKY CHARMS and coffee leave a decidedly offensive aftertaste upon coming back up. I didn't have any mints or a toothbrush handy at the shop either, so I tried to mask the vomit-breath with saltwater taffy.

It didn't work.

In retrospect, of course, it was the least of my problems. But since I had no control over the uniformed officers standing around my counter and inspecting a scene straight out of *The Silence of the Lambs*, I had to hyperfocus on *something*. I unwrapped another piece of candy.

"Did you call Calvin?" Max asked from where he sat on the floor, his back against the bookshelves situated in the farthest corner of the shop. Dillon was parked between his legs, enjoying the nervous scratches Max was giving him and not really all that concerned about the morning's proceedings.

I turned from where I stood at the midpoint between the officers and Max and said, "No." I tugged the taffy from the wax paper. It stretched into long tendrils and stuck to my hand. I raised my thumb and index finger to suck them clean.

"Why?" Max protested.

"I think it might constitute as crossing a professional line."

"Yeah, because you've *zero* experience doing that," Max said, voice dripping with sarcasm.

"Things are different now."

To say the least.

I rubbed the last of the sticky candy residue against my trouser leg.

"I don't like this," Max continued. "When Sebastian has a reverse Ichabod Crane situation, Calvin and Quinn show up. That's how it works. The universe has established this."

"I'm one money-order-made-payable-to-the-City-Clerk away from really pissing his sergeant off," I explained. "I have to follow proper channels these days. That means starting with 911, and letting the NYPD decide which lucky detective team is investigating this mess."

I turned my head just then to watch a third uniformed officer enter the shop. He muttered some nicety to the man standing guard at the door before immediately making his way toward the counter where a female officer stood.

I turned to Max and held both hands out, indicating for him not to move. "Stay here." I started after the newcomer.

The cop was tall. Broad shoulders, dark hair, and thick eyebrows. He was watching me approach while quieting the radio emitting gibberish from his belt.

"Hi," I said. I held out a hand. "I'm the owner. I called—"

"Sebastian Snow," he answered for me.

I slowly lowered my hand. "Er—yeah."

"You've got a reputation."

"I've been told that before."

"I'm sure you have."

I got the distinct impression this officer did not find me to be a charming sonofabitch.

"Now, I know you like to play amateur sleuth, Mr. Snow," he continued, hands on his utility belt. His accent was *so Brooklyn*, it was practically a stereotype.

"I've recently retired."

"I don't think you're funny."

"Okay."

"And I don't think you're cute."

"Good."

"Being a cop is a serious job," he said in a chastising tone. "And when civilians stick their noses into our business—"

"I'm pretty certain I called you folks for help," I interrupted.

The female officer leaned over the counter and whispered something to my new biggest fan.

"I know who he's dating," Dickhead retorted. He pointed a finger at me. "And this ain't got nothing to do with you being gay."

"Thank God," I said humorlessly. Because I hadn't heard *that* before.

"I wouldn't care if you were engaged to my sergeant. You shouldn't be allowed within a hundred feet of a crime scene."

I tugged my sweater closed and crossed my arms over my chest. "So did you want to question me, or should I skedaddle and leave you to all this, Mr. Holmes?"

Dickhead's nostrils flared like an enraged bull. He closed the space between us and stared me down—which didn't work because I've been around the block a few times with cops—then something in his facial expression changed. Faltered, maybe.

"What're your eyes doing?"

"Moving," I answered, my tone more dry than white bread left on too high a setting in the toaster. My Dancing Eyes condition was hardly noticeable as an adult, but still they wobbled involuntarily at times. "I have achromatopsia. Sometimes my eyes move strangely when I get stressed."

"You're stressed?"

"Yes, Officer," I said with a *hint* of mockery. "I've only had one cup of coffee and found a head in a box."

"Your stressed is pretty calm, Mr. Snow."

I shrugged. "Hysterics won't change the situation. Although, I did vomit, if that'll make you happy."

"For Christ's sake, Rossi," the female cop said, loud enough for me to hear. She leaned over the counter a second time and asked, "Do you know the deceased, Mr. Snow?"

I stared at her, at Rossi, then back to her again. "Do I—know—*the head*? We're not acquainted, no."

Rossi started to speak, but the bell over the shop's front door chimed for the umpteenth time and gave him pause. He looked around me, raised his lip, and all but rolled his eyes.

"Calvary's here," he muttered.

I turned around.

Rescue came in the form of Calvin Winter.

My most favorite detective of the NYPD.

Not that I was biased or anything.

He marched across the showroom floor, making a direct beeline for me where I stood at the base of the elevated counter with Rossi.

"Calvin—" I started, hoping I sounded cool and relaxed and not utterly relieved that despite our soon-to-be legally recognized relationship, he'd still been the one shouldered with another case involving yours truly.

But Calvin cut me off by grabbing my shoulders and pulling me into a bone-crushing embrace. His heavy coat was damp from melting snow. The wool was itchy and cold against my skin, but the discomfort was eased by the familiar warmth and hard body under the layers. Sure, I'd been in bed with this handsome man only a few hours ago, but I didn't think I'd never *not* find comfort in the scent of Calvin's earthy cologne or the ever-present cinnamon on his breath from obsessive mint-popping.

He'd shown up like a knight in shining armor.

"I called 911," I stated, pulling back and adjusting my glasses.

"I know you did."

"I obeyed the chain of command and everything," I said lightly in an attempt to bolster the mood.

Calvin gently took my hand and gave it a firm grip. "You're okay?" he confirmed, voice a low whisper.

I nodded. "I'm glad you're here, though," I admitted, just as quietly.

He only let go, with a hint of reluctance, when Quinn Lancaster reached the counter. Calvin's gray eyes shone like the cut and polished edges of a gemstone. They reflected everything he carried inside him—frustration, concern, that touch of chronic weariness, but also his newly found happiness. And relief. Relief that his dumbass, trouble-prone fiancé hadn't been shot or run over or suffered so much as a papercut before he'd gotten to the scene. The dim lighting of the shop created shadows on Calvin's face, produced from the hard lines and angles of his cheekbones and jawline. Clusters of freckles across his cheeks, nose—even lips—stood out in stark relief from his pale complexion.

Beautiful, in an unconventional sort of way.

Calvin cleared his throat, squared his shoulders, and said to Officer Rossi, "We'll take it from here. If you can direct CSU and the ME when they arrive? Thank you."

Despite the dismissal, Rossi lingered a beat. But when the staring contest with Calvin proved to be going nowhere fast, he let out a breath and unhurriedly left us.

I looked between Quinn and Calvin. "He's a charming individual."

"He's a brownnosing SOB aching for a promotion to detective before he's learned a thing or two *about* detecting," Quinn grumbled.

"Ah."

Calvin motioned to the counter and the remaining officer standing guard over the box. "Dispatch gave us a rundown of the report so far." He looked at me. "But please explain in your own words why I'm seeing you after breakfast instead of at dinnertime."

"Speaking of breakfast—it's back there," I said. "So watch your step."

Quinn made a sound of disgust.

"A courier service dropped off a package this morning," I started. "Just before nine."

"Which service?" Calvin asked, retrieving the small notepad he kept in his inner coat pocket.

I shrugged. "I didn't really take note."

Calvin frowned a little. "Why not?"

"I wasn't expecting a human head."

"Seb's off his game!" Max shouted from across the room.

Calvin ignored my assistant. "What about the courier's name?"

"No."

Calvin tapped his pen against the blank page. "Seb—"

"I'm not trying to be difficult. You know on any given day I might have up to a dozen packages coming and going from here. Sometimes a mystery delivery slips in."

"What *can* you tell us, then?" Quinn interjected.

"The package came with a letter." I motioned at the counter. "It's still there."

Quinn shot Calvin a quick look before moving around us both. She took the stairs, stepped over the vomit, and went to the register to examine the note. "I, hereby known afterward as Party A, am looking to hire Sebastian Andrew Snow, hereby known as Party B, to recover a most unusual article lost to time and neglect."

"Yeah. See, that's not weird," I stated. "I get asked to hunt down strange and rare artifacts all the time."

Calvin made a sound of agreement. After all, he'd been dating a small-business owner who once couldn't shut up for an entire day about the quality of a taxidermy violet-capped wood-nymph hummingbird and its hand-carved perch, circa 1860, that he'd gotten at an estate sale in Queens. Whether Calvin liked it or not, he knew the ins and outs of my antique store.

"Upon said article's salvage, Party A is prepared to reward Party B with *a most substantial sum*," Quinn finished.

I pointed at her. "*That's* the weird part. The note never says what they want me to find. Or why. Or what the compensation is."

Calvin shut the notepad. He tucked it into his coat and leaned over the countertop to study the note for himself.

From Calvin's telltale tics to hearing what was *not* said between cops, I'd become pretty adept at understanding murder scenes without verbal explanations. Unfortunately—for me or them, I wasn't certain—the silence, *the look* between detectives, was one of recognition. Something about this event, be it the letter or the head, was familiar to both Calvin and Quinn.

Merry Christmas.

"Am I a victim or a suspect?" I asked.

They both turned to me with mild surprise.

I was about to break a very strict rule Calvin had been enforcing in our house since May.

No work talk.

His, not mine.

It was part of the wean-Sebastian-off-sleuthing thing, which I didn't find terribly necessary after being shot. Even *I* had my limits. But I abided by the no crime-solving discussion decree because I didn't enjoy being the source of Calvin's stress. He dealt with enough bullshit at work. There was no reason for him to talk about murderers roaming the streets after he'd loosened his tie and removed his service weapon for the day.

And I'd been doing pretty well for half a year. I had the occasional slip of Twenty Questions when I'd seen something interesting in the media, but I'd become especially mindful of being a harassing busybody since Calvin proposed to me.

No takebacks and all that.

But in the middle of December, I worked seven days a week due to the holiday rush. I was also planning a wedding—something I knew literally nothing about. Murder and mayhem were the furthest things from my mind. The fact that this particular crime scene matched another of Calvin's cases, in *some* fashion, was extremely disconcerting. And I felt justified in my need to inquire.

I was shaken by a sensation I hadn't experienced in a long while—the one that would tie my guts up in knots when I realized I'd overlooked an important clue. It was an anxiety of sorts. Unique to me. Had Calvin behaved different at home over the last few days? No. I didn't believe so. He'd worked late, but this wasn't unusual when he had new cases. Had there been anything in the newspaper that hinted toward the details of said new cases? Again, no.

"Seb."

I blinked. "What?"

"Stop," Calvin said firmly.

"But I—"

He took a step closer. "I can see the cogs turning, baby."

I put my hands up, like *I'm innocent, copper! Innocent, I tell ya!*

The front door opened again. Calvin turned, and I peered around his hulking form. Neil Millett, my ex-boyfriend and detective for the city's Crime Scene Unit, was being directed to the counter by Officer Rossi.

Hmm.

This, in and of itself, was not strange. After all, with less than fifty CSU detectives to serve the five boroughs, there was going to be crossover. Neil had ended up a key team member on several of Calvin's cases over the past year. So seeing him walk toward us, bundled in a coat I'm sure was *the* style this season, with his shapeless Crime Scene Unit jacket thrown over it as an afterthought, didn't concern me very much.

In fact, it didn't concern me at all. Neil and I had parted ways on… er… less than amicable terms, but had curiously enough circled back to something positive. We'd finally settled into the relationship we were always meant to have—a bickering friendship. And Calvin was cool with it. He was not a man easily prone to jealousy or insecurity.

Really, the only disconcerting detail was the look of expectancy on Neil's face as he drew near.

Had he been anticipating a crime scene today?

Predicting it'd involve me? Or the Emporium?

No. If Neil thought that, so would Calvin, and I wouldn't be here this morning. I'd have been somewhere else—somewhere safe—and the entire situation would have been explained to me. I would not be standing a mere four feet from a decapitated head and my own now-thickening vomit.

It brought me back to the look Calvin and Quinn shared.

Recognition.

Neil seemed to only just notice me as he stopped at the stairs. "Nancy," he said by way of greeting.

"Bess," I countered.

"What are you doing here?"

I crossed my arms and took a look around the Emporium as if I had no idea where I was. "Is this… *my* shop?"

Neil said, "I mean, it's Monday. Shouldn't you be closed?"

"I'm getting my money's worth on the rent."

"Holiday rush," Calvin answered for me.

Neil stared at me while jutting a thumb at Calvin. "See how difficult it was to give a straight answer?"

"I'm anything but straight," I replied.

Neil let out a breath, made a motion with his hand, like *I already can't with you*, and started up the steps beside the register. He set his kit down, bent down beside it, and removed a pair of latex gloves. Neil put them on as he stood.

Quinn pointed at the box. She said something about the head, but too quietly for me to hear. I squinted and watched her lips.

Bit—more. Bit more. Bit more toe.

Bit more than a toe.

Calvin shifted to the right and loomed over me. "Nice try."

"What?" I asked quickly—innocently.

"I know you read lips, Sebastian."

"Oh."

Calvin frowned.

I shoved my hands into my pockets and briefly looked over my shoulder toward the book corner. Max had gotten to his feet. He'd wisely put Dillon on a leash so the dog didn't run through our surprise crime scene in order to greet his human. "You shutting me down, Detective?" I asked, turning back to Calvin.

"I know it's your busiest time of year."

"What's money matter? Now I have time to pick up our Christmas tree. It may end up being a Charlie Brown, though."

"It wasn't that long ago I threatened to arrest you for being a smartass," Calvin warned.

"And instead you put a ring on it," I said, raising my left hand and tapping the matte tungsten band with the tip of my thumb.

Calvin grunted. "Come with me." He walked across the floor, up the farther set of stairs, and into my office.

Crap.

I reluctantly followed, then pulled the door shut behind me as I entered the cramped, closet-sized space. "I'm sorry for—"

Calvin put a hand on the doorframe and leaned in close. "I need you to think carefully."

I raised an eyebrow. "Okay…."

"In the past week, have you had any unusual customers?"

"You've seen my clientele, Calvin."

Wrong answer.

"Baby. I'm serious," Calvin said in a borderline exasperated tone. "Has anyone stood out as… overtly strange? Any requests that made you do a double take? Business transactions that went south?"

"Why?" I countered. "Am I actually in some kind of trouble?"

"Sebastian, answer the question."

"*No*. I can't think of anything. Ask Max if you don't believe me."

"I believe you," Calvin replied.

"I hear a *but*," I countered.

Calvin shook his head. "I wish I didn't."

"*Believe me*? No offense, but that's a surefire way to guarantee a cold shoulder for at least two—three days."

"I don't mean it like that." Calvin lowered his hand. He absently unbuttoned his winter coat. "If you were withholding information, I'd actually have something to work with on this case."

I cocked my head. "So this is connected to another murder?"

Calvin answered by saying nothing.

"How so?" I prodded. "The note or the body part?"

"Please don't start poking around."

"I'm not," I replied. "The deerstalker is hung up for good."

Calvin shrugged off his coat and draped it over the back of my desk chair.

"I'm only asking for clarification," I began, "because I would like to know if I'm in some sort of immediate danger."

"You didn't recognize the deceased?"

I shook my head. "No. Not that it'd be easy to—he was missing an eye and I think a few front teeth. I didn't study it much more beyond that." I stared at Calvin. "Did *you* recognize him?"

"No," Calvin murmured. He stared at me again.

Neither of us wanted to say it. Speaking it out loud gave substance to the situation. We'd already survived too many murder mysteries together in one year. *Bizarre* mysteries. Where the outcome had hinged on my insight of peculiar characters from a century long since passed.

True, I had landed myself a soul mate due to those unfortunate events, but now that the red thread was firmly tied between us, I really had no reason to accept a fourth dance with the devil. Between us, we had two more bullet wounds than this time last year, and I'll be the first to say they aren't as sexy or romantic as fiction portrays them to be. No more for me, thank you.

"Son of a bitch," Calvin swore, very quietly. He raked a hand through his thick, fiery hair.

"We've got to stop meeting like this," I said coyly. "People will talk."

"Hate to break it to you, sweetheart," Calvin eventually said, "but they've *been* talking."

"No shit. Apparently even beat cops know of me." I leaned back against the door. "I have *no* interest in worming my way into this case… but I'm still curious. You know that, right?" I asked, voice low.

Calvin let out a breath and nodded. "Yeah."

"I can't help it."

"I know."

Mysteries were always going to enthrall me—even taking my near-death experience into account. I think I was hardwired to solve puzzles. My ego thrived on proving I knew a thing or two about *everything*—and if I didn't, you'd bet your ass I'd make myself the most informed person on the scene. So for as gruesome and unnerving as this morning's event had been, it was also temptation of the worst kind.

Interrogatives, burning with regard, buzzed in my mind.

Who sent the head?

Unknown.

What did it mean?

A threat. Or perhaps a clue.

Where had the murder taken place?

Unknown.

And when?

While I hadn't given the head much consideration before blowing chunks, the presence of blood in the bag suggested decapitation happened hours after death, versus days. Had it been more than, say, ten hours, the liquid would have coagulated and solidified inside the body and produced next to no bleeding, despite severing major arteries.

And perhaps the most important of the Five Ws: *Why?*

No damn idea. But since it appeared to involve me… this Collector was undoubtedly looking for something antiquated, weird, and *clearly* felt it was worth killing for.

"What can you tell me about that drawing on the note?" Calvin asked.

"I'm torn between the Eye of Providence and some wackadoo conspiracy theory, or the 1800s Pinkerton National Detective Agency logo."

"It's not a reference to anything? Or anyone?"

"If it is, it's not obvious to me," I said. "But the handwriting is Spencerian script."

Calvin cocked his head a little.

"Cursive from the nineteenth century. It's accurate too. Someone did their homework."

Calvin looked away and studied my desk and the shelving overhead, as if the answer to his latest quandary resided somewhere among the clutter of reference books, binders of inventory, accounting files, and office supplies.

"I can't say if you're in immediate danger, but based on past events, I'm not taking any chances." He turned to me.

"Stalker, vigilante, or art thief," I said, ticking off past players on my fingers.

Calvin enclosed his hand over mine. "I know you don't like it, but is your father home today?"

"Maybe."

"Give him a ring? I'll have a black-and-white drive you over."

POP ENDED up being home and with no plans of his own until later that afternoon. I kept our conversation brief. No reason to explain over the phone what I could lie by omission about to his face. Not that lying to my father was something I found particularly enjoyable. In fact, it rarely worked to my benefit. Pop could smell my shit from a mile away.

But he was in his sixties, and I had no desire to be the reason he had a stroke.

It's the thought that counts, at least.

Donned in coats and scarves, Calvin saw me and Max out the door. The sky was still spitting big fat snowflakes. The air froze my lungs on every intake and settled around me in a jagged, razor-sharp cloud with every outtake. Our steps crunched loudly along the salt-coated sidewalk as we walked away from the shop front and a parked NYPD Crime Scene Unit van that advertised a crime, probably gruesome, had occurred on the property.

"He needs to get to Brooklyn," Calvin told an officer as he pointed at Max.

Max handed Dillon's leash to me. "Thanks, Calvin."

He nodded. "Let Sebastian know when you get home safely."

"10-4," Max said with a salute. He spared me a look. "Don't get into trouble, boss."

"Me? I'm hurt."

Max snorted. The cop opened the back door of the cruiser for him, and Max walked to it, got inside, and gave us both a wave before the car pulled onto the road.

Calvin motioned to the second cruiser. "It's a good thing we've got this routine down pat."

"Sebastian sits on his ass and Calvin catches the bad guy."

"You got it."

"Make sure you lock up the shop when you're done," I finished. I gave Calvin a hug and took a step away with Dillon before my name was called. I turned and, despite sunglasses, needed to shield my eyes to look at the Emporium door.

Neil stepped outside, sans jacket, with his camera around his neck. He yanked his latex gloves off as he walked toward us. "Be honest with me," he began.

"This slim-cut suit you've been sporting for the last month is sure to bring all the boys to your yard," I answered.

Neil gave me an incredulous expression, glanced at Calvin, then drew out, "Thank you?"

"Sure. Lose the PPE, though."

He tucked the used gloves into his suit coat pocket.

"Unless you're looking for a cop groupie," I continued.

"I meant," Neil interrupted, "about the package."

I stared at him. "It's pretty self-explanatory."

"You have a tendency to conveniently misplace details so you can snoop into the matter yourself," Neil pointed out.

"I've stopped doing that," I told him while patting my abdomen, where I was now rocking one hideous scar.

"Yeah."

"Boy howdy, do I remember that tone," I stated.

Neil looked at Calvin again. He let out a held breath, and it puffed like a cloud of smoke.

Calvin shook his head in response to the stare, which I caught from the corner of my eye.

"If he knows—" Neil started.

"*No*," Calvin said in his don't-fuck-with-me voice, which I'd say no one ever wanted to be on the receiving end of. I speak from experience on the matter.

I waved my hand between the two, breaking their showdown. "I'm *right* here."

Neil lifted his camera and began to press buttons on the menu. After a moment, he removed the strap from around his neck and turned the digital screen for me to see. "What do you think?"

"*Millett*," Calvin barked.

"It's an ear," I stated, staring at a photo taken of a drawing on a sheet of paper. Antiquated in appearance. Similar in style to the eyeball rendition left on my own note.

"No shit, Sherlock," Neil answered.

"I'm sorry," I said dryly. "Was I supposed to glean a deeper meaning behind van Gogh's love note?"

"You could try," Neil said. "I'm in the doghouse now. Make it worth it."

I rolled my eyes and took the camera from his hold. I brought the screen closer and stared hard at the drawing. It was a very good piece of art, as far as I was concerned. Done by a professional. Or a gifted amateur. But it went beyond an understanding and respect for realism. It was almost… clinical. Not a drawing of an ear, but the study of one.

"There's no color in this, right?" I asked.

"Black ink," Neil confirmed. "Probably a run-of-the-mill ballpoint pen, judging by the strokes left behind. I'm having it analyzed."

I shook my head after another moment and handed the camera back. "I don't know what it's supposed to mean."

"Happy now?" Calvin asked Neil.

Neil glowered and put the strap around his neck again.

"Did it have a message included like mine?" I asked.

Calvin put one strong hand on my shoulder, turned me toward the awaiting cruiser, and essentially severed any and all ties I had to the investigation. "I'll give you a call later this evening."

Chapter Two

"Kiddo!"

"Hey, Pop," I said. I reached the landing of the hallway stairs and saw my dad—William Snow—standing in the open doorway of his apartment. "How're you?" I gave him a brief hug.

"Fine, fine. Come in." Pop ushered me inside, took another peek into the hall, and shut the door. "No Calvin?"

"No," I agreed, bending down to unclasp Dillon's leash so he could go play with Maggie before the giant pit bull came to greet me with her usual tackle and slobber. "Working."

"Then New York's in good hands," Pop said with a chuckle.

I straightened, took off my coat and scarf, and hung them up. I removed my glasses case from my messenger bag, swapped out sunglasses for regular ones, then set the bag against the wall.

"Good grief, Sebastian," Pop murmured, tugging on the sleeve of my button-down shirt.

"It's not that wrinkled."

"I know you know what an iron is."

"Who has time to iron?"

"Apparently not you." Pop made a sudden face. "Did you brush your teeth this morning?"

I put a hand over my mouth at the reminder of vomit breath and started across the room. "I'll be right back." I went down the dim hallway and turned into the bathroom. No spare toothbrush, but my finger and copious amounts of toothpaste worked just as well. I swished some mouthwash afterward for good measure, then used my hand to wipe excess water from my unshaven face. I dried my mouth and chin on the sleeve of my shirt.

Huh. It *was* pretty wrinkled.

I shrugged and left the room.

"Minty fresh," I declared, joining Pop again.

"Thank goodness," Pop said as he busily filled the coffee maker with water. "I really thought at thirty-three, I wouldn't have to remind you of the necessity of basic grooming."

"I'm thirty-four."

"That's right," Pop said, shaking his head a little, whether at his mistake or my age, I wasn't sure.

"Anyway. I did brush my teeth this morning." I walked to the kitchen area on the left of the spacious apartment layout, opened a cupboard, and removed two mugs. "But something happened and I blew chunks."

Pop set the pot down with a minor clatter and looked at me. "Are you sick?" He did the parent hand-on-forehead maneuver.

"I'm fine."

He was still frowning. Then recognition lit Pop's features, and he sighed while shaking his head. "Oh, Sebastian…."

"I didn't do anything."

Pop put a hand on his hip, the other tapping the kitchen counter.

"*Honest.*"

"Where's Calvin?"

"He's working," I insisted.

"At the Emporium?"

"Er…."

"I simply don't understand how so much mayhem can befall a single individual," Pop said as he flipped the coffee maker on.

"Apparently I've got a reputation on the streets."

"What kind of reputation?"

I shrugged. "Busybody, know-it-all, I guess."

"And habitual dead-body discoverer."

Couldn't argue with that.

Business had been booming for the last twelve months, but it wasn't merely because waves of folks were suddenly discovering a joy in tangible history. I'd been briefly mentioned in the media after crashing Good Books to stop loose cannon Duncan Andrews from killing innocent patrons. I'd definitely been discussed publicly after uncovering the murderous rampage NYPD officer Brigg had gone on. And revealing Pete White to be an art and antiques thief, followed by being shot in the Javits Center—let's say that while I was in the hospital, I briefly required a security detail.

Even taking these past events into account, my private life was still surprisingly private. I mean, yeah, people knew I was the gay, antique-hoarding amateur sleuth. And yes, my fiancé had gone from the back-back-back of the closet to sort of finding himself a reluctant poster child the NYPD used to showcase their diversity. But outside of crime scenes,

Calvin and I managed not to have any serious issues. I suspected word of my crotchety disposition had made the rounds along with my inability to let a mystery rest.

I was an acquired taste and not to most people's liking. For once that was doing me a favor.

I moved around Pop, fetched cream from the fridge, and added a splash to both mugs. "At least I didn't trip over this one," I told him. "And it wasn't even a whole body."

Pop was frowning. A lot. The kind of face that adults warned kids would stick if they held it for too long. He opened a cupboard and took out a plastic container of black-and-white cookies. He placed several on a plate and handed it to me. "Are we making a repeat of last Christmas?"

"*No*." I walked the cookies to the dining table near the bay windows, the curtains drawn tightly shut. "No reimagining of Poe tales. And Calvin likes me a lot more this year than last. Hey, Dad—is it a hard-and-fast rule that wedding tables need centerpieces?" I turned.

Pop was watching me. Silent.

"Because they're kind of expensive," I added.

The coffee garbled.

Dog toys squeaked from the corner of the room where Maggie and Dillon were pawing through a box.

"There was a logical transition in subject matter."

Pop raised a hand. "I've got experience in deducing your thought process, kiddo."

Point A to Point Q, as Calvin liked to tease.

"Let's focus on the bigger issue." Pop turned and poured the coffee into our mugs.

"I don't know anything about centerpieces." I obediently shut up and sat at the table when Pop walked across the room with the beverages and gave me The Look.

"Tell me what happened," Pop said, sitting beside me.

I gave him the most accurate account I could, starting with the courier and ending with Neil's bold defiance of Calvin's direct order not to share any prior crime-scene details with me that might have linked the events. I did my best to leave out the grislier details, though, both for Pop's benefit and my own.

The bloated tongue protruding from the mouth.

The missing eye.

The fluids pooling in the thick plastic.

I shuddered a little and did my best to disguise it as a shiver from the cold. I picked up my mug and took a long sip.

Pop broke a cookie apart. He took a bite of the darker piece and then said, "So who thinks this unfortunate incident at the Emporium is linked to another homicide case? You? Neil?"

"All of us, I think," I replied as I put the cup down on the tabletop.

"But you don't know the other victim?"

"I don't know *this* victim," I answered. "I know nothing about whatever case Neil and Calvin worked on prior to today, but it seems at least the note I got is similar to another one out there."

Pop considered this. "If you were involved, even unknowingly, in this previous case, Calvin would have said something, wouldn't he?"

"I'm certain. I'm here now because he doesn't seem to know what's going on and didn't want me alone. Not that I have to be pushed to visit with you," I hastened to add.

My dad smiled a little, but it was a distant expression. "But that seems to suggest you've been randomly targeted."

I leaned back in the chair. "Maybe. Not that my dance card has many names on it, but I'm sure Calvin is looking into past acquaintances and customers to deduce whether there's overlap with whoever the previous victim was." I finally reached for a cookie.

Pop looked at me. He didn't say anything for a long, increasingly uncomfortable moment.

"What?" I finally asked. The frosting of the cookie was warming and softening in my hold.

"What if it's not *you* who's been targeted, per se, but your reputation?"

"You don't think Calvin will find a common individual to link the events?"

Pop solemnly shook his head. "The wording of your message implies they could have contacted anyone with the right… magnetism. 'An intriguing proposition for a most curious man.' That's very particular verbiage."

The thought that this lunatic could be any random face on the streets—in a city of eight million people—was alarming. If a connection could be traced to a sour customer or… fuck, I don't know, an old high school classmate… that made Calvin's job ever so *slightly* easier. There was an established timeline. A relationship. A perceived link between Calvin's previous homicide and the one currently in a box on my counter.

And with that association—no matter how tentative or absurd—there was bound to be a motive.

If I, Sebastian Snow, the frumpy-dumpy guy who lived on the fourth floor of a multiuse in the East Village, was not a clue in this case, what did the detectives have to work with? The head, of course. Somewhere in New York City was a body bound to match it. Then there was the plastic. It was thick and heavy, maybe used in an industrial environment. And the note. Hopefully the pen wasn't as common as Neil suspected. Or perhaps the Collector left a fingerprint behind on the packaging.

But if the physical clues didn't provide anything of real use—then what?

That left us with the reputation of Sebastian Snow. And by all accounts from the media over the last year, he was most definitely a curious man who had a compulsion for intrigue, mystery, murder, and to quote one newspaper, "a complex fascination with the morbidity of a bygone era." Translation: I could speak at length about the fascinating relationship Victorians had with death, and apparently that was weird to some folks.

The point was, Pop might have been on to something.

This *Collector* was looking for something old, lost, and strange. Their words. And I'd been portrayed as a man who could uncover that very sort of thing. Maybe the vagueness of the note was done on purpose. To arouse curiosity. To ensure I sank my teeth into the mystery.

Reputation could be the connection between me and the other homicide. Maybe the first victim was a curious person too. Maybe they hadn't solved the puzzle in time….

I swallowed audibly.

I was absolutely not getting involved.

But that didn't mean I couldn't at least share this concept with Calvin. If nothing else, it'd be something for him to mull over in between interviews, paperwork, and cups of shitty precinct coffee.

"Father knows best," I finally said.

MUDDER NYC missn toe.

I sat in Pop's living room, squinting at the screen of my phone. I pushed my glasses up with my knuckle and tried that internet search again. I carefully pecked out with one finger: *Murder NYC missing toe.*

I couldn't be certain what those well-drawn body parts on the notes implied, but I found it particularly odd that my own message had an eyeball and the bagged head was missing one eye. Simple logic would suggest the photo of Neil's ear corresponded with a severed ear on a real body. I wondered if that was the only photo of a mysterious drawing on Neil's camera, or if there were others. Like of the toes Quinn spoke of. If I had a teeny tiny bit more information on what Calvin was working on prior to this morning, I might be able to give him more than my wild two cents to run with.

But I wasn't sleuthing. Not really.

I was sunk into the couch cushions with my feet propped up on the coffee table. I was going nowhere fast.

And I didn't really suspect I'd find much on the internet. This seemed—if anything—to be the sort of crime the police would try to keep out of the papers, lest they spook the bastard behind it. Unsurprisingly, Google pulled up a plethora of articles tagged with *murder* and *NYC*. Some were years old but sensational enough to remain at the top of the search results. Homicide had been steadily on the decline in The City That Never Sleeps, but until that number hit zero, Calvin was still gainfully employed. I thumbed through the sound bites of urban atrocities before taking pause at one posted five days ago—last Wednesday.

Human Remains Mailed to AMNH Staff.

Color me intrigued.

I clicked the article and scanned the contents. On Wednesday morning, a staff member of the paleontology division at the American Museum of Natural History received some kind of delivery that included unspecified human remains—and not the ancient sort. There wasn't much more information beyond that. The museum staffer wasn't named, and the lead detective on the scene—Calvin, I'd bet—had directed the news outlet to the Chief of Detectives for comment.

I wished Neil had shown me a photo of the entire note, and not only the drawing….

Regardless, this was too coincidental to not be related to this morning's adventure. *That* much was for sure.

But I didn't have a connection to the museum. I loved it, visited quite a bit, and of course had discovered a dead exotic dancer in one of their displays…. But did I know anyone who worked in the field of paleontology? Personally or professionally? I was drawing a big blank on that. The article added weight to Pop's suggestion that it was my reputation that had been targeted and not *me*-me.

My phone's screen blackened, rang obnoxiously, and *Calvin Winter* popped up. I quickly accepted the call. "I swear you're a mind reader," I said upon answering.

"Yeah? Why's that?"

"I was thinking of you."

"In a positive light, I hope."

"Professional context. But if you'd rather, I can imagine you stark naked."

The distinct murmur of Quinn's voice was much too close for this to have been a private phone call.

"I'm on speaker, aren't I?" I concluded.

"Yup," Calvin answered.

"Hi, Quinn," I called.

"Sebastian," she replied.

"We're caught in a traffic jam at Columbus Circle," Calvin continued, not missing a beat. "I just wanted to check in with you."

Huh. If they took a right onto Central Park West and headed uptown for almost twenty blocks, they'd land at the Museum of Natural History. Funny how that works.

"Uptown murder?" I asked casually.

"Some follow-up interviews."

"Can I tell you something?"

A few car horns blared in the distance before Calvin said, "I know you will. Further discussion is a matter of topic, isn't it?"

I glanced to my right. Before delving into internet snooping, I had honest to God pulled out my battered spiral-bound notebook that was my "wedding planner" and wasted time drawing squiggles around the to-do list.

I put my fingertip on the scrawled note to myself and said, "Did you know that 'purchase undergarments' is part of a wedding itinerary?"

Calvin was quiet for a beat. "I really don't think that applies to us."

"Sure, I know. But I'm having to make this up as I go, and most of these to-do lists are for brides."

"Uh-huh."

"There's a whole industry dedicated to specialized bras for wedding dresses," I continued.

Calvin's silence was palpable confusion.

"They make adhesive bras," I concluded. "Which… sounds pretty awful."

"Almost lost my nipple to one of those," Quinn stated. "Had a rash for three days from the residue."

Calvin cleared his throat. "Well, thank goodness we aren't in the market for one."

"Are you going to the Museum of Natural History?" I asked quickly.

"How did—" Calvin paused, mentally backtracked. "Sebastian."

"It was a logic jump."

"No, it wasn't."

"It was," I insisted. "It's in the news. Someone in the paleontology division was mailed human remains."

Silence.

"Last Wednesday."

Still silence.

"And I'm going to go out on a limb and suspect the undetermined remains were phalanges. I was thinking about the museum," I said without taking a breath for subject transition. "I'm certain I don't have any connection." I put my feet down on the floor.

"You found a crime scene in February," Calvin replied.

"But here's the thing I wanted to tell you." I stood from the couch, knees cracking as I straightened. "If you're looking for a tangible relationship between me and this other event, I don't think you're going to find one. I don't have any friends or acquaintances who work there. I have no relationship to anyone in the field of paleontology. The body of Meredith Brown was found in the museum only because it related to P.T. Barnum."

"What's your point?" Calvin asked.

"I didn't have a relationship to Barnum either," I answered. "But my reputation did."

"No association, but also not a random target," Calvin replied. "Is that what you're trying to say?"

"Basically." I moved around the couch, watching as Pop came from his bedroom, winter boots having replaced his house slippers. "Obviously without knowing either of the victims or the staffer who received this first package, it's impossible to contrast and compare to determine something more sinister, like a serial—"

"Stop right there, sweetheart," Calvin interrupted.

"You say *that word,* and I'm going to come kick your ass for an hour," Quinn warned.

Realizing what I'd nearly said out loud, and with my father standing only a few feet away, I grasped for something—*anything*—to counteract the bad luck I was about to bring down upon the NYPD.

"F-fair thoughts and happy hours attend on you," I quickly said. A theater superstition, but lucky Shakespeare was lucky Shakespeare, right?

Pop was staring at me curiously.

The tension over the line was thick enough to cut with a knife.

"I'm going to let you go," I told them both.

"Please find another method of self-entertainment," Calvin replied.

"Jack off and take a nap," Quinn called.

Calvin sighed a little at that, then added, "I love you."

"Love you too," I mumbled before ending the call.

Pop walked to the coatrack, pulled on his jacket, and asked, "What's with *The Merchant of Venice*?"

"Warding off some misfortune," I said. "Where're you off to?"

"Maggie and I have a lesson at Exotic Animal Haven around one o'clock." He looked at the still-closed curtains by the dining table, as if to judge the weather. "With the snow, I want to leave a bit early. Afterward, we've got some socializing to do at Puppy Pals. I should be back around five…." Pop put on his scarf and gloves. "Will you still be here?"

"I suspect that'll be the case," I answered.

Pop nodded. "I'll pick us up something for dinner."

"No, no. I'll cook something."

"Twist my arm," he said with a chuckle. "You'll be okay alone?"

"Sure. How much trouble can I get into?"

Houston, we've had a problem.

CHAPTER THREE

TO ANSWER my own question: a lot.

I could get into an excessive amount of trouble, sitting at Pop's with zero, zilch, and nada to keep me occupied. I *did* try working from home. I had shop emails to answer, calls to make, and some research to do, but hunched over my laptop with an internet connection seemed like a rabbit hole of bad ideas. I supposed I could have more seriously done wedding prep, but to be honest, I'd have rather stuck a fork in my eye. Not that I didn't want to get married. That I wanted very much. I simply didn't have the sensibilities to give a crap about all the details that were apparently supposed to make the big day even more magical.

I mean, color palettes? Mood boards? Lighting designers?

For Christ's sake, I'd marry Calvin standing in my skivvies out front of Macy's.

Romance I could do. I thoroughly enjoyed syrupy-sweet declarations of love. Hell, after a year, I still practically swooned when Calvin called me his baby or sweetheart. And I liked flowers and candlelit dinners and hand-in-hand walks through the park in the rain with the best of them. But there was something about weddings that didn't feel all that romantic. More like an obligation. Fulfilling a civic duty. I liked date nights with my fiancé because it was just *us*. We did it for no one *but* us.

Weddings meant company. It meant *in-laws*. And if that reason alone wasn't enough to kill the mood… weddings meant a whole lot of folks staring at the happy couple through a magnifying lens as we went through preplanned and rehearsed motions. It didn't seem spontaneous and loving in that respect. It seemed tedious, if the planning was anything to go by.

I don't know. I found the act of being married romantic. The mere thought of spending my life with a guy who *gets me* was an actual dream come true. And I'd pay serious cash to see Calvin dressed to the nines. But weddings themselves?

Meh. My planner was full of more doodles than actual plans, and it was bumming me out.

Max had suggested more than once over the last two weeks to give in and hire a planner, which, yeah, was probably a smart move if we wanted to get hitched sometime in the next decade… but it brought me to my other problem.

Money.

New York City wedding planners came with price tags that gave me hives. This hoopla was already going to be expensive enough, but to shell out how many more thousands for someone else to make the phone calls and decide between periwinkle or lilac? I supposed I could tell them to do the entire thing in shades of gray so we could skip the color details entirely….

Anyway. Point was, owning a business with as niche a market as mine, I wasn't a millionaire. I was well off and successful, all things considered, but I sure as fuck didn't have extra Benjamins hanging out in my wallet. If I did, I'd be paying off the excessive hospital debt a lot faster. My dad had offered to help pay for some of the wedding, but he was a retired college professor—he wasn't bringing in the cash. And that left Calvin, who was absolutely not footing even one penny more than what I could meet him at, differences in our salaries be damned.

I shut the notebook a bit more forcefully than intended. I turned in my chair, pushed my glasses up, and stared at Dillon, fast asleep on Maggie's bed. I could abide by the rules of dog—when in doubt, take a nap. But I wasn't tired. I could tell Quinn I took her up on the suggestion of jacking off, but doing it alone was no fun. Not when I had a brick wall of man to play Adult Twister with.

So what was I left with?

Human toes at the Museum of Natural History.

"No," I said firmly. "No, no, *no*." I stood up. "It's Christmas. Focus on that. I could make myself useful and order a tree." I picked up my phone from beside the notebook, typed in *Christmas trees NYC*, and dialed the first business that came up.

"Skippy's Trees," a man said, half the greeting already spoken before the receiver had been fully moved into position.

"Yeah, hi, do you offer delivery on Christmas trees?"

"Complimentary delivery and installation to Manhattan, the Bronx, Brooklyn, and Queens," he quickly spouted off, for what I'm sure was the hundredth time today, alone. "Additional fees required for delivery to Staten Island. No delivery available for Long Island and Jersey."

"I'm in the East Village," I supplied.

"So you want a tree or what?"

"Er—yeah."

"Fraser firs are available from four to twenty feet. Except we're sold out of five footers."

"Six feet, I guess."

"You want tree-removal service too?"

"Yes."

"Okay. Hang on."

I hung on.

A printing calculator whirred and buzzed over the line as the man added up the fees owed. "Two fifty."

"Two hundred and fifty dollars?" I clarified. "You know the tree will be dead in a matter of weeks."

The seller ignored that and responded with "One sixty for the tree, eighty for removal, and then miscellaneous taxes. You want the fir or not?"

I sighed and rubbed my forehead. "Sure."

"I got delivery availability tonight."

"That wo—oh no. I'm not home tonight. Maybe."

"Don't work with maybes, buddy. Either tonight or… I got Friday night open."

"I should have gone into the tree business," I answered. "Sounds like it's booming."

"Better fuckin' believe it," he said with a laugh. "Tonight or Friday?"

"I guess it'll have to be tonight."

I gave Skippy's Trees our address, paid over the phone, and promised to meet his van by 7:00 p.m. on the dot. After ending the call and checking the time *again*, I was thrilled to see I'd managed to waste a cool *eleven minutes*.

Now I needed to keep myself out of trouble for at least another three hours until Pop returned.

The clock on the wall was the only thing making noise in the apartment.

Ticktock.

Ticktock.

Ticktock.

I sighed dramatically.

I DIDN'T last until 5:00 p.m.…. I understood that Calvin didn't want me alone until he had a grasp on the homicide situation, but unless he was going to get me some hired muscle, it simply wasn't a reasonable request. Pop had his own commitments, and more to the purpose, what was my sixty-four-year-old father going to do if shit hit the fan? I'd be protecting *him*, not the other way around. And since I'd been climbing the walls by four o'clock, I made the decision to step outside and do something more constructive with my time.

The dog needed a walk. I had to pick up some groceries for dinner with Dad. And then there was the tree delivery later in the evening. The way I saw it, no matter where I went, there were people. Help. Witnesses. I'd be safe from whatever Calvin was unsure of.

Dillon loved exploring outside of our immediate neighborhood. There were new trees—apparently better trees—to leave doggy communication on. After a very thorough investigation of every available trunk on Bleecker Street between Mercer and the Bowery, he was satisfied enough to let me do some quick food shopping. The stores I used to frequent with my father as a kid were no longer in business. The city ebbed and flowed with the comings and goings of trends and who could afford the leases on business properties. Unfortunately it was the mom-and-pop shops that ultimately suffered under change—quaint storefronts that once supported a hardworking family had been replaced with high-end clothing or jewelry boutiques that I *never* saw customers in, yet somehow they remained open.

Luckily there was still Wheeler's Deli. It'd been open since the seventies. The little sun-faded awning and subtle window decal were nearly lost from view in the current scaffolding of constant city construction. I was mildly surprised, upon stepping inside, that the shop owner recognized and remembered my name, even though I hadn't made it a habit of buying groceries there since leaving the family nest. Must have been the eyebrows and nose. Pop's "best features," as he called them.

I stayed long enough for the usual chitchat of "this fucking weather" and "how's the family" and "really, they're still alive?" before purchasing a loaf of freshly baked bread, an onion, and a bag full of decent tomatoes. When I got back to my dad's place, using my copy of his key to get inside the building, I had enough time to chop the onion, peel tomatoes, and start tossing spices into a pot before he walked through the door with Maggie.

"Hey, kiddo."

"Welcome home."

"Smells good. What're you cooking?" Pop asked, unhooking Maggie's leash before removing his winter clothes.

"Thought I'd make some tomato sou—*Maggie*!" I shouted when she nearly took me out with a fifty-pound run-and-jump sneak attack.

"Down, girl," Pop ordered, not even needing to raise his voice for her full obedience. She turned, trotted back to his side, and slobbered his hand affectionately. "We've talked about this. *No jumping*," he chastised quietly.

I pointed a wooden cooking spoon at her. "You're not a princess—you're a devil."

"Hey," Pop said with a smile. "She just likes you."

I grumbled and stirred the bubbling soup. "Neither of these dogs listen to me," I said, inclining my head absently to where Dillon was in the living room.

"You need to be more assertive."

"I should have pushed you to get a cat," I corrected. "A big fat one that does nothing but lie on the windowsill all day and cast judgment from afar."

Pop was chuckling as he joined my side. He picked up the loaf of bread, made a sound of appreciation after inhaling the yeasty freshness, then fetched a serrated knife to begin cutting smaller portions for our meal. "You sound hangry."

"I get grouchy when I'm bored."

"What did you do while I was out?"

"Rearranged your spice cabinet."

Pop paused. He opened the cupboard in front of him and stared at the hanging rack on the other side of the door, where he did his best to keep all of his spices in a centralized location. "So you did."

"It's done by theme."

"I can see that."

"Calvin did it in our kitchen. He does most of the cooking anyway—did I tell you a few months ago that I accidentally put chili powder in a recipe instead of cocoa powder? Because they were alphabetized at the time. The texture looks the same to me. I guess the colors aren't."

"That's true," Pop said with a simple nod. He shut the door.

I turned the burner off, grabbed the ladle on the counter, and poured soup into two bowls. "I'm heading home after dinner. Warden hasn't called with an update, but I have a hostage situation to negotiate at seven o'clock for a Christmas tree." I picked up the bowls and walked to the dining table. "Oh. I cleaned your record collection too."

"There's over a hundred vinyls," Pop protested from behind me.

"Yeah."

SKIPPY'S TREES ran their delivery and installation service with an efficiency that was impressive even by the New York standards of needing something yesterday. I'd barely turned the key in the lock of the front door when someone called from the street, "You waiting on Skippy's?"

Holding the door open, I looked over my shoulder. A van was double parked, hazard lights flashing like a lighthouse in the dark. "Yeah. Are you delivering for Snow?"

The driver checked what I thought was probably his phone. "Sebastian? 4B?"

"That's me," I confirmed.

The driver went around the back of the van and was joined by a second individual from the passenger side. They removed a huge, tightly bound pine and started across the sidewalk toward me. I pulled Dillon out of the way, opened the door wide, and let them enter the building first. I heard something crinkle on the floor as they walked through the threshold, and upon following them inside, I stepped on whatever they had. Bending down, I retrieved a small padded mailing envelope with a few dirty, wet shoe impressions left on it.

Well, shit. I looked back at the front door as it fell shut. The mail carrier must have forgotten this and shoved it through the old-fashioned mail slot instead of entering the building again. I placed it on top of the individual mailboxes fastened to the wall for the recipient to find—

"Son of a…." I grabbed it and brought it close.

Sebastian Snow.

"Figures." I shook the envelope lightly. No sound. I shrugged and raced after the guys, who were already up the first flight of stairs.

Once we reached the fourth floor, I moved around them, unlocked our apartment, and went inside to switch on the nearest lamp. "Between the bookshelf and couch would be great," I said, pointing farther into the room.

They murmured acknowledgment and set to work removing the netting and getting the tree mounted in a base.

I unclasped Dillon's leash, tossed the unfortunate piece of mail on the table, and hung up my coat and scarf. I changed into my regular glasses and put my shoulder bag in its usual I'm-too-lazy-to-find-it-a-real-home place on the floor. I turned around to shut the door that'd been left open and yelped in surprise at Calvin standing in the threshold.

"Holy—*fuck*, Cal. You scared the shit out of me." I put a hand to my chest.

He had a very distinct frown on his face as he entered the apartment. His gaze flickered over my shoulder to the fuss happening behind me, and then he said calmly, "I just came from your dad's."

"I had to meet them for delivery," I said, jutting a thumb backward.

"Is there something wrong with your phone?"

"I don't think so." I went to remove it from a pocket.

"That was sarcasm, Sebastian. I didn't ask you stay at your father's for shits and giggles." He paused when one of the guys announced they were finished. Calvin reached into his back pocket, removed his wallet, and took out a few bills for a tip. He offered the money as the men made for the door.

"Hey, thanks," one said with a nod. "Happy holidays."

Calvin was quiet until the door shut behind him. He looked at me again.

"I meant to call," I said. "I got distracted." A likely excuse if there ever was one. "Max phoned while I was walking home—he'd heard some '90s band on the oldies radio station and was having a crisis over being twenty-three."

Calvin didn't respond as he removed his winter jacket. He unbuttoned his suit coat, tossed it over one of the chairs at the table, and unbuckled his shoulder holster. He set his SIG P226 aside.

"I'm sorry," I said.

Calvin reached up, scrubbed his face briefly with both hands, then steepled his fingertips together and rested them against his mouth. He stared at a framed print on the wall of *Un bar aux Folies-Bergère* by Édouard Manet. An interesting painting. Firmly rooted in the Realism movement. Not my taste—I leaned more toward Romanticism and the escape its themes provided. But ever since Calvin had seen this painting in one of my reference books, he'd been fascinated by it. I'd asked him, after we obtained a print, what it was about the barmaid that moved him.

"I'm not an art critic, baby," he'd said with a chuckle.

"So what?"

He'd taken a deep breath and considered the painting for some time. "There's a... duality in her that I relate to, I guess. Her reflection in the mirror shows her fulfilling a behavior expected of her. A public persona. But we—the onlooker, *not the customer—see her emotions head-on. A moment of… resigned melancholy." He'd stared for another moment. "The private human underneath."*

"The play is the tragedy, Man," I'd answered.

"I know you didn't want me alone," I continued. "But I didn't think it'd be a—"

"He's gone missing," Calvin interrupted.

I blinked, glanced around the room, then asked, "Who has?"

Calvin looked at me. "Frank Newell."

"I'll take 'People I Don't Know' for five hundred, Alex," I said with a shrug.

"He works at the Museum of Natural History," Calvin said reluctantly.

I raised both eyebrows. "Let me guess. He loves dinosaurs."

"Assistant Curator for the Division of Paleontology. Last Wednesday he received a package with human remains inside. We're still trying to identify the victim." Calvin walked back to me, took my hands, and pulled me close. "Frank didn't show up to work on Friday, and by Saturday afternoon, his girlfriend reported him missing. There's been no ransom note, no phone call from possible kidnappers, no nothing. He's… gone."

"I'm getting that queasy feeling in my stomach, like when you tell me I've narrowly missed imminent danger," I answered.

"*I* suspect this is a repeating pattern. That perhaps there was a missing person before Frank—maybe they became the remains that were delivered to him."

I swallowed with some difficulty. "Uh… huh. And so… what? You think I'm going to go missing in two days' time?"

Calvin's expression could have been chiseled from stone. He gave nothing away.

"Except that wasn't Frank in my box," I stated.

"Correct."

"Who the fuck was it?"

"We're working on that. If these events happen spaced between two days, we've got a lapse between Frank and you."

"Enough time to kill Jack-in-the-Box."

"We're cross-referencing every colleague, employer, friend, and family member of Frank Newell's we can find."

"Because you think his disappearance is related to the decapitated head, and therefore related to me?" I concluded.

Calvin took a breath. "I suspect you're right. There is *something* that links these events, but it's not going to be tangible or obvious."

"When did all of… of *this* occur to you?"

Calvin put his hands firmly on my shoulders. "About an hour ago. I stepped out to come talk to you. Sweetheart, it wasn't my intention to scare you, but this is why I don't want you alone."

"Because some nutcase is going to kidnap me, chop me up, and put me under someone's Christmas tree wrapped in a big bow?" I shouted, acting the scene out with my hands for further emphasis.

"That won't happen," Calvin said with authority.

"Cal, you can't—"

"It *won't*, Sebastian," he said again. "But in order for me to protect you, I need to know you're safe. I'm trying to line up police protection for you."

"*What*?" I moved around him, walked farther into the living room, and said over my shoulder, "This is insane!"

"No, this is smart." Calvin followed behind me. He grabbed my hand and turned me around. "Tell me you wouldn't do the same, if our roles were reversed."

I wanted to protest—even tried to. But it came out as nothing more than an indignant sputter. Of course if I had even the *vaguest* hint that Calvin's life was being threatened in this way, I'd be demanding all sorts of protections be put in place. He was my partner. My soul mate. The love of my life. And… sometimes I had to remind myself that I was those same things for him.

The problem was, I had an ego that tended to overcompensate when I was backed into a corner. Too many years of putting on a brave face and wielding sarcasm like a sword still made it hard to admit my own weaknesses. To show how raw my fear could be.

Even to Calvin.

"How am I supposed to do my job under supervision?" I asked.

"It won't be hard. Pretend it's me."

"Should I take my police protection out on a few dates first, or can we skip the formalities?"

"Seb, knock it off."

I pulled my hand from Calvin's and waved both. "Come on! What the fuck kind of reaction did you expect? You went to work this morning, leaving me here to finish a bowl of soggy Lucky Charms without a care in the world. Then less than twelve hours later, I'm being told to go underground because someone referring to themselves as *Collector* is looking to accumulate parts of me?" I leaned over to rest my hands on my knees and took a deep, shaky breath.

We were both quiet after my outburst.

I closed my eyes when Calvin's shoes appeared in my line of vision. His hand came to rest on my back. "Sorry," I whispered at the floor.

"It's all right," he answered. "I'm scared too."

I reluctantly raised my head. His face was blurry over the rims of my glasses. "I hate that I do this. Every time some clusterfuck occurs in our lives, I fight you tooth and nail when you're only trying to do your job."

"I know."

My scowl deepened.

Calvin moved his hand to cup my chin, forcing me to stand once more. "You're smart and strong and fiercely independent."

"I wasn't looking for an ego stroke."

"Weren't you?"

After a brief hesitation, I huffed, leaned forward, and rested my forehead on his shoulder. "Guess it helps," I mumbled into his armpit.

He wrapped his arms around me.

I inhaled the last traces of his fading cologne.

"I don't like fighting with you," Calvin said at length. "I've come to understand, after twelve months and three major homicide investigations, that I expect you to react in your calm, problem-solving sort of way to every established danger, and that's not fair. You're not a soldier and you're not a cop. You haven't been trained for this. We all react differently when our backs are to the wall."

"Please don't make excuses for my bad behavior."

"I'm not. I'm making an observation." Calvin tightened his arms around me. "Humans are not one-sided."

"Like the barmaid?"

He tilted his head, resting his cheek against my hair. "Yeah."

I didn't let go for a long time. Not until I was certain I was done shouting and wouldn't possibly break down into tears as an alternative. I was definitely scared. I didn't want to be decapitated and left in someone's mailbox. I had long-term husbandy plans with Calvin and wanted to see those through until we were old, stooped, and counting liver spots.

Calvin was offering a tight smile as I stepped back. "You okay?"

"I'll manage," I replied. "What now, Major?"

"I think a hotel would be wise. I don't want you here, and I've got to get back to the precinct." He added after a moment, "And this way we don't need to inconvenience your dad."

I didn't like the idea that our home couldn't be considered secure. And spending money on a hotel wasn't turning my mood around any. But I did agree—avoiding Pop's couch would be a plus. I didn't want to upset him by explaining the full extent of potential danger I was in.

"Dillon too?" I asked, pointing to the pup, who'd been obediently sitting through our flare-up, hoping to eventually get some attention.

Calvin nodded, already reaching for his cell. "There's a chain hotel just south of Times Square that's pet-friendly."

"Oh boy. My favorite neighborhood," I said dryly.

Calvin smiled, staring at his phone's screen. "Go pack."

"For how many days?"

"A few."

I nodded, turned, and walked to the stairs. I started up to the loft, but paused, looking down at Calvin still standing in the main room. "What about you?"

He glanced up while putting his phone to his ear. "If you can fit a clean suit in the bag, that'd be appreciated."

I went to the bedroom. Calvin's deep voice drifted up to the loft, but I ignored the temptation to pick out individual words and instead focused on packing for an undesired staycation. I grabbed a duffel bag from the closet, threw in some of my usual work clothes of trousers and sweaters, and added a pair of jeans on the off chance I was feeling wild and crazy later in the week. I removed one of Calvin's suits and a few button-down shirts, took more care in folding them than I had my own, and tucked the clothes into the bag. I returned from collecting our toiletries in the bathroom to see Calvin coming up the stairs.

"I've got a room booked for three nights," he said upon reaching the landing.

"Will we need it that long?"

"Hopefully not."

"I'm gonna need you to instill some more confidence, Detective."

Calvin's mouth quirked a little, but he didn't correct himself.

I shoved the handful of products into the bag, zipped it closed, and looked at Calvin. "You won't spend the entire night at the precinct, right?"

Calvin slid his hands into his pockets. "Right," he agreed, maybe a bit reluctantly, but I could have been projecting that hesitation.

"I don't care if you wake me up," I insisted. "I just need to know you're getting some sleep."

"Okay."

"You know why this entire thing sucks?" I asked suddenly.

"I can think of a few reasons."

"We haven't had sex in six days."

Calvin snorted. "You keep track?"

"Not intentionally."

He laughed a little and approached me. Calvin put his hands on my hips and tilted his head down to kiss my mouth.

"I start getting weird," I murmured as Calvin pulled back a bit.

"I think you mean *horny*."

"Maybe. Right now I'm really turned-on by your hands."

"Some people have a thing for hands."

"And your freckles."

"You're right. That's weird."

I laughed and kissed Calvin again.

He drew both hands up, then quickly popped open the buttons on my shirt and caressed bare skin with his strong, blunt fingertips.

"D-do we have time for this?" I whispered against his lips.

"We're going to make time," he answered. Calvin quickly finished with my shirt but didn't bother to tug it off before he fastened his mouth on my throat and gave a hard suck.

Since meeting Calvin, I'd learned that I was never going to be too old to enjoy a good old-fashioned hickey and the combination of pride and embarrassment that typically accompanied such love marks the following day. I shuddered as concentrated sensual delight ricocheted up and down my spine like my body was a pinball machine. I leaned into Calvin, wrapped my arms around his neck, and gave his thick hair a bit of a tug.

He let up on my throat and roughly pressed our hips together. I groaned as Calvin rubbed his dick against mine, the material of our pants creating a frustrating barrier that needed to be dealt with immediately. As if reading my mind, Calvin looked down and opened the button and fly of my trousers. He pushed them from my hips, and his touch roamed, giving appreciation to my ass, dick, balls.

I swallowed hard.

"Get on the bed. On your stomach."

Oh, thank God.

Sometimes there was nothing better than getting rode hard from behind, completely at the mercy of another man's speed, angle, hold.

I kicked off my loafers, shimmied out of my pants and boxer briefs, sat down on the bed, and rolled onto my stomach. I turned my head and watched Calvin. He loosened his tie, shucked off his pants, and opened the drawer of the bedside table. It took every ounce of self-control not to thrust into the bedding while I waited.

Lube and condom procured, Calvin got onto the bed and settled between my legs as I spread them. He smoothed one hand over my ass and murmured, "You're so gorgeous."

But he didn't indulge me nearly as much as he used to.

Instead, he waited.

He waited because he knew I could—*would* say it these days. Sure, my self-esteem had been slowly chugging along in an upward trajectory all these months, but what had really put life into perspective for me was that extremely real heart-to-heart I'd had with my own mortality. Sex with someone you love was so… life-affirming. It simply wasn't the time to let hang-ups and old embarrassments get the best of me.

Not anymore.

Not ever again.

"Cal…."

"Say it," he ordered.

"Spank me."

Whack.

I moaned loudly, no consideration given to the mirrored loft of 4A on the other side of the wall. 4A hadn't liked me since the Moving Image case, when JD Malory and I had fallen through his open door and landed on top of him during a scuffle. There wasn't any face left to save, so whatever. I was going to be loud.

I pushed up on my knees a bit, raising my ass. "Ah—*again*. Spank me again."

Calvin hit the other cheek. He repeated the action several times, with sharp, fast strokes that left my ass tingling and burning. It wasn't *pain* pain—not the traditional sensation, anyway. There was certainly an element of uncomfortableness to having your ass spanked, but with it was such a powerful release of endorphins, arousal, and the realization that, whatever the hell it was I seemed to get out of this sexual punishment, Calvin got the same in giving it to me.

A perfect partnership.

"Oh my God," I cried. I pushed my hips back down, thrusting hard against the mattress and shuddering. I felt like every single molecule in my body was buzzing with stimulation.

"Feel good?" Calvin asked, a smile in his voice.

"Y-yes," I mumbled into the pillows.

He grabbed my hips and hoisted me back up on my knees. Calvin spread my cheeks apart and licked me, hard and fierce.

I moaned loudly and fisted the sheets.

Whack.

I gasped. "C-Cal!"

Whack.

"Holy fuck! Again—please!"

Calvin let up, breathing heavily. He smoothed his palm over both asscheeks and then smacked.

Harder.

A lot harder.

One more of those and I'd actually come from this and nothing more.

But Calvin stopped touching me.

I looked over my shoulder and shoved my glasses up my nose with one hand. "Why'd you stop?" I sounded desperate and didn't even care.

"Because I don't want you finished and spent yet." Calvin uncapped the lube and coated his fingers in a generous portion. He reached forward and pressed his middle finger in to the knuckle. "You've got the tightest ass…."

I swallowed and rocked back into his touch as Calvin added a second finger. "You like it?" I asked, voice dropping a bit quieter.

Calvin growled, a dangerous combination of playfulness and possessiveness. "Oh yeah." He leaned over, grabbed the collar of my shirt, and pulled me up enough so that we could kiss. He let go after a moment, removed his fingers, and tore open the condom package.

I repositioned myself on the bed, waiting with… not trepidation, but that minor hesitation I could never shake before bottoming. I liked this position in bed—I preferred it, really. But those nerves were always there, if even for a moment.

"Deep breath," Calvin murmured. Then the head of his dick pushed in, forcing itself past the tight ring of muscle.

"*Jesus Christ*," I swore.

Calvin held my hip with one hand and made a soothing motion up and down the links of my spine with the other. It'd never been like this with my previous partners. Calvin was so different from them. Even this—the smallest expression of care—left such an impression on my heart and memory. Each gentle stroke of his callused palm against my skin was a reminder that Calvin cared for my physical enjoyment.

That he respected me.

Cherished me.

"You okay?" he asked, and I could hear the stress in his tone from keeping still.

I nodded. "Move."

Calvin tightened his hold a bit, thrust forward, pulled back, thrust in again, until his entire cock was buried in my ass. He moved his hands up to my shoulders, my body prone and ready for the taking. He pulled out slow, a delicious burning pleasure I could feel from ass to balls to toes, before shoving in roughly.

"Fuck!" Calvin shouted. "God—so good. Your ass was made for me."

I gave up any semblance of a struggle for dominance, which was typical play to get Calvin all hot and bothered, and let him pound into me. His grip on my shoulders kept me from flying right off the bed on those thrusts that hit *just right*, and his balls slapped my ass with every forward motion. The air around us was heavy with the heady scent of male, sweat, and sex, and the quiet was disrupted by gasps, pants, and incredible dirty talk coming from the handsome redhead taking me for one hell of a ride.

I didn't even realize I'd been holding my breath until Calvin's hand reached under and gave my overlooked cock a few quick strokes. I took in a shuddering lungful of air, balanced on one hand, and reached down to continue jerking myself.

"That's it," he said in a deep, gorgeous voice. "My cock makes you so hard."

"C-Cal! I can't—"

Finish the sentence. I don't think my brain has gotten oxygen in at least five minutes.

Calvin put his arm across my chest and hoisted me up, back against his own chest. "Let me watch you come," he whispered in my ear.

I stroked quickly, the tunnel of light growing brighter, blinding, and then it was like fireworks on New Year's. Cum splattered my stomach and dribbled down my fist. I fought for air as I leaned my head to rest on Calvin's shoulder. With my clean hand, I reached back, fumbled, and got ahold of his tie. I gave it a jerk over my shoulder, and he grunted.

Calvin kept fucking me, kept shoving into my tightened ass and shuddering muscles. He wrapped his hand around my wrist, raised it, and sucked on my sticky fingers.

Calvin's rhythmic thrusts faltered as he licked my hand. His breathing turned jagged, intensified, and then I felt him spend inside me. I kept a grip on his tie, holding us flush against each other as he finished with the same tidal wave washing over him.

"HUH."

"What?"

I tapped the StepTrack on my wrist, looked up, and watched as Calvin hastily redressed in front of the full-length mirror on the wall. "That burned ninety-six calories."

He smiled into the reflection as he adjusted the knot of his tie.

I stood from the bed, finished tugging my trousers into place, and buttoned them. "I have a question. About the wedding."

Calvin smoothed his shirt a few times. "You know, as long as you're there and I'm there, details like flower vases and cake toppers don't seem so important." He turned and walked toward me. "Don't you think?"

God, yes.

But I instead said, "You haven't mentioned anything about inviting your family."

Calvin didn't respond, but his expression stumbled as if he had spoken.

"I killed the postsex mood, didn't I?"

A brief, *reluctant* smile crossed Calvin's features. He looked down, took my hand, and ran the pad of his thumb over my ring. "I haven't decided yet," he said before meeting my gaze. "Getting married isn't about them. It's about you."

"It's about us," I corrected.

"*Us*," he echoed in quiet agreement. "What I mean is… I love you. You've been my family since the beginning. It's not…." Calvin stopped. He looked down at my hand again. "I don't need to feel guilty for their reaction to my coming out."

"That's true," I murmured.

"I am not obligated to extend an olive branch in the form of invitation to an event they've openly and viciously criticized in the past. It's one thing—what they say to or about me—but I *will not* allow that behavior to be directed toward you."

"I shouldn't have brought it up—"

"No. It's all right. I do need to decide either way," Calvin said. He brought my hand up, kissed the ring, and let go. "Give me a bit longer to think it over."

"One crisis at a time," I agreed.

"Right." Calvin checked his watch and swore quietly. "I need to head back. Finish getting dressed, and I'll drop you off at the hotel." He moved around the foot of the bed, grabbed the bag that'd been knocked to the floor during our impromptu tangle in the sheets, and headed downstairs with it.

I puffed my cheeks as I let out a deep breath. I'm not sure why I thought *now* had been a good time to bring up the estranged family. Sex and bigoted in-laws didn't exactly go hand-in-hand. Although, replace sex with murder, and yeah… I could see the connection. I figured it had been lingering in the back of my mind since earlier in the day, when I'd honestly tried to do some wedding prep.

I still wasn't sure how I felt, beyond supportive of Calvin's decision—no question there. The petty asshole in me wanted the Winters to attend so I could kiss their son in front of the entire world and show them I was the person who made him happier than he'd ever been. When I was more rational about it, of course I was not enthused about the idea of Retired Colonel Dickhead giving me stink eye the entire event.

Catch-22.

"Seb?" Calvin called from the living room.

I hastily buttoned my shirt, bent to yank my loafers back on, and walked to the stairs. "Yeah?" I started down, looking over the railing to the right as Calvin put his weapon on.

"What's this?" he asked, with his free hand raising the envelope I'd tossed onto the table.

"USPS must have shoved it through the mail slot. I stepped on it when I got home."

Calvin set it aside and put his suit coat on. He adjusted the collar and gave me a sideways glance as I joined him. "They delivered without postage?"

I grabbed the envelope and looked at it. After stepping on it in my haste to see the delivery guys upstairs, I hadn't taken notice of the lack of stamps or confirmation it'd been processed through any post office. There didn't appear to be a return address. I flipped it over—nothing on the back either.

I didn't want to jump to any paranoid conclusions, although I didn't think I'd be blamed for doing so. Still holding the envelope, I asked without looking at Calvin, "Do you want me to open it?"

"Wait." Calvin walked toward the front door, turned left down the hall to the kitchen, and returned a moment later with a small kitchen knife. He carefully cut along the top of the envelope as I held it with the tips of my fingers.

Once Calvin finished, I dumped the contents onto the tabletop. A plastic Ziploc bag with some kind of mush inside fell out, followed by a folded piece of paper. I set the envelope aside, picked up the baggie, and held it up for both of us to examine.

"That's a human eye," Calvin stated.

Chapter Four

Or rather—it *was* a human eye.

After being trampled by two beefy delivery guys lugging a giant pine tree, followed by me and a dog, there wasn't a lot left to its original form.

"Eye goop," Neil said before snapping a photo. "Just great."

Calvin stood a few feet farther into the living room, conversing with Quinn on his cell. Two police in uniform stood in the open doorway of our apartment. Another member of CSU was downstairs with a third officer, investigating the building's front door and resident mailboxes.

I crossed my arms and studied Neil. No suit. He'd since changed into a long-sleeve sweater and a pair of dark jeans. "For not being the one on the receiving end of some seriously fucked-up, serial-killer, body-part-collector bullshit, you're in an awfully foul mood this evening."

Neil shot me a sour look.

I shrugged. "Trying to put life into perspective for you."

"I'd just gotten off duty. I was in the middle of something."

"Something sounds nice. Did I mention there's a person wanting to cut me up into bite-size pieces?"

Neil paused, tilted his head back, and closed his eyes. I knew the stance because it was one thing that he and Calvin had in common: the tendency to count to ten before deciding whether to take an argument with me to the next level.

When Neil opened his eyes again, I asked, "Feel better?"

"Nice hickey," he retaliated, and not quietly.

I put a hand to my neck. "Shut it."

Neil took another photo of the eye soup before setting his camera aside. "Have you looked at the note yet?"

I shook my head and took a wary step closer. "I wasn't allowed."

With gloved hands, Neil picked up the paper and carefully unfolded it. In identical Spencerian penmanship was one sentence:

A most peculiar war of intellect began and ended with a skull.

A Collector.

Underneath that—another drawing of an anatomical body part.

Neil was silent.

"A battle of wits," I stated.

"Between who?"

"And to what length?" I said, instead of answering. "I mean, are we talking Odysseus crossing enemy lines inside the Trojan horse, or a game of questions between Rosencrantz and Guildenstern?"

"I don't think the note is suggesting a work of fiction," Neil replied.

"No, I don't believe so either," I answered. "I only mean, a war of intellect can be both a literal or figurative battle. This note is extremely vague."

"Well, which one involved a skull?"

"Do I look like fucking Wikipedia?" I shot back.

Neil clenched his jaw. He looked over my shoulder toward the living room, then said, very quietly, "I'm going to tell you about our other case because I think—*for once*—you being involved is a good thing."

I shook my head and put my hands over my ears. "I don't want to know."

"Tough shit."

"La, la, la, I can't hear you."

"Hey! Encyclopedia Britannica!" Neil snapped. "Listen to me."

I lowered my hands. "Are you going to tell me about Frank Newell going missing? I'm aware. Why do you think Calvin is bringing me to a hotel?"

"Okay, fine. Did he also tell you this is the exact same message Frank got? Along with a delivery of human toes?" Neil waved the note for emphasis.

"The toes I knew about. Calvin… didn't mention the note," I said stiffly. Then a curious thought occurred to me. "Was this the only message Frank received?"

Neil shot Calvin another glance before murmuring, "No. He received two—"

"With another body part?"

"Yes," Neil said slowly.

"Have you confirmed both—er—pieces were the same victim?"

"DNA evidence confirms this, yes. But we still don't know who—"

I waved a hand to stop him. "What did the second note say? Do you remember? When did you find that one?"

"Hold up on the inquisition." Neil took a breath. "The second package was left on the tire of his car in a parking garage. It was found Wednesday evening. Same day as the first one that was delivered." Neil retrieved his camera and started sifting through images stored on the memory card.

"Did you guys request video surveillance from the garage?"

"Wow. I bet that never occurred to Winter." Neil turned the camera screen toward me. "This was his second note."

A picture of now-familiar handwriting on plain paper said:

You have forty-eight hours. Hope you're satisfied.

A Collector.

At the bottom was a drawing—a clinical rendition of the lower portion of a human foot.

Okay. One thing. Well, two things.

Fuck.

First thing.

"Look at how the drawings correspond to the packages. It's basically showing you what to expect. His first note had a drawing of an ear, but the delivery was toes. This second note has a drawing of toes. So I'm guessing the package left in the garage had a severed ear?"

Neil nodded. "Indeed."

"It's the same as with me." I reached to grab the note on the tabletop, then thought twice of doing so without latex gloves. Instead, I hovered my hand over it. "This morning at the Emporium, I had a delivery of a human head and a drawing of an eyeball. Tonight at home, I received said eyeball and a drawing of… what are these, molars?" I squinted a little at the picture in question, then looked at Neil, watching the wheels in his head begin to turn. "I'm going to get at least one more delivery, don't you agree? And I bet it'll have teeth. If it has a sketch of a head, that'll bring the packages full circle."

"Frank only had two messages."

"Yeah. It seems like the Collector is adjusting their approach. Maybe because Frank failed in retrieving the artifact in question…."

"Or because you're *you*," Neil said. "And your brain doesn't tick like most people's."

I scratched at my bristly chin. "That certainly gives more weight to the theory that it's my reputation being targeted."

Neil cocked his head. "Come again?"

I didn't stop thinking out loud to explain to him what Calvin and I already feared to be the truth. "The first letter was an invitation to my curiosity. The second a temptation to my critical thinking."

Neil raised an eyebrow. "And… the final message?"

"I suspect it'll be similar—the countdown begins."

"To find a skull," Neil stated.

"Maybe."

"What kind of skull?"

"I'm a snoop, not a clairvoyant," I answered.

Calvin cleared his throat.

I turned around to see that not only had my handsome detective finished with his call to Quinn, but he'd likely been standing behind me and listening for a good minute. "Oh. Calvin. When did you get here?"

"*Smooth*," Neil muttered.

Calvin stared at us. "Any other details of the case you want to share with an unauthorized individual, Millett?"

That annoyed Neil. Not that it was difficult to do. But his feathers were all a-ruffled that evening. "Was Frank Newell *not* confidential information?" he countered.

"I explained to Sebastian who Mr. Newell was so that he'd understand why I'm requesting police protection."

"I told you this morning, and I'll tell you again," Neil said sternly, "keeping him out of this mystery is going to create more problems than simply asking for his help."

"I don't *want* to be involved," I protested.

"Yes, you do," Neil shot back.

"I mean, yes—but I won't—wait, my help with what?" I asked suddenly, holding up my hands like I was putting on the brakes.

"No," Calvin said to Neil with finality. "We're done and not having this discussion again." He looked at me briefly. "Grab your coat, sweetheart."

I bit back a comment about them marking territory by pissing on my floor, and went toward the front door to fetch my coat from the rack. I glanced back, not surprised to see Calvin had assumed the hands-on-hips pose of authority as he continued to speak with Neil. When I grabbed for my scarf next, I caught one of the female officers in the open doorway staring at me.

"*Men*," I said with a shrug.

She snorted, shook her head, and laughed a little.

I detoured briefly to the kitchen in order to collect the dog's bowls and a bag of food. When I left the dark room and walked back down the hall, Calvin was straightening from putting Dillon's leash on. I took it from him while he tossed the duffel bag over his shoulder.

"Usually I'm the one running low on sugar, spice, and everything nice," I stated as we left the apartment.

Calvin followed me into the hall, tactfully ignoring the jab. "Millett will finish up here while I drive you to the hotel."

"All right."

He declined further comment after that.

We went down the three flights of stairs to the ground floor, where Calvin took the lead in order to have a brief word with the CSU detective and uniformed cop at the front door. I then followed him outside and along the sidewalk to his parked Ford Fusion. I settled Dillon in the back seat and climbed into the passenger's as Calvin started the car. Cold air briefly blew out of the vents before it began to warm.

Calvin finagled the car from the side of the road and took off toward First Avenue. He hung the first left onto East Eleventh, then turned again uptown upon reaching Third Avenue. He adjusted the temperature controls with one hand.

"Need the heat higher?" he asked.

I shook my head. "It's fine." I glanced to the left as Calvin settled back in his seat. Light from streetlamps bounced off the windshield, cutting abstract shapes across his strong profile. "Hey. Uh—I'm not causing some kind of issue between you and Neil, am I?"

"No, Seb."

"Because you could have fooled me."

"Millett seems to have selective amnesia," Calvin eventually said, "and thinks we'd benefit from having you professionally consult on this case."

"Is that a slam?"

"Against you? It's not meant to be, no."

"I find it difficult to believe Neil wants me on this case more than what the Collector has already forced me into."

"You're smart," Calvin said simply.

"That never stopped him from telling me to sit down and shut up in the past."

Calvin tapped the wheel absently. "Yes, well… you might have an exasperating method of sleuthing, but that doesn't diminish the knowledge you've provided on past cases."

"Are *you* asking for my assistance?"

"Nope."

I grunted. "Why not?"

"Because I don't gamble with human lives. You're already in too deep—*I know*, not by your own choosing," he added when I made a sound of protest.

I looked at Calvin again when he stopped at a traffic light. "Can I tell you something about that note?"

"Which one?" He met my gaze. "The one addressed to you, or the one Millett insisted upon showing you?"

"Erm… both."

Calvin looked at the road. "What about them?" he asked warily.

"Don't they seem strange to you?"

"Obviously." The light changed, and Calvin took his foot off the brake.

"I think we can come to the conclusion that 'a most unusual article lost to time and neglect' is likely to be a skull, based on the follow-up message. Now, what this war of intellect reference is, I can't say. Nor do I have any idea what sort of skull the Collector may be searching for."

"What about a dinosaur skull?" Calvin asked. "Frank *is* a paleontologist."

I made a face, propped my elbow on the door, and leaned my head against my hand. "That's possible."

"What? A long-lost dinosaur skull doesn't intrigue you?"

"It does," I insisted.

"Did you not have a favorite dinosaur growing up?"

"*Troodon*."

"Mine was *Stegosaurus*."

"You know *Stegosaurus* was one of the dumbest dinosaurs? I mean, in relation to its brain-size versus body-size," I explained.

"Thanks for breaking a seven-year-old boy's heart," Calvin replied.

"Suppose it *is* a dinosaur skull," I continued, "for lack of any other lead. We should assume, based on the initial message, this is already a found artifact."

"Not something yet to be unearthed in the sandstone hills of Wyoming, is that what you're trying to say?" Calvin asked.

"Hmm. Once found, since lost."

"Paleontology was all the rage in the 1800s," Calvin suggested. "Perhaps that's the incentive toward contacting you."

"Egyptomania and anthropomorphic taxidermy were also hip," I countered. "But yes, if we're talking about a dinosaur bone specific to Victorian America, then… I can see why my reputation would encourage the Collector to reach out. But I'm going to admit right now, I don't know much about dinosaurs beyond what I read in books as a kid."

We'd hit Midtown by then. Traffic slowed to an evening crawl as we crossed avenues. I reached into the messenger bag at my feet, took out my sunglasses, and replaced my regular lenses with them. The closer we got to Times Square, the more commercial storefronts glowed in the night, the brighter the advertising, and the more blinding the visual noise.

"Frank's second message is strange."

"Of course it is." Calvin hit the brakes suddenly. A biker, bundled up in enough winter gear to look like the Michelin Man, zoomed past without a care. Calvin shook his head and started driving again.

"'I hope you're satisfied.' That phrase doesn't make any sense in the context of the forty-eighty hour warning." I scratched the back of my head. "It stands out like a sore thumb."

"A double meaning?"

I shrugged. "A reference, perhaps."

I mulled over possible allusions, ultimately coming up empty-handed as Calvin pulled to the curbside in front of a hotel on West Thirty-Seventh. He got out of the car, walked around the front, and was stopped by a doorman telling him he couldn't park there. Drop-off only. Calvin flashed his badge as I climbed out of the passenger seat. I overheard him explain he'd be inside for only a few moments, to which the employee reluctantly agreed after studying Calvin's credentials.

Dog and duffel bag accounted for, the two of us walked through the sliding glass doors. Calvin checked in at the front desk, retrieved our room keys, and was directed to the elevators around the corner. There was a little dining area—now dark—for breakfast in the mornings, and a small bar setup on the opposite end of the room, with one tender and two young women giggling over martinis. I followed Calvin into an open and awaiting elevator.

He pressed 6 with his thumb, and the doors silently shuttered.

I reached for his hand. Calvin slid his fingers through mine. He gave me a brief squeeze. Not so strong as if to say he feared the worst, nor so little as if saying it'd all blow over. Just enough.

The doors opened on the sixth floor, and we stepped out. It was very clean and eerily quiet. Calvin checked the room card in his hand again, then walked to the left, turned a sharp corner, and stopped outside of 6112. He scanned the key, and the lock gave. He walked inside first and held his hand out to indicate staying where I was. Calvin quickly checked the bathroom, around each side of the double beds, and then briefly peeked through the curtains.

He turned on the floor lamp in the corner of the room and said, "Come in."

I let Dillon in, and the door fell shut behind me. The dog immediately jumped onto the nearest bed and flopped back dramatically against the pillows.

I glanced at Calvin and pointed to the bed beside the window. "I guess this one is ours."

He smiled a little, set the bag beside the desk, and approached me. "I have to go. It'll be late by the time I return," he said, handing me one of the key cards. "Call room service if you need anything." Calvin gave me a kiss.

"Okay." I turned and watched him go to the door. I took a breath. "Hey. I like you."

Calvin glanced at me as he stepped into the hall. "I like you too."

I ACTUALLY did leave the room, intending to grab a beer at the bar downstairs. But when the elevator doors opened on the ground floor, the drunken laughter of the two martini-sipping ladies filled the otherwise silent dining area and reminded me why I never drank at bars. I went back upstairs and instead ordered a Guinness and slice of cheesecake from room service.

"What're you eating?" Max asked on speaker phone.

I sat on the bed, legs crossed under me, the television on mute, with a wedge of dessert balanced on my fork. "Cake," I said before taking a bite.

"You've been mailed human remains, have potentially picked up a new stalker, the police have you under protection, and you're sitting in a hotel room drinking beer and eating cake?"

"Yeah."

"You're living your best life, man," Max said.

"Thanks."

"So this guy knows your home address?" Max asked next.

"I guess it wouldn't be so hard to deduce," I answered. I took another bite of cheesecake. "At least when it comes to shadowing someone whose mode of transportation is walking."

"That and you're a creature of habit."

"What do you mean?"

"You take the same exact route to work every day," Max explained. "You walk on the right-hand side of the street—"

"That's not weird. The sidewalk on the right is about half a foot wider, and there's less overhead construction."

"Uh-huh. And you get to work at the same time, unless you were treated to the morning bump-and-grind. In which case you have a tendency to roll in around nine o'clock, all flushed, with your hair uncombed, and wearing mismatched loafers."

I glared at the phone beside my knee. "Funny."

"Only because it's true."

I leaned back, grabbed the beer off the nightstand, and took a sip. "Anyway. The real conundrum is that Neil is encouraging bad behavior."

"Calvin is too. At least a little," Max said.

And he had a point. If Calvin wasn't remotely interested in my being a part of this case, he wouldn't have actively discussed the handwritten notes on the car ride to the hotel. He wouldn't have told me details about Frank Newell beyond "he's missing, so you may, by extension, be in danger."

"That's true," I said in agreement. I set the beer down. "But Neil is outright showing me crime-scene photos."

"Has he been dropped on his head recently?"

"I don't know. But he's pretty insistent that I'd actually be beneficial to the investigation."

Max made a sound under his breath. "I admit I'm intrigued, but defying Calvin in this instance seems like a pretty surefire way to end up on his shit-list for life."

"I don't like that list," I answered.

"Who would?"

I stuffed the last wedge of cheesecake in my mouth and said between bites, "Have you ever read the phrase, 'Hope you're satisfied'?"

"What do you mean?"

"Like in a historical context. That's what Frank's second note said. I don't think it's an original phrase from the Collector. I think it's a reference, or a quote even."

"Nothing comes to mind." I heard the sound of a keyboard after Max fell quiet for a moment. "It's a song. 'Hope You're Satisfied,' by Betty and Dupree."

"Etta James," I replied. I picked up the remote and flipped channels to something not so bright and flashy. World Poker Tournament? Sure.

"It says Betty and Dupree," Max was saying.

"That was a onetime release under aliases for Etta James and Harvey Fuqua. It's a good song. You should listen to it."

"Well… anyway. That's all that shows up when you google it."

I sighed. "I feel like I should recognize it."

"Me too. You're oh-for-two today."

"Not that I don't appreciate your support…," I began. I climbed off the bed and picked up my beer. "But I'm going to finish this overpriced Guinness and get some sleep. I don't know if we've been cleared to open the Emporium tomorrow, so enjoy your day off."

"Cool. Lock your door, boss."

"Already done."

"Check the closet."

"What's going to be in it, an ironing board?"

Max snorted. "This is *you* we're talking about. Check the damn closet."

I rolled my eyes and walked across the room, beer in hand. I opened the door. "Nada," I called loudly.

"All right," Max answered. "Give Calvin a kiss for me."

"Will do."

"With tongue."

I shut the closet door and walked back to the bed. "No."

"Squeeze his butt."

"Max."

"Just one cheek!"

"*Good night*," I said sternly, ending the call.

I glanced at the second bed. Dillon thumped his tail lazily at me. Sighing, I finished the last sips of beer, tossed the bottle, and got undressed. I put on pajamas, brushed my teeth, and took out my contacts before turning off the lights and television. I blindly stumbled to the bed and crawled under the blankets.

The room was so quiet. So *not* our apartment. And I had a sudden pang in my chest for all those gentle sounds of life that I'd come to associate with home and heart. The ticktock of the wall clock downstairs that echoed all the way up to the loft. The hiss and ping of the old radiators coming on at night. The muffled laughter of 4A, who talked way too loud on his phone.

I missed the domestic calm Calvin and I had finally obtained in our lives. I could admit that, *even now*, mysteries were more captivating than the contentment of nine to five, but if it were a choice between Calvin or a good mental exercise? I'd take my big redheaded fellow any day. And that said a thing or two, considering I'd nearly died more than once simply to prove I was intelligent.

Should have told him I loved him before he left.

I rolled onto my back. I closed my eyes and thought about Frank Newell's second message.

Hope you're satisfied.

I thought about my own notes.

Recover a most unusual article lost to time and neglect.

A most peculiar war of intellect began and ended with a skull.

The clues were all there, waiting for me to piece them together. And based on both mine and Frank's circumstances, the Collector believed this was enough to figure it out.

Spencerian script told me post-1850s and pre-1920s. The attempt at antiquated verbiage suggested this person was zeroed in on the nineteenth century. An unusual… *skull*… that both began and ended a war. There were plenty of battles, skirmishes, and all-out actual wars the Collector could have been referencing in the given time period. There was the Civil War, for starters. The Spanish-American War. And countless atrocities against indigenous people.

Except none of those seemed to fit this particular description.

Because they weren't *peculiar wars*. Peculiar implied not a literal, but a figurative war. A legitimate battle of the minds. A dispute over a dinosaur skull….

I HAD a strange dream that night. *Real strange.*

I'd been at the Museum of Natural History, in the hall of permanent dinosaur exhibits. One of the skeletons on display was… there was something wrong with it. There were people, just out of the corner of my eye, arguing about the fossil, but I couldn't pick out their individual comments. It was only after what felt like hours in the dream that I'd come to a simple conclusion: the dinosaur's skull had been placed on the wrong end of the body.

I also determined I could fix it myself.

Walking forward, unrestricted by the usual barriers that didn't appear to exist in the dream, I reached up and plucked the head off the tail. But when I turned it around in my hands to study the details, it was the decapitated head from the Emporium.

The one milky eye rolled around before focusing on me. The mouth moved, showing the gaping holes where several teeth had been yanked out. The bloated tongue licked at chapped lips.

"Dixon. Dixon. Dixon. Hope you're satisfied!" it said.

"*DIXON*!" I shouted, jolting awake like you do from a falling dream, and scaring the ever-loving shit out of myself. The sudden jump startled the body draped across my chest, and before I realized what was happening, I fell off the edge of the mattress I'd been teetering on. "Son of a fuck!" I cried, hitting the floor.

"Jesus Christ!" Calvin said from above me, breathless.

The lamp on the bedside table was switched on.

I slowly pulled my legs out from the tangle of sheets, finished my ungraceful landing onto the carpeted floor, and then buried my face into the bend of my arm.

"Seb?" Calvin asked after a beat, his voice shaky.

"Present," I muttered. I slowly sat up on my knees, turned, and squinted.

Calvin was sitting up in bed, a hand pressed against his bare chest as he struggled to calm his breathing. Waking him suddenly or making loud noises were still triggers of his PTSD that we'd been diligently working on. But Calvin was beginning to make progress on taking control of those fight-or-flight responses. Consistent therapy and the presence of Dillon were finally producing positive headway in his life. In fact, said dog must have moved to my bed during the night and was currently sitting beside Calvin, licking his free hand.

The anchoring action kept Calvin *here*. In New York. In our hotel. He looked at the dog and pulled Dillon closer.

I cleared my throat. "I had a bad dream. What time is it? When did you get here?"

Calvin glanced at the clock on the bedside table. "It's four in the morning. I got in about an hour ago."

I climbed to my feet, knees cracking. "I'm sorry." I leaned over the bed to kiss him. I missed his lips, catching the corner of his mouth.

Calvin put his hand on my jaw. It still shook slightly as he redirected the kiss.

"Oh my God," I mumbled against his lips.

He pulled back a bit. "What?"

"Samuel G. Dixon. Hope you're satisfied!"

"I need you to use complete sentences."

I grabbed my glasses off the table, walked across the room, and picked up my messenger bag from the floor. "I know where the phrase is from!" I took my laptop out, set it on the desk, and powered it on. I pulled out the computer chair to sit but turned to look at Calvin. "No! I know—*wait*. Oh shit. This is big."

He was staring at me as if that fall to the floor had done some actual damage to my brain. Even Dillon had his head cocked and ears up in apparent befuddlement.

"I fell asleep with that phrase in my head. The meaning was right in front of me the entire time. I simply wasn't *thinking*." I turned when the computer sounded its start-up jingle, typed in the password, then looked at Calvin again. "I had a dream about a dinosaur skull—like what we talked about."

Calvin rubbed his jaw and nodded for me to continue.

"In my dream I realized the skull had been put on the wrong end—on the tail. So I was going to fix it. Anyway, the skull turned into decapitated Jack-in-the-Box, and that freaked me out and woke me."

"Who's Dixon? You shouted Dixon when you woke up."

I finally sat in the chair and rolled it toward the foot of the bed. "I did a project junior year of college on illustration plates and how the printing industry for books and newspapers was shifting to accommodate a growing population during the second half of the nineteenth century. One of the books I cited in the report was…." I snapped my fingers a few times and then tapped my forehead. "Fuck… oh. *Vertebrata of the Tertiary Formations of the West*. It was written by paleontologist Edward Drinker Cope, and—where're you going?" I asked as Calvin climbed out of bed.

He said nothing but held up a finger to indicate he needed a moment while walking to the stand beside the desk. He collected a disposable cup, went into the bathroom and filled it with tap water, then returned and poured it into the tiny coffeepot. He popped one of those K-cup knockoff brands into the top and turned it on. The machine gurgled, sputtered, and then began brewing.

"All right. I'm listening," he said quietly. Calvin looked down at me and combed his fingers through my sleep-mussed hair before giving me an encouraging smile.

"Cope was brilliant. But he was also a total asshole." I spun around in the chair, opened a web browser, and did a quick search for the photograph I had stored in my long-term memory. It was found easily with a few keywords. "This is a picture of the study in his home the year he died."

A picture, dated 1897, showed a room with large bay windows letting in daylight, completely packed to the gills with books, endless stacks of paperwork across multiple desks and chairs, as well as scientific specimens.

Calvin rubbed his eyes and studied the screen for a moment. "Okay," he said at last.

"When I was doing research about his bible—as the *Vertebrata* was called—I came across this story about Cope doing dissections on snakes at the academy in Philadelphia he was a curator for, and bringing the organs to his home to study without permission. The executive officer of the board—Dixon—asked him to return the missing items, which Cope did by leaving them on his desk, soaked in alcohol solution, with a note."

"Hope you're satisfied," Calvin concluded.

"Right." I smiled. "I *knew* that phrase was familiar."

Calvin reached for the cup of coffee and took a sip of the undoctored beverage. "So this Cope guy…." He looked down at me again. "Did he steal a skull too?"

"Here's the good part," I declared. "The thing in my dream, about the skull? That's a true story. It sparked the Bone Wars."

Chapter Five

Calvin slowly sat down on the edge of the bed. "The Bone Wars?"

"A period of intense fossil-hunting in America. Hmm… 1870s to 1890s. I'll get you the specific dates," I said, putting the computer on my lap.

"It can hold," Calvin insisted. "It wasn't an actual war, though."

"No. I mean, not technically. Scientific rivalry between Cope and another paleontologist named Othniel Charles Marsh. They literally spent their entire professional careers and wealth trying to sabotage, embarrass, or one-up the other."

"Over dinosaurs," Calvin stated dryly before taking another sip of coffee.

"People kill for less."

His eyebrows went up, and he nodded while swallowing. "That is true. So do you think *this* is the war of intellect the notes are referring to?"

"It must be," I replied. "The quote is a direct reference to Cope. The whole rivalry thing spiraled out of control because Cope had reconstructed a skeleton and placed the head on the wrong end. Marsh called him out on it, and totally humiliated, Cope tried to collect all copies of his recent scientific publication with the error. His attempted cover-up was later found out."

"Sounds like a man with an exceptionally fragile ego," Calvin murmured.

I did another search of the internet and quickly found the story in question. "*Elasmosaurus*."

"What?"

I pushed my glasses up my nose and looked at Calvin. "That was the fossil."

"*Elasmosaurus* would be the skull that 'began the war'?"

"Certainly could be viewed that way."

"And what about the one that ended the war?"

I shrugged. "I'm not certain. But between the two men, they found something like a hundred specimens. That's a lot of potential skulls."

Calvin stood. He took another drink before setting his almost-empty cup beside the coffeepot. "Interesting."

"Yeah?"

He nodded, put a fist to his mouth, and suppressed a yawn. "It gives us an insight to the sort of knowledge and background of the Collector. It might open a few new avenues of inquiry."

"It doesn't explain the reason this person mailed human body parts and included anatomically correct drawings," I replied.

"No, it doesn't."

"Cope *was* an artist," I suggested. "I mean, nothing to the extent of those clinical drawings, but he drew reconstructed fossils."

"Hmm…." Calvin rubbed the back of his neck briefly and then gently took my computer from my lap. "Okay."

"Okay?" I echoed.

He put the laptop on the desk and closed the top. "Let's go back to bed."

"What? No. I'm really on to something with this." I reached out for the computer, but Calvin took my hand.

"I'm a little tired, Sebastian."

Calvin's admissions of perceived physical weaknesses were about as rare as my own confessions when it came to fear and uncertainty. There was always a significant weight behind his words. Because *a little tired* meant he was absolutely wrecked. It reminded me of last December during the Nevermore case, when I'd found him asleep on the landing of my stairs, waiting for me to come home. That was one of the first hints I had about how hard Calvin worked himself and how dangerous that pattern of behavior was for his health.

"All right," I said.

I stood and went back to the bed with Calvin. I set my glasses on the nightstand and turned off the light. He climbed in beside me, rolled close, and draped his big body over my own. I liked when he did that—found comfort in my arms. And his weight was sort of like my own anchoring to reality.

Every so often, I had to be brought back to Earth.

I WOKE up to Calvin leaning over me, turning off the alarm clock that was set to a quiet radio station. He sighed and dropped back down on top of me.

I grunted. "Big guy… I can't breathe."

Calvin smiled against my neck before sitting up a little. "Sorry. You're comfy."

"You mean squishy."

"I mean perfect." Calvin kissed the side of my head.

I turned and squinted at the LED numbers of the clock. "Is it really seven o'clock?"

"Yes."

"Dammit."

Calvin made a sound of agreement under his breath. He pushed the blankets back, swung his legs over the edge of the mattress, and got to his feet. He chuckled as Dillon all but flew off the bed, barked excitedly, and ran to the hotel door.

"I'll be right back," he told me, putting on yesterday's clothes and grabbing the dog leash.

"I'll be here," I answered, rolling onto my stomach.

When the door shut behind them, I lifted the pillow over my head to burrow underneath. I shut my eyes and dozed in and out of semiconsciousness a bit longer. The problem with being woken enough for me to form words was that there was typically little hope of falling asleep again. My brain was already problem-solving, asking questions, going over to-do lists….

I pushed up from the mattress and cocoon of moist, wet heat accumulating under the pillow. I got to my feet, stumbled to the bathroom, popped in my red-tinted contacts, and had started brushing my teeth when Calvin returned. I poked my head out of the room and squinted, watching his out-of-focus form pour kibble for Dillon and then strip naked. I moved from the doorway, bumping against the counter as I allowed Calvin to step inside. He pulled the shower curtain back, turned on the water, and got in.

I spit into the sink, rinsed my mouth, and asked, "Got room in there for a plus-one?"

"Sure," Calvin answered. He opened the curtain once more in invitation.

I shucked off my pajamas and climbed in behind him. I put my fingertips on Calvin's back and pressed against the rock-solid muscles. Flexing. Powerful. A warrior's body. In a previous lifetime, he could have been a muse to classic Greek sculptors.

"What're you thinking about?" Calvin asked over the water. He had his head in the stream, washing out shampoo.

"Greece."

I picked up the complimentary soap and washcloth and lathered it up. I put it on Calvin's chest as he turned and wiped water from his face. I got his chest hair nice and sudsy before moving on to his arms. *This* made my mind calm. Helped to slow everything in my head down. Allowed me to take a moment and smell the roses, so to speak. I'd nearly reached a state of absolute tranquility as I scrubbed, focusing on nothing more than the warm water and bubbles soaking freckle-splattered skin, when Calvin wrapped a hand around my throat. My breath caught when he squeezed lightly, and I looked up.

Calvin dragged his thumb across my lower lip. "Lather yourself," he said just loud enough to be heard over the spray.

I swallowed against his hand, then lowered the cloth from his body, reached down, and began to soap my dick. I hadn't been hard, hadn't even considered a morning romp, but the way Calvin's gaze followed my movements, the way his eyes narrowed as he appraised—*approved*—I might as well have woken up with this flagpole.

"Now me," he ordered, giving my neck another gentle squeeze.

I didn't respond. I wasn't meant to. I blindly reached for Calvin, never looking away from his face, using touch alone to determine when he was properly soaped up. I dropped the washcloth to the floor, where it landed with a wet *splat*.

Calvin closed what little space was left between us. He kept his hold on my throat and took our erections into his other hand. He tightened his grasp and gave us a quick, hard stroke. The angle wasn't quite right, had I been jacking myself off, but his hard cock wet and rubbing against mine more than made up for it. Calvin kissed my mouth. He seemed to savor every breath I gasped for when he applied pressure to my neck.

"Good," he murmured.

I reached up, putting my hands on his shoulders before moving them to his wet hair to give a tug.

Calvin kissed me again, tongue soft and warm and so fucking delicious. "You really are *perfect*," he said. He sounded breathless. He sounded in love.

Calvin was the Watson to my Sherlock.

The jelly to my peanut butter.

Knight to my prince.

Calvin had me tilt my head back with the lightest touch of his thumb on my jaw. He kissed and nipped my lips, chin, earlobe. "You gonna come, baby?"

I weakly nodded. "*Y-yes*."

He sped his hand up and squeezed my neck again while saying in my ear, "Say my name."

I looked at his face—the strong angles, sharp eyes, and constellations of freckles. That one second between us held suspended. As if time stopped. And despite knowing twelve months ago that I'd found my soul mate, this force felt like a sudden revelation. It took my breath away. I loved Calvin. More than I could ever say. And his name was sacred.

"*Calvin*," I whispered.

Something in his expression changed. Maybe it was hard to tell without my glasses on. Or maybe it was simply one of those emotions that was… undefinable. Because despite having over one hundred thousand words in the English language, none of them seemed to explain the reaction I'd witnessed from Calvin upon speaking his name.

He let go of my throat, leaned in, and kissed my mouth firmly.

My hips jerked into his strong touch once, twice—then I was shuddering and spending in his hand. I broke the kiss, wrapped my arms firmly around Calvin's neck, and clung for dear life as my knees threatened to send me crashing to the shower floor. He grunted and kept stroking our cocks. I squirmed and panted. It was too much. A physical overload bordering on painful. I groaned, but it came out as an embarrassing whimper, and I had to pull back from his touch as Calvin spurted cum onto his hand and my stomach.

He sagged a little under my grip, sighed, and gently let us go. He smoothed one hand up and down my back.

"I love you," I murmured.

"I love you too, Sebastian."

"WHAT DO you think triggered your dream?" Calvin asked. He sat on the edge of the unmade bed, tying his oxfords.

"A generous portion of cheesecake and beer," I answered while pulling a sweater on. "That seems like a good combination for a nightly disturbance."

"Ah." Calvin stood. He buttoned his cuffs before beginning to knot the tie around his neck. "Do you want to go to work today?"

I paused from trying to wrestle the sleeve of my button-down shirt, which was bunched up in my sweater. "Is this a trick question?"

"No."

"Then yes. Of course."

Calvin finished with his tie. He walked to the mirror on the far end of the room to check his appearance. "I got approval for your police protection last night. So long as you don't stray from the officer's side and promise to check in with me throughout the day—"

"How did you swing it?" I interrupted.

Calvin turned around. "Swing what? An escort?"

I nodded. "I didn't call yesterday morning because I figured your sergeant would have suspended you for getting tangled up with me again. Now he's approved diverting resources for *me*?"

"Things are different than they were ten months ago," Calvin answered as he walked toward me. "Hell. Even two months ago."

"Say it ain't so."

He put his hands on my shoulders. "Threats against a cop's fiancé are taken into… greater consideration than those against his nosy boyfriend. I know that's not fair."

"Such is life," I answered.

Calvin looked like he wanted to say something else, but the hotel phone rang. He went to the bedside table and picked up the receiver. "Hello? … Speaking. … Oh. Good. I'll be right down. Thank you." He hung up and patted my arm as he passed to go to the door. "Speaking of your protection…."

"I'll be here," I said for a second time that morning.

Calvin saluted over his shoulder before the door fell closed behind him.

"Thank God," I muttered before glancing at Dillon on the second bed. "Because we were going to have to have a come-to-Jesus moment if he thought I'd sit in this room all day twiddling my thumbs." I slipped my loafers on, dancing from foot to foot as I tugged the backs over my heels.

A cell phone rang. I patted my pockets and looked around the room before picking up mine from the desk. The screen was dark. Not me. I turned again and rushed to the nightstand for Calvin's phone. If it was Quinn, I was comfortable answering. Any other number I'd let go to voice….

Marc.

Hold up.

Marc, as in, *Marc Winter*?

My blood pressure rose with each ring. To my knowledge, Calvin's older brother had not phoned *once* since he'd come out to his family last Christmas. His father had called maybe two or three times, but it'd always been in regard to Calvin's uncle and nothing more. Never had any of his immediate family members attempted to make amends.

So what the hell was this about?

Had Uncle Nelson fallen ill again?

Maybe something had happened to Calvin's asshole, homophobic father?

And then, because I was a semidecent human being, I immediately felt guilty for giving life to such a thought. I swore and tapped Accept.

"Uh—Calvin Winter's phone." I winced.

Acute silence and hesitation echoed on the other end. Finally a voice asked, "Calvin…?"

"No. This is Sebastian Snow. His—er—" I froze up before blurting out *fiancé*. It wasn't my place. Marc might be my future brother-in-law, but this announcement needed to come from Calvin, in whatever method he felt was best for delivering it. "His guy," I eventually said. I smacked my forehead.

His guy?

Christ.

"His boyfriend," I corrected. Wow, did I sound like a complete dunce.

"Oh." More silence. "My name is Marc. I'm his… I'm Calvin's brother."

"Yeah. I mean, I know. Your name is in his address book."

"Is Calvin available?"

"No." Okay, maybe a touch hostile.

"When would be a better time for me to call?"

"Uh…." I ran a hand through my still-damp hair. "Can I ask what it's in regard to?"

"It's personal," Marc answered coolly.

"I see." I shoved my hand into my pocket. "It's not my intention to stir up drama by saying this, but now probably isn't a good time."

He let out a long breath over the line. "With all due respect, Mr. Snow, this is my brother's phone number. Not yours."

I took a play from both Calvin's and Neil's handbooks—count to ten.

Unfortunately I only made it to three.

"He's in the middle of a homicide investigation," I answered, more curtly.

Another pause from Marc. "All right," he said, drawing the response out. "Look… I'm calling because I'm in the city for business all week. And I would like to see Calvin."

My gut was saying no. Not no, but *hell no*. Don't let this familial pressure bog Calvin down during a case that's already got him stressed-out. But how did I relay that importance to Marc without simultaneously undermining the man I loved? For someone related by blood, I was fairly certain Marc knew little or nothing of how the atrocities of war left their mark on Calvin. And he definitely wasn't aware of the effort Calvin put into bettering his health, or how his family suddenly parachuting into his life would probably have an adverse effect.

I had my suspicions that, in the Winter household, Calvin was a decorated military officer to boast of. *Heroes didn't suffer. Heroes didn't have scars*. So in retrospect, it was of little surprise that Calvin refused to admit for so long that he had PTSD. He'd been conditioned to lie about his sexuality for forty years—what was a little extra emotional and mental trauma added to that?

God. It made me feel sick to imagine growing up in such a way. But it also made me all the more thankful that I could share my own dad with Calvin, give him the loving father figure he never had.

"Marc?"

"Yes?" he asked warily.

"Can we meet first? You and me? Calvin really is in the middle of a case. A high-profile one," I added, which was a lie, but whatever. "I'm on my way to work—my shop is in the East Village. Snow's Antique Emporium. Can you be there by nine?"

More silence.

I heard the distant ping of the elevator down the hall.

Fuck.

"Marc?" I asked insistently.

"I… suppose—"

I cut him off, quickly gave him the street address, and said goodbye before hanging up. I brought the phone closer and opened the recent calls list. I swiped and deleted the record of Marc's call at 7:42 a.m. before putting the phone back on the nightstand as the door opened.

I turned around and gave Calvin a smile, which I felt sort of slide off my face and hit the floor when a plainclothes Officer Rossi followed from behind, shutting the door as he entered.

"Oh" was all I got out.

Calvin gave me a look before saying, "Seb, this is Officer Nico Rossi. Rossi, I believe you already know Sebastian Snow."

Rossi nodded stiffly. "Yes, sir, I do."

"Rossi has been assigned as your protection," Calvin continued.

"Lucky me," I answered. I looked Rossi's way as Calvin collected his cell and put his jacket and scarf on. His posture indicated he was about as thrilled to be assigned babysitting duty as I was for him to *be* the babysitter.

"Text me when you reach the Emporium," Calvin said as he stood in front of me, buttoning his coat.

I quickly turned my gaze to him and nodded. "Text, yup. Will do."

"I'll give you a call around noon. And remember, anywhere you go, Rossi goes. Clear?"

"Crystal." I took the front of Calvin's coat, tugged him closer, and stood on my toes to kiss him.

Calvin smiled. "See you tonight." He kissed my temple before turning.

Rossi sort of startled to attention and gave a quick nod to Calvin. It was one of those knee-jerk reactions that suggested he wasn't uncomfortable—per se—but that he was at least uncertain if his response to two men kissing should be… different, I guess. Like he didn't realize our affection was exactly like any other couple and he could be as engaged or apathetic as he wanted to be.

"Regular intervals," Calvin said to Rossi.

"Yes, sir."

Once Calvin left the hotel room, I looked at Rossi while crossing my arms. "This will be fun."

CHAPTER SIX

I NEEDED food. And coffee. But I wasn't looking to share a meal in the downstairs lounge with Rossi, so I forwent a semidecent breakfast in favor of eating whatever snacks or leftovers were squirreled away at the Emporium.

We exited the hotel, took a right, and caught a cab at the corner of Ninth Avenue for the long trek downtown. I sat in the back with Dillon—Rossi opted for the front with the driver.

"Pleasure to see you again, Rossi," I finally said.

He didn't respond.

"Sorry it was you who got saddled with this." Sorry for him or for me—the jury was still out on that.

"I offered my services," he said in a clipped tone.

I raised an eyebrow, stared at his right shoulder and arm, and the sort of blurry reflection of his face in the side mirror. He was looking down—texting on his phone, I think. "Couldn't get enough of my charming personality, huh?"

He once again declined further comment.

Ah-ha. I got it.

"Detective Winter has some serious pull in the NYPD," I said casually. "Keeping his fiancé safe during this investigation would definitely put you on the right trajectory for a promotion to detective."

Rossi met my gaze in the mirror.

His silence was… loud. But when he ultimately didn't rise to the bait, I dropped the line of inquiry. It was stupid, bureaucratic bullshit anyway. If I had the patience for those kinds of games, I wouldn't have taken the chance at opening my own business. I did make note to myself that Calvin would need a heads-up about Rossi's personal motives. However, considering Quinn's choice of words yesterday regarding him, I figured Calvin already knew the angle being played. He was much better at reading people—dead or alive—than I was.

I shut my eyes and sagged back against the car seat. The drive took a while as we fought the morning rush. The taxi raked in waiting fees as we sat in gridlocked traffic until finally managing to get out of the hell that was Midtown. When the car came to a sudden halt that suggested it really needed to get its brakes checked, I cracked open one eye.

The woven metal gate was rolled down over my storefront, and the Snow's Antique Emporium lettering stood out against an otherwise dark window display. Good Books was already open for morning business. I shifted in my seat to pull my wallet from my back pocket.

"Here you are," I said, passing a bill through the window to the driver. "Keep the change." I opened the door, took Dillon's leash, and climbed out of the taxi.

Rossi shut the passenger door and turned to me as the car pulled onto the road. "May I speak freely to you, Mr. Snow?" Breath puffed around Rossi as if he were an angry dragon.

"Knock yourself out."

"I volunteered for this duty because when a psychopath attacks a cop or a cop's—"

I smiled.

"*Significant other*," he finally decided upon, "it's an attack on all of us."

"That's very noble of you," I answered.

"It has nothing to do with Detective Winter."

I made a sound that was more snort than laugh. "Either way, at least I know you've got a vested interest in my overall well-being." I opened my messenger bag, fished out my ring of keys, and walked to the gate. I unlocked it, crouched down, and hoisted the gate up and over my head.

"Mr. Snow?" a third voice broke in.

I turned to my right.

Rossi moved across the sidewalk and stood between me and some guy straight out of *Mad Men*. "I'm going to need you to step back, sir," he said, hand going to his coat.

The stranger had a perfectly parted and slicked haircut combined with round tortoiseshell glasses. He was clean-shaven. And based on his trousers and expensive-looking oxfords, he had a suit on underneath the winter jacket. Even though he looked as if he'd stepped off the set of a period film, I could see the family resemblance now. The shade of hair was the same gray as Calvin's. The height, the build, and while not quite as many—the freckles.

"Wait, hold on," I protested, reaching a hand out for Rossi. "Marc?"

Confused, wary, and on the verge of raising his hands up like he'd been told to freeze, Marc said, "*Yes*."

"It's okay," I told Rossi. "He's Calvin's brother."

Rossi lowered his hand from reaching for his concealed weapon.

"Is this how you always greet people?" Marc protested, looking at me but pointing at Rossi, as if he were hired muscle.

"Not typically," I answered.

Even if Rossi hadn't nearly drawn a gun on Marc, the man seemed wound especially tight. A palpable, edgy mood. It was a curious thing—how familiar his bulk was, and yet how incredibly foreign his characteristics were. Marc had none of Calvin's usual cool or calm. He didn't have that sort of relaxed stance Calvin would often assume when he was listening—the one that still conveyed he was the man in charge and to be respected. Marc's energy was much more… *in your face*.

It made me feel forced into a corner.

I'm sure Patrick Swayze would have had something to say about that.

"So," Marc continued, "you wanted to speak with me. Here I am."

I glared a little, turned to the Emporium, and unlocked the door. I leaned inside to tap the code on the security panel, then silently held the door for both men to enter. Rossi did so without question. Marc was hesitant but ultimately stepped past me and into the store.

I knew I could have been more polite. More thankful that he came to speak with me before Calvin… but I wasn't an ass-kisser. Not even—no. Correction. *Especially* not to Calvin's family. They'd abandoned him last Christmas. Left him alone after being shot, with no one to care about his life but me. And where had they been when I got wrecked by Pete White in May and Calvin *needed* an emotional crutch? Not here, that was for fucking sure. A real family makes themselves known in times of need. And my ex-boyfriend was willing to come by the hospital and make sure Calvin was resting and feeding himself as he stressed at my bedside, while Calvin's own flesh and blood had no idea. Because they hadn't cared to know.

So screw the niceties.

I pulled the door shut, removed Dillon's leash, and switched a few bank lamps on as I walked through the shop. I dropped my bag and winter attire onto the register counter, walked to the bathroom in the back, and called over my shoulder, "Excuse me for a second."

I closed the door, flipped the toilet lid down, and sat. I took a deep breath before leaning over and putting my hands in my hair. I hadn't actually considered what I was going to say to Marc. It'd been an instinctual thing—to protect Calvin. I had to be careful, especially if this was an honest attempt being made on Marc's behalf to reunite the family. But I also couldn't—*wouldn't*—be a pushover.

My brain felt like a library card catalog, and I was in a mad rush to find the *one* title that would help me navigate this sensitive situation with relative success.

Filed under social sciences. Should I start with 302.2—Social interaction, communication? 305.3—Groups of people, by gender or sex? Hold up, 306.7 has a footnote—*for problems and controversies concerning various sexual relations, see 363.4.*

"This is why no one likes you," I muttered while raising my head. "You're in the bathroom making Dewey Decimal jokes to yourself."

I removed my phone from my pocket and sent Calvin a text to let him know I'd arrived safely.

I felt a little queasy as I stood again, but it was nerves. I left the room and poked my head around the corner. Rossi was standing beside my closed office door, leaning against the wall. He texted on his phone with one hand and occasionally raised his head to watch Marc. Marc hadn't moved very far from the front door, but he was looking around the showroom floor with obvious curiosity. I tried to imagine seeing this place for the first time through his eyes. Cavernous, jam-packed with oddities from a previous century, hectically decorated for the holidays, and run by a sarcastic oddball fucking his brother.

The thought, while self-deprecating in delivery, was certainly true.

But then, in that same second, I realized: I didn't care.

I was exactly the guy he saw, and I wasn't trying to be anything more.

I was a weird, cynical, borderline-asshole shop owner, and the only damn person whose opinion mattered besides my father's was Calvin's.

Marc was not Calvin.

And it was that awareness that put confidence into my step. Maybe Calvin would be upset. Upset that I weaseled my way into a conversation he should have been having, but I had nothing to gain and Calvin had everything to lose. Sure, if Marc was cruel, the words would hurt me. I was human. But I didn't have a history with him for those words to tear me apart and make me bleed. They'd be superficial wounds.

Nothing I hadn't heard before.

I squared my shoulders and made my way through the maze of displays. "Sorry about outside," I said to Marc, stopping about two feet away from him. "Rossi is a cop. He's been assigned to protect me."

The tightness of Marc's mouth softened a little. "Oh… ah… I see."

I glanced at Rossi, who quickly looked at his phone again, and pretended he couldn't hear us. "So you want to see Calvin."

"Yes."

"Why now?"

"What do you mean?"

I shrugged. "Is it the convenience of being in the city?"

"No. I live in Philadelphia. I travel to New York for business quite often."

Wow. Wrong answer.

But Marc was still talking. "With the holidays approaching, it seemed like as good a time as any to at least reach out."

"So for the last twelve months," I began, "Calvin has been patently ignored by your entire family, with the exception of his ailing uncle, because your conscience hadn't acquired enough guilt yet? Amazing what 'tis-the-season does for some folks."

"It was not my intention—"

"I somehow doubt that."

Marc was being surprisingly composed, all things considered. He put his hands into his coat pockets and stared at me. "When Calvin was in the hospital last year, he said he had met an antique dealer while working a case."

"Uh-huh."

"A man."

"Oh yeah. An educated, successful businessman, who has never cheated on his taxes." I smiled sardonically. "What a delinquent."

"I never forgot your name when he told us," Marc finished.

"We like using an ampersand," I replied.

Marc took a deep breath, then slowly released it. "Calvin obviously felt you were worth giving up his family over."

"*No*," I said sternly, pointing an accusing finger at Marc. "Don't you dare. Say what you want about me. Whatever you've got, I guarantee I've heard worse. But don't you think for one moment I'm going to let you emotionally guilt or blackmail Calvin over one of the hardest decisions he's ever had to make for himself."

"What was that?"

"Allowing himself to be happy," I said. "*You* made a conscious decision when you walked out of his hospital room. And you've continued to consciously make a decision each day you haven't picked up a damn phone to call him."

I had to stop. I realized I'd been taking a step forward with every word I spoke, and had breached Marc's personal space. It was kind of startling to realize how much anger had been building up inside me toward a man I'd never met, never spoken to. I wasn't doing a hell of a lot to make myself likable either, but that didn't matter.

I didn't matter.

"Your brother is an incredible person," I said, voice low. "And I feel like… you have no clue."

"I'm here," Marc answered. "Aren't I? I want to fix this."

"Fix your relationship or fix *him*?"

The bell over the Emporium door chimed. "Good morning!" Beth Harrison of Good Books called cheerfully as she shuffled inside.

I looked at her. "Now's not a good time," I stated.

"There is nothing either good or bad, but thinking makes it so," Beth answered. She put her bejeweled glasses on with one hand, the other hugging two items to her chest. After giving the room a brief assessment, she asked, "Who died in here?"

"What?" Rossi asked, quickly coming to attention.

"*What*?" Beth echoed.

I held my hands up for everyone to stop. "Figure of speech, Rossi."

Beth narrowed her eyes and gave Marc a visible once-over. She turned to me, jutted a thumb at him, and said accusingly, "You never told me your gorgeous fiancé had an equally gorgeous sibling."

"Beth!" I shouted.

"*Fiancé*?" Marc protested.

Beth held her hand out to Marc as if she were royalty. "Beth Harrison."

"You and Calvin are engaged?" Marc sputtered.

"Oh my God," I groaned. I took my glasses off and covered my face with my hand.

Beth made a face. "Was it a secret? You're wearing a damn ring, Sebby."

"And he hadn't noticed. Thanks, Beth."

She huffed and walked toward me. "I brought you something."

"A tire iron?" I put my glasses back on.

Beth's brow furrowed. "Why would I bring you that?"

"So I can knock myself out?" I smiled sweetly.

"You're so dramatic." She plucked the book nestled between her chest and a manila envelope. "I picked this up yesterday at a yard sale in Queens."

I brought the cover close. *Miss Butterwith and the Dear Departed.*

"I know you already own it," she continued, tapping the cover. "But look inside."

I opened the book and on the title page was a scrawled name. I glanced up over the rim of my glasses. "Is this really Christopher Holmes's signature?"

"Feel better?" she asked, a smirk growing across her face.

"How much?"

"Bring my account up to date, and we'll call it even."

"Like hell. You owe me close to a grand."

"Mr. Snow," Marc interrupted.

I held a finger up, to which Marc made a sound of offended protest. I nodded my head at the envelope Beth still clutched. "Is that for me too?"

"Hmm? Oh, it's your mail."

"What?"

"It'd been stuck between the links of your gate this morning. I took it with me." She handed it over.

I quickly set my autographed cozy mystery aside and snatched the envelope. "No postage," I stated, studying both the front and back.

Beth was nodding. "This is a nice neighborhood, but we still live in New York City. I mean, hell! I once saw a man attempt to steal a refrigerator off a delivery truck."

I turned away and started for the counter, zigzagged around displays, and bolted up the steps. I set the envelope beside the register and crouched. I tossed boxes and bags aside, knocked over a roll of gift wrap and spools of ribbon, before standing with a letter opener.

"What's going on?" Rossi asked. He pocketed his cell and approached my right side.

"*Mr. Snow*!" Marc finally sounded pissed and as if he were ready to strangle… well, me.

I sliced across the top of the envelope and unceremoniously dumped the contents out. Half a dozen human teeth skittered across the countertop. The discoloration on them was sure to be blood.

"Son of a bitch," Rossi whispered.

A plain sheet of paper rested message-up. Spencerian script twisted my gut into a knot so tight, I had to gasp for air.

The Wars could have come to an end.

But he lost his head.

Party A now allots Party B forty-eight hours in which to retrieve the artifact (see message #1.) Failure to safely procure said article within the determined timetable will forfeit Party B's right to the collection of a most substantial sum—*Calvin Liam Winter—hereby known as Party C.*

Hope you're satisfied.

A Collector.

And underneath… the rendition of a human skull.

Chapter Seven

No.

No.

Absolutely fucking not.

My hands shook as I struggled to free my cell from my pocket. I chose Calvin's name from the list of recent contacts and put the phone to my ear.

It rang and rang and rang.

But no response.

That was normal, though. Because Calvin was working. And sometimes he couldn't answer.

This was New York City.

Crime happened.

People died.

And it was Calvin's job to investigate the situation.

That was all. Because anything else—anything more—would absolutely be too fucking absurd to even consider.

Rossi reached out for the note on the counter, but I lowered the phone and grabbed the letter opener with my other hand.

"Don't touch it," I threatened.

"Those are *human* teeth." He motioned at molars with his own phone. "I'm calling for backup."

I raised the letter opener like a dagger and held it out at Rossi. "Just be quiet and let me *think*!"

"I can arrest you right now," Rossi retaliated.

"Sebby," Beth called.

"Put that thing down before you hurt someone," Rossi continued.

"*Sebby*." More insistent.

I clenched the letter opener and phone so tight in both hands, I was surprised neither broke. I felt completely overwhelmed, like my system was about to combust from the onslaught of sensory stimulation. At once, my dim and cozy shop was too bright, the unrelenting voices were too loud, too harsh, and as I struggled to breathe, all I could think was that the incentive to solve this case had never been about money, extortion, or even allowing *me* to live—it'd been about Calvin.

Because I was not like most men.

I'd never gotten caught up in past mysteries for fame or fortune. My own safety hadn't even been a factor. To the dismay of the Collector, I'd dug my heels into the ground hard this time, refusing to budge and taking my retirement from sleuthing seriously. They'd prodded my ego in all the right ways, but my future with Calvin was more important than their mystery. *Finally*. But whoever this Collector was, they got smart. They dangled in front of me the only motivation in this entire goddamn world that would make me walk barefoot through fire.

Calvin.

"Everybody *shut up*!" I screamed as the seams that held my sanity together unraveled faster than I could stitch them closed.

A pin could have been heard falling a hundred yards away in the silence that followed. I dropped the letter opener to the floor and gripped the edge of the counter. My extremities felt cold and tingly—a dire warning of imminent dry heaves and a possible blackout. I fought to take a deep breath, but I could barely manage more than a gasp.

Was I having a panic attack?

A heart attack?

Stroke?

"I got a text from Calvin," Beth said quietly.

I raised my head. She was holding her phone up, waving it back and forth. From where she stood—all the way across the showroom—she had no idea what this note from the Collector said. Beth had no clue at all what was transpiring at that very moment.

I'd just tried calling Calvin. Why didn't he answer? Why did he text *Beth*?

Beth turned her phone around again, studied the text through her bifocals, and read aloud, "Don't involve the cops." She glanced at me. "The hell does that mean?"

I immediately called Calvin again. It rang three times and then stopped as if it'd been answered.

No one spoke.

"Calvin?"

No response.

"*Calvin*?" I choked. "Where are you? Please—who is this?"

All I heard was the faintest of breathing. Then I picked up the honk of a horn. A muffled voice. The static caused by wind hitting a microphone.

Outside.

"Forty-eight hours to find *what* skull? You've got to tell me that much," I tried. "Let me speak to Calvin. I need—*please*. Is he okay?"

Still… no reply.

"I can't stop the police from investigating," I begged. "He's a detective. They're going to pull all of their resources to find him." I gripped the phone. "You've *kidnapped*—Major Cases has jurisdiction, for Christ's sake! I'll play your game. I'll solve whatever mystery you want. But this is between us. *Right*?"

The Collector chuckled. It was a faraway sound. Detail-less.

"Let me talk to Calvin," I shouted, tears of rage rolling down my cheeks.

There was a loud *clank* through the connection, then a distorted *plop*.

Beep.

Beep.

Beep.

THE CITY was closing in on me as if I were stuck in a perpetual loop of the Vertigo Effect.

In the alley between Beth's shop and mine, crouched against the brick wall, I closed my eyes and lowered my head. The sickening motion continued.

I was usually good at keeping calm.

It took a lot of turmoil to really shake me, to break me down.

I had a nearly perfect outer armor, a remnant from growing up. Because when you're the weird kid, the awkward kid, the kid chosen last, or the kid sitting alone, you've got to protect yourself. That shell had been built out of intelligence and wit. History and words were my weapons.

If I couldn't beat them physically, I'd beat them mentally.

And it'd worked. For a long time. Too long, really. Because I was still doing it as an adult.

Study the evidence, follow the clues, put together the puzzle, and prove I'm smart.

I'm useful.

I'm *better* than what I look to be.

The difference between then and now was that Calvin knew when I was acting. It was still frightening to be seen naked and for what I was. Because the leftovers of childhood were still with me, in a bag I couldn't seem to release my grip on. Insecurities I didn't want Calvin to see through the lens of bullies long since past. Insecurities I didn't *ever* want him to feel or think about me.

But I'd had a complete meltdown in the Emporium. I hadn't felt that raw and utterly obliterated inside since summer, when I'd briefly broken the dam in front of Pop. What had happened—the screaming, the crying—I couldn't cope with an audience realizing that kind of terrifying intensity existed inside a grown man.

It was like standing onstage.

The house was full. Lights blazed down from the batten.

And I, the one-man show, had forgotten every word of my soliloquy.

"Sebastian?" The crunch of shoes on frozen ice and snow paused to my left.

I raised my head, took a deep breath, pushed my sunglasses up my nose, and glanced at the open alleyway.

Neil had entered. He continued forward, each step echoing through the enclosed space. He stopped beside me, tugged his trousers up a bit, and crouched against the wall in a similar fashion. He didn't say anything.

"He *laughed*," I whispered. My lower lip wouldn't stop quivering. "The Collector…." I shook my head, took my sunglasses off, and passed a hand over my face.

"I talked to Max," Neil said after a lengthy span of silence. "On a hunch."

"What hunch?" I whispered.

"The Collector texted Beth." Neil shifted and removed his own cell. "Max confirmed receiving the same message as her from Calvin." He offered his phone.

I put my glasses on, hesitated, and took it. "What?"

"Look," Neil murmured, nodding his chin at the device.

I brought the screen close and squinted.

Sender: Calvin Winter (Det.)

Back off.

I turned my head to Neil. "When did you get this?"

"9:11 a.m." He took the phone back. "Same as Max and Beth."

I knitted my brows together. "What does it mean?"

Neil tucked the phone into his pocket. "It means… this Collector is aware of *who* in Calvin's list of contacts is considered a personal relation to both of you." He stared at me once more. "Quinn got the same message as me."

"No," I said, shaking my head. "Calvin's address book is exhaustive. Beat cops, administrators, crime-scene crews, lab technicians, medical examiners—"

"I called your father," Neil said, stopping me.

"You what?"

Neil was grimacing. "William received the same text." He finished very quietly with "Like Max and Beth."

I quickly pushed to my feet.

Neil stood too. "Sebastian—"

"*No*," I said, louder for those in the goddamn back. "This is… it's *insane*, Neil. The possibility of some batshit crazy motherfucker out there who—who's kidnapped my fiancé off the streets of New York City as if he were some drifter, never to be missed."

Neil looked down at the ground.

"And now they've sent threats and warnings to the closest people in my life?" I jabbed Neil hard in the chest. "Threats that if I don't do this alone, if I seek police assistance like any rational citizen would, Calvin will… what? *Die*?"

"Seb."

"Do you understand *why* I might not want to accept this as gospel?" I said, poking him harder as hot tears blurred my vision once more.

Neil grabbed my wrist and held it firmly. "I'm sorry."

"I don't want your goddamn apology! I don't want sympathy. I—I want Calvin to answer his phone and tell me he's okay!" I felt hollow. Like my soul had shattered from the cold after the fire inside was snuffed out of existence.

Neil turned, looked at the alleyway entrance, and then sighed. I don't know what I was expecting from him. To tell me to buck up? Stop crying? Simply walk away from me? But he didn't do any of those.

Instead… he hugged me.

Neil put his arms around my shoulders and pulled me into a rough and stiff embrace against his chest. I'd hugged him a lot, once upon a time. But it was different now. Neil wasn't a lover. He was an awkward, closeted friend who simply wanted to make me feel better and didn't know how to go about managing that.

I gripped the back of his coat as I quietly lost it for the second time.

"Do you know why I hated Calvin for so long?" he murmured, putting a hand on the back of my head.

I snorted. "God. *This* is a conversation I want to have."

"It wasn't because I felt stolen from. I'd lost your affection months before the two of you ever met. I was careless. I know that now." He stroked my hair a few times. "It was because… he was never intimidated by you."

"What?" I muttered against his thoroughly snotty and tearstained jacket.

"You're the whole package, Sebastian. Romantic. Loyal. Brave. Calvin's met you every step of the way. And this time last year, he was… like me. But he saw the stars in you, and he reached." Neil pulled back. He put his cold hands on my face. "I never dared. I was—I still am—intimidated by you."

"I'm a fucking mess," I declared.

"You're always a mess. Whether it's not combing your hair for days on end, or…." He glanced down at the front of himself. "Covered in snot."

"*Thanks*," I muttered, wiping my nose with the sleeve of my coat.

"You're *smart*," Neil whispered. "Smarter than me. Smarter than Calvin. But he didn't let that hold him back. He knew how to embrace all the wild shit you've got up here." He tapped the side of my head before grabbing the collar of my coat and holding me tight. "Now it's my turn."

"The hell are you talking about?"

Neil reached one-handed into his coat and pulled out his badge. "See this?" He tossed it to the ground. "The Collector told me to back off. *No cops*. Fine. I'm not a cop."

"Have you lost your mind?" I protested.

"Sebastian. The NYPD has no clue what's going on. *Fuck*. There were guys reading CliffsNotes during the Nevermore case in order to keep up with you. We need *you* if we're going to even pretend to reach Calvin within forty-eight hours." Neil slowly released his grip on me. "No matter what, I'll have your back this time. I promise you that."

I… didn't know what to say. I didn't know what to do.

Neil's career had always been the most important part of his life. It was how he defined himself. How he found self-worth when I think he otherwise had a pretty shitty opinion of himself. And to see his badge tossed to the ground was particularly shocking.

"What're you doing, Neil?" I asked, voice very quiet.

He squared his shoulders. "I'm being the man I wish I was." In an even rarer move, Neil smiled—lopsided, a little boyish, but always handsome. He reached out and gave my chin one of those attaboy nudges with the knuckles of his fist.

The scrape of boots crunching on ice sounded from behind Neil. He bent and retrieved his badge as Quinn rounded the entrance and walked toward us.

She pointed a finger at me as she approached. "You're upset. I get it."

"I—"

"But I need you to count to ten or take a shot of gin or do whatever the hell it is that'll calm you down." Quinn paused and made a motion with her hand to indicate Neil and me. "Because you two are my brain trust now, and every second counts."

"What do you expect me to do?" I asked.

Quinn snapped her fingers. "Do the damn thing you always do."

"What *thing*?" I retorted.

"Tell us the origin of 'brain trust,'" Neil quickly suggested.

"Ah… the phrase was originally patterned after the term used to describe economic consolidation in the latter half of the 1800s. It was associated with politics by the turn of the century and is most famously connected to the Franklin D. Roosevelt administration."

"*Great*," Quinn stated dryly, putting her hands on her hips. "Now I need facts relevant to our current crisis."

Facts.

Focus on the facts.

Quinn was still talking. "Ms. Harrison has your dog. I sent Marc on his way. The ME is inside collecting the teeth. So let's hear it."

"Calvin left the hotel at 7:50 a.m."

"Are you certain?" Quinn asked.

"Yes." I nodded. "I left with Rossi a little after eight to come here."

"Did you see Calvin's car?"

Now that I thought about it, no. I hadn't seen Calvin's Ford Fusion parked anywhere on the hotel's block. "No, but I don't know how close he parked to the hotel after getting off work last night."

Quinn was already on her phone. "ATL on a navy blue Ford Fusion, last seen around Thirty-Seventh and Eighth—might still be parked in the neighborhood."

"You said the Collector laughed," Neil continued. "This person called you?"

Quinn turned her head away from us as she concentrated on the call. "Yes, that's correct. New York license. Plate number…."

"I phoned Calvin," I corrected Neil as Quinn rattled off more information regarding Calvin's car than I ever knew about myself. "The Collector never spoke." I watched Quinn end her call and finished, "You need to track Calvin's cell."

"That was the first step I took," she answered. "Hopefully this motherfucker hasn't turned it off, so we can get an accurate ping on his location."

"I think it might have been tossed," I said. "But I can tell you the Collector was outside when they answered my call."

"Outside doesn't narrow the scope," Quinn said sternly.

"All right, all right." I closed my eyes and hyperfocused. I tried to catalog all of the clues I could, which wasn't many, about that one-sided conversation, when all at once, a very simple thought occurred to me. "Calvin knows the Collector."

"Excuse me?" Quinn asked.

I opened my eyes. "Think about it. This wasn't some dark alley at two in the morning where he could have been jumped without a witness. Calvin's a big guy—with military training, no less. Who could coerce someone as wide as a doorframe, during morning rush hour in *Midtown*, without drawing an audience? The only logical conclusion is he knows the Collector. He'd trust this person, was probably even asked to get into a car with them."

"It makes sense," Neil murmured, turning his attention to Quinn.

"It implies someone in law enforcement," she hissed.

"So *what*?" I replied. "Dirty cops exist. Remember Brigg and Lowry? One tried to blow me up, and the other nearly had me swimming with the fishes."

"Calvin knows too many people," Quinn argued.

"We'd only need to consider those who also know Sebastian," Neil corrected.

"Just about all of New York City knows about the NYPD's tumor," she said.

"I'm benign, thank you," I retorted, crossing my arms.

"Max, Ms. Harrison next door, and Sebastian's father all got texts in regard to keeping the police out of this," Neil explained, ticking the names off his fingers.

Quinn's eyes darted from Neil to me. "Anyone else?"

"I don't *like* anyone else," I answered.

"Calvin *knows* a lot of people," Neil said. "And Sebastian is *known* by a lot of people, but because of these messages sent to non–law-enforcement individuals, we need to focus on who may be aware of the interpersonal relations shared by them both."

Quinn narrowed her gaze at me, waiting not so patiently for an explanation.

I shrugged. "We have a strict no-work-talk rule at home. *You* would have a better idea than me."

Quinn's phone rang then, and she had it to her ear before the jingle could come to a full stop. "Lancaster." She made a sudden about-face for the street. "The cell towers pinged the phone and got a triangulation!" she called over her shoulder. "Let's go!"

THE FINANCIAL District.

I slammed shut the passenger door of Quinn's car and raced after her on the sidewalk. Along with two police cruisers and vans from both the Crime Scene Unit and Department of Environmental Protection, we'd managed to completely block the thoroughfare of Nassau Street. Obnoxious honking came from behind us as drivers were forced to merge onto John Street, backing up traffic for several blocks. The area directly ahead was taped off to pedestrians, and more LEOs swarmed in by the minute.

It seemed word was officially out that one of their own was in trouble. If it hadn't been for the warnings to keep the police *out* of the search, I'd have felt a hell of a lot more hopeful.

A second call for Quinn had come in while she'd been driving us from the East Village to the coordinates provided—Calvin's car had been located. It was parked a block and a half from the hotel, with no indication that he'd ever reached it that morning.

"It makes no sense that Calvin would have been grabbed all the way down here," I called after Quinn. I nearly plowed into a woman exiting a sandwich shop, skidded sideways, and not so gracefully managed to avoid crashing into a sidewalk sign advertising the nail salon next door.

"He wasn't," Quinn agreed. She flashed her badge at an officer, lifted the crime-scene tape, and impatiently shouted for me to follow. When she finally came to a stop, it was beside the DEP truck.

The air crackled with the radios of uniformed officers, communicating in jargon that hardly made sense even if one *could* decipher the conversation amongst all the static. Two city workers in hard-hats were pulling out crowbar-looking tools from their truck. I shielded my eyes from the glare of the midmorning sun as I scanned the rest of the scene. Neil had driven behind us from the Emporium in his CSU van, but just then, he'd hopped out of the open back doors in a full bodysuit.

"What the—" I bit my tongue when the DEP guys hooked their tools to the grate of a catch basin beside the sidewalk and hoisted the heavy cast-iron frame up.

I leaned over for a look. The hole was about ten feet deep and at least half-full of dark, stagnant water. Runoff from the road no doubt included additives such as motor oil and human piss, dead leaves, cigarette butts, candy wrappers, soda bottles, and used condoms, to name a few of the more savory ingredients.

Neil approached me, tugging a hood down over his head.

I reached an arm out and slapped him square in the chest. "You're not seriously climbing into the witches' caldron, are you?"

"It's one of the more exciting aspects of working CSU," he answered before pulling a respiratory mask over his face.

"But wait," I protested. "*Why*? I know dropping a waterlogged phone into a bag of rice can work wonders, but you should consider Calvin's a lost cause."

"We need it as evidence, Sebastian," Quinn said firmly.

I made a face and glanced back at the hole. "Neil's fingers are going to fall off if he touches that toxic waste."

"Hence the sexy PPE," Neil said, voice muffled by the mask, before he stepped onto the street.

Quinn was watching Neil climb into the basin as she said, "Calvin's car never left Midtown, yet his phone was discarded in the Financial District. It gives us a few clues."

"Like what?" I asked.

I had to not think of Calvin as *Calvin*. Merely… a puzzle to solve. It was the only way I could do this—the only way I could investigate and get my sleuthing ass caught up in more mayhem without having another emotional episode cripple me. I focused on the moment. The details. The… *Christ*… rancid smell coming from the water as Neil's body distorted the contents and released odors.

"This close to the Brooklyn Bridge," Quinn started, making a motion over her shoulder without looking up, "leads me to suspect the Collector wants to get out of Manhattan. And if I were them, I most certainly wouldn't take the chance at having a kidnap victim in my vehicle when I pop out to make a few threatening text messages before ditching the phone." I felt her eyes on me for a brief moment. "Right?"

"Makes sense," I whispered before covering my nose and mouth with my sleeve. "All it takes is getting pulled over for a taillight out, and *bam*!—cops find an unconscious detective in the back seat or something."

"So what's that say?" she pressed.

"If the Collector is smart, they would have dropped Calvin off at a safe house—or maybe even—" I stopped. Saying his name was hard. I forced myself to swallow the lump building in my throat. "The same place the headless body might have ended up. Or maybe… where Frank Newell currently is."

Neil tossed a rat carcass up from the basin, the partially decomposed body landing on the asphalt with a *splat*.

"I will give the benefit of the doubt as to this individual's intelligence," I said, clearing my throat. "Because they've already killed two, possibly three people, and have taunted the police without being caught. I say they'd move *away* from their safe zone in order to ditch the phone."

"Between Calvin leaving the hotel and you speaking to the Collector on his phone, that gives us under an hour and twenty minutes to account for."

I perked up and turned to Quinn. "Take the traffic into consideration…."

"And we have a working search radius," she concluded.

"How's it smell down there, Crime Scene Guy?" One of the city workers laughed as he leaned over the basin and called down to Neil.

I didn't hear a response from the Third Circle of Hell, but based on the chuckles from the DEP gentlemen, I suspected Neil had flipped them off while standing up to his hips in refuse.

I took my phone from my pocket and turned the screen on. Half a dozen missed calls from Max. I ignored them and opened the maps application. This close to the East River, the streets were turned into wind tunnels and the temperature was noticeably lower than neighborhoods north of here. My fingertips were frozen, making for a few frustrating attempts as I zoomed in on streets. Pop-ups began appearing on the screen to warn of heavy traffic areas.

"If we allow the Collector… say, ten minutes for making a drop-off… that's still just over an hour to get as far as they can, then turn around and reach the Financial District. *Quinn*." I looked up. "That doesn't narrow the scope enough. Calvin could be in Dumbo *or* Brooklyn Heights. The Collector could have made it seem as if they wanted to leave the borough to give us a false trail. In which case, Calvin might actually be in *Tribeca*."

"Seb."

I calculated how much time had passed since I opened the package of human teeth, and typed it into a timer app. "We can't search that much ground in… forty-six hours and forty-two minutes."

Quinn looked at me. She grabbed the front of my coat, dragged me away from the commotion of the basin, and said in a hushed tone, "I need you *here* and *now*, Sebastian."

"I *am* here. But I—"

Her mouth formed a thin, grim line. "Calvin's my best friend." She put her hands on her hips and avoided my eyes, instead scanning the scene over my shoulder. "September twenty-eight—twenty-two days after I was promoted and we were assigned to work together—he saved my life. Drug dealers don't like being hauled in for questioning by cops. Imagine that." Quinn reluctantly returned her gaze to me. "I made a stupid mistake. Didn't clear behind the door. Next thing I knew, the barrel of a semiautomatic is resting on the back of my fucking head. Anyway… Calvin's a hero. To a lot of people. Including me."

I barely nodded.

"But this isn't the same situation. I can't save him with brute strength alone. The Collector contacted *you*. Let's not forget that." She reached up and flicked my forehead with her thumb and forefinger.

"Ouch."

"Keep your head on. We need it." She walked back to the side of the road.

I turned around. Neil was climbing out of the hole, the lower half of his jumpsuit covered and dripping in a foul-smelling, dark-colored slop. I walked to the edge of the sidewalk.

Neil lifted his mask up and over his head. He handed it off to a nearby officer and squelched toward us. He held what was once a working iPhone. "What color was Calvin's phone?"

"*Really*?" I asked.

Neil corrected himself and directed the question at Quinn.

"Red," she answered. "The limited-edition one that came out a few months ago."

Neil turned the phone, showing what I had to assume was a red backing. "The serial will confirm—but I'm happy to make an intuitive leap and say this is Calvin's."

"You really stink," I muttered.

"Yeah," Neil answered in a very matter-of-fact tone.

Tires squealed at the end of the block, and the three of us turned. An unmarked car with lights flashing had parked diagonally along the street. Two figures got out of the front, but I couldn't make out any details at this distance.

"Shit," Quinn swore. "My sergeant."

"Who's the other guy?" I asked.

"Rossi," she answered with a growl. Quinn moved around me to take a line of defense. "Sir—"

"I want him out of here, Lancaster," Sarge ordered, pointing at me as he joined the hubbub.

"But Mr. Snow is—" she started.

"The whole reason the best detective in my precinct is missing," he finished.

"*I* didn't kidnap him," I protested.

Quinn held up a hand as if to tell me *now is* so *not the time to open your damn mouth*. "Mr. Snow is an expert in his field, sir," she tried again. "His knowledge has helped our department crack several cases in the past."

"I know all about Mr. Snow," Sarge said. "I read the reports, remember? He's a smartass busybody. I never should have allowed you and Winter to take the call at his shop yesterday."

Rossi had slinked beside the sergeant by then, keeping one step outside the volatile circle. I had a sickening feeling that this little beat-cop, wannabe detective was the reason Quinn's boss, who I'd been told was a stern but good man, was having an intense, public blowup.

"That incident was directly related to John Doe at the museum," Quinn argued. "As well as the disappearance of Frank Newell. It's *our* case. We had to respond."

"And one misinterpretation of the evidence due to clouded judgment leaves us up one sleuth and down a decorated officer!" Sarge barked.

My fists were clenched so tight, the tips of my fingernails were digging holes into my flesh.

"All of the evidence pointed to a repeat of the Newell situation," Quinn said. "The body parts, followed by similar messages, indicated that Mr. Snow would go missing in forty-eight hours. We had no way of knowing until an hour ago that the perp's plan was to snatch Calvin!"

"Assigning police protection probably spooked our perp," Rossi spoke, directing an accusing finger at me. "He had to change his usual MO—hence grabbing Winter instead."

"*Our* perp?" Quinn repeated with a laugh that made my soul shake. "You aren't a damn detective, Rossi."

"*Lancaster*!" Sarge butted in.

"The Collector was forced to make amendments to their original plan because of me," I interjected. "But *not* because you were following me," I added, looking at Rossi. Before Sarge was able to take a breath, I continued. "They know me—at least a little. Enough to know they needn't bother offering money as a reward. I would have engaged for the history aspect and puzzle alone. The threat was merely incentive to do it… faster."

"Then why didn't you snoop?" Rossi retorted. "You've had no problem 'helping' the NYPD in the past." He actually used air quotes when he said that.

"I told you, I've retired," I stated. "I made a promise to Calvin, and I wasn't going to let the Collector push me. They must have realized that…."

"This isn't your case anymore," Sarge said to Quinn. "I don't give a damn about Spencerian script or dinosaur bones or angry paleontologists. Mr. Snow's expertise is no longer required."

"But sir—!" Quinn tried.

"You can't ignore those details!" I objected.

"Getting Winter back is the priority now," Sarge said over both of us. "The Chief of Detectives is already getting heat to involve the damn Feds."

"You can't let the FBI take over," I pleaded, desperation in my tone going unchecked. "The Collector warned for the police to back off. It *has* to be me!"

"And if the chief finds out I've let Winter's compromised and *civilian* fiancé run amok, it'll be my ass," he concluded. He jutted a thumb over his shoulder. "Get out."

THE HISTORY.

The clues.

The Collector gave me—gave Frank Newell—the tools necessary to figure out this puzzle. Each word written, each gruesome package mailed, were all deliberate hints in a word game that would bring Calvin back to me.

The Collector wanted me to *think*.

This person was different from all of the others. Not an obsessive, delusional stalker like Duncan Andrews. Definitely not a vigilante like Brigg. And they didn't seem to be a money-hungry thief like Pete White.

They were brutal. Methodical. Smarter. At least… they wanted me to view them as more intelligent. Better than all the rest. The pièce de résistance of my sleuthing career.

Declining official escort, I walked from the immediate vicinity and left the clusterfuck of traffic and police presence behind me. Anger toward the sergeant had gotten my blood pumping, and I was feeling particularly fiery. He was ignoring the most important facts of the case. I knew it was because he wanted to find his officer and felt he needed to look at a bigger picture, but *this*—I looked over my shoulder at the mess of vehicles, flashing lights, and law enforcement running this way and that—this wasn't how we'd find Calvin.

No one in the NYPD wanted a dead cop. No one wanted to give a press conference about how their golden goose detective was kidnapped and *murdered*.

I understood that.

But Quinn had been right. The Collector had contacted *me*. And now I needed to make that the Collector's first mistake.

Because maybe I wasn't an action hero like Calvin, but I *was* a know-it-all who ran headfirst into danger. I had an undeterrable curiosity and an inability to give up. That alone made me one serious pain in the ass. But couple that with having the love of my life torn from my grasp?

They'd taken up battle with the wrong color-blind sleuth.

I jumped over a puddle of slush at the end of the block and raced across the street as the crosswalk hand began flashing. I pulled Max up in my phone's contacts once I reached the other side.

He picked up on the first ring. "Boss! I called you like a hundred times!"

"Five," I corrected.

"What's going on?" he continued. "Neil called me a while ago—Calvin sent me some bizarre text—but when I asked Neil what it meant, he was a total jackass and wouldn't tell me anything."

"Max," I interrupted. "Listen to me. The Collector—ah, the person—"

"Oh, Jesus," he groaned. "He's got a serial-killer nickname now."

"*Listen*," I hissed before taking a deep breath. "Calvin's in trouble. *A lot* of trouble. The Collector took him, and I have less than forty-eight hours to save him."

I could hear Max's voice shaking as he said, "I d-don't understand."

"I think I was the original target," I explained. "But I wasn't budging."

"Calvin," Max whispered, piecing it together on his own.

"Right," I said, clipped. "Because now I'm fucking invested in the mystery."

"But what was that text message?"

"We're assuming the Collector sent those from Calvin's phone after he was taken. The phone was ditched. Neil pulled it out of a drain in the Financial District."

"Holy shit," Max said, voice still panicky. "This is some fucked-up Hollywood bullshit!"

"You saw the message. No cops. But try telling them that," I said in a mocking tone. "I have to find Calvin before the law-enforcement pressure makes the Collector act earlier than planned." I was breathing hard, pace short of an all-out sprint. "I need help," I pleaded. "I've been tossed curbside, even after Quinn fought her sergeant to keep me involved, and—"

"Let's get this guy," Max returned. "What do you need from me?"

The relief of those words hit me like a brick to the face. I slowed to a brisk walk and took a deep breath. "Calvin told me an assistant curator at the Museum of Natural History, Frank Newell, received a package of human remains last Wednesday," I explained. "That's where the case began. The same man was reported missing on Saturday by his girlfriend. As far as anyone can tell, he's simply vanished."

"Dead," Max muttered.

"I think so," I admitted. "But he wasn't our head. So something happened to an additional person between Wednesday and yesterday. I need to figure out what."

"Are you going to go to the museum?"

"Yeah. To try to get Frank's supervisor to talk to me. While I do that, can you try to get some information on his girlfriend?"

"How, pray tell?"

"The Face-stalking thing you do."

"Dude. I can try, but do you at least have her name?"

"No."

"Job?"

"No."

"Absolutely anything useful?"

"No."

"*Great*," he said.

"Text me what you find," I replied.

"Will do. I'll meet you in the city."

"Max?"

"Yeah?"

"Thanks," I murmured. "I mean it."

CHAPTER EIGHT

I SPARED the towering dinosaur fossils in the Theodore Roosevelt Rotunda a second look as I stood in line at the ticket counter in the Museum of Natural History. An epic reimagining of a herbivore defending against a sharp-toothed predator. They weren't real fossils, of course. The soaring display would have been too heavy. Plaster castings.

They seemed more important today.

"*Mommy.*" A young girl in line behind me was insistent on getting her mother's attention. "See! Look! That one's *Barosaurus*."

"Oh, I see it. The tall one?"

"Yes. And the carnivore is *Allosaurus*," the girl continued, speaking in a tone as if she were defending a dissertation.

I smiled a little, reminded of my own childhood and how I tried to teach Pop everything I ever read. He was always a sport about it, even if he'd already known that F. Scott Fitzgerald's father's first cousin once removed was hanged for conspiring to assassinate Abraham Lincoln.

"Next in line," a cashier called.

I moved quickly to the next teller. "Hi. I, uhm, have a bit of a strange request."

The man behind the computer raised his eyebrows. "Okay…."

"Your fossil halls," I began. "Specifically dinosaurs…."

"Yes, sir," the young guy said with a smile and sudden upbeat tone. "It includes six permanent exhibits of—"

I waved a hand. "No, I know about the halls. I mean, there's an assistant curator who works in the department. His name is Frank Newell."

He made a sort of exaggerated expression. "I wouldn't know that, I'm afraid."

"It wasn't a question," I answered. "I'm telling you that there is. I need to talk to his supervisor."

"Sir," Ticket Boy said, starting to get a bit snotty. "Our academic staff isn't available to answer questions from the general public. They're all very busy."

I frowned, noticed a name tag, and squinted a bit. "Chad." I stared at Chad. "Look. Frank Newell was reported missing four days ago. It's vital I speak to his boss."

Chad licked his lips, huffed, then squared his shoulders. "Are you a cop?"

"No."

"Then, *sir*… you need to either purchase an admission, or I'm going to have to ask you to leave." Chad was one head bob away from wagging his finger in my face.

I begrudgingly slid my credit card across the counter. "One adult."

THE HALL of Ornithischian Dinosaurs was pretty crowded. Not that I could complain. I mean… dinosaurs were pretty cool. I stood in front of a *Stegosaurus* display, hunched over with my magnifying glass to read the information plaque.

Scientists once thought Stegosaurus *had two brains because its head was so small….*

Poor Calvin. Of all dinosaurs to adore growing up, he'd chosen the one that paleontologists said simply *had* to have a second brain, because there was no way such an animal could have managed with one the size of a walnut.

I smiled a little as I straightened my stance. I didn't know what to do with the apparent dead end so soon into my sleuthing. I needed to talk to someone who knew Frank. Preferably someone who would also know a thing or two about whatever skull would have brought an end to the Bone Wars. But Chad wasn't sympathetic to my plight, and up here in the hall, the security guards overseeing the crowds either told me to fuck off in various levels of politeness, or feigned deafness in order not to have to deal with annoying visitors. Paid too little to give a shit, I figured.

A young woman walked past me then, an ID badge hanging from her sweater and a few binders tucked under one arm. She had a certain kind of bubbliness to her step, with a warm smile that suggested she was the sort who simply *loved* her job. An academic who hadn't yet lost the joy for research and had it replaced with bitter cynicism.

"Hey!" I rushed after her. "Ma'am?"

She paused midstep and turned to look up at me. "Yes?"

"Sorry to bother you," I began, doing my best to match a smile to her sunny disposition and not come across totally cranky and riddled with anxiety.

Her gaze faltered.

Not working. Okay, skip that. "Er—do you work here? I mean, in paleontology?"

"Oh! Yes, I do!" Her hand instinctively went to her badge, suggesting she was quite proud of herself. "Three weeks now. Is there something I can help you with?"

I tucked my magnifying glass into my front coat pocket. "Would that mean you know Frank Newell?"

Her eyes widened a little. "Dr. Newell?"

"Doctor, yes, sorry."

"Have you heard from him?" she asked, her voice dropping low and eyes darting around the hall.

I had to tilt my head to the side to catch her words, they were so quiet. "Not… exactly. I'm looking for his supervisor. I guess that would be the division's head curator?"

"Dr. Logan Thyne," she answered.

"Dr. Thyne," I repeated with a quick nod. "And is he around?"

She cautiously shrugged. "Maybe? I mean, he's always here…. He could be in a meeting or hosting an educational class or—"

I put my hands up to stop her. "I understand. He must be very busy. But I'm here because…." I hesitated to throw out too much information. I didn't know who any of the potential suspects were or what details Calvin shared with anyone prior to his disappearance, but she had made it very clear she was at least aware of him being MIA. "I'm concerned. Regarding his extended absence."

"Are you a friend of his?" she asked but with a sympathetic tone that hinted she was more than ready to believe me.

So I lied.

"Yes."

She pressed the binders to her chest, cast her eyes to the ground for a moment, then said, "Stay right here. Let me see what I can do."

I watched her hurry through the hall and vanish among the crowd at the entrance of the room. I began to sweat in my winter coat, and the weight of the messenger bag flung over one shoulder was giving me a weird ache on that side. I focused on those minor annoyances to distract myself from instead counting each wasted second via my heart slugging against my rib cage, threatening to burst right out of my chest.

The fear, adrenaline, excessive warmth, and lack of breakfast were really starting to make me light-headed. I glanced around for a place I might have been able to sit for a moment, when a strong, booming voice said, "A man waiting by the *Stegosaurus* wishes to speak with me. Who? Who's here to waste my time? *You*?"

A man in a dark suit, spectacles a bit too small for his face, and jowls at odds with his age—like he'd never smiled once in his life—stopped before me. My spunky young friend came to a halt behind him and took a deep breath, as if she'd been chasing him the entire way.

"Am I looking for you?" he asked me.

"Dr. Thyne?" I countered.

"Yes. I know who I am. Who are you?" he impatiently prodded.

I thrust my hand out quickly. "Sebastian Snow."

"Your name means nothing to me," he answered, not bothering to shake.

"Yours isn't all that impressive either, buddy," I shot back.

Thyne's eyes grew. He sniffed loudly and began to walk away.

"*Wait*! Hold on." I dodged a visitor and skidded in front to cut the good doctor off. "I'm sorry," I said, swallowing my pride. "Let me start again. My name is Sebastian Snow, and I'm looking into the disappearance of Dr. Newell. I believe he works for you?"

"Let me see your badge."

"Well… I'm not a cop."

"Then how are you investigating *anything*?"

I hesitated, but that split second of silence gave Thyne the opportunity to move around me and continue walking. "Sonofa—" I darted to the side and blocked him for a second time.

"I am not looking to have a dance with you. Move aside. I am a very busy man." Thyne looked over his shoulder. "Ms. Gould, I hope next time you'll fully consider the definition of *emergency*. Perhaps you need a copy of Merriam-Webster?"

"*Dr*. Gould," she timidly reminded him.

Thyne snorted. "We'll see."

Oh, good. A bully. I knew how to deal with those sorts. I snapped my fingers at Thyne. "Hey. Have you been interviewed by the NYPD?"

Thyne startled and looked at me. "Did you *snap* at me, Mr. Snow?"

"Was it Detective Winter?" I continued without pause. "Red hair and freckles?" I raised my hand up over my head. "About this tall?"

Thyne's expression, once an impassible wall, began to show cracks. "How do you know that?"

I quickly took my cell phone from my pocket. I opened the photos folder and chose a picture after a moment of consideration. I turned the screen toward Thyne. Gould craned her neck to look over his supervisor's shoulder at the image—a selfie of Calvin sitting comfortably across the length of the couch and me between his legs, leaning back against his chest. I'd caught Calvin midlaugh, so he was a bit blurry. I wasn't much of a photographer, even with a phone that'd cost a grand and boasted having a state-of-the-art camera. But still. Unadulterated joy on Calvin's face was a picture to be cherished.

"Here. This is Detective Winter, do you agree?"

"Yes," Thyne said, drawing the single word out.

"He's my fiancé and has been investigating the murder involving your coworker." I lowered the phone.

Thyne took a deep breath, straightened his posture, and slid his hands into his trouser pockets. He looked around us, watching the crowd move like the coming and going of ocean waves. "I fail to understand what I have to do with this."

"I need to ask you some questions. It'll take ten minutes."

"*Mr. Snow*—" he began, the frustration returning.

"My fiancé has disappeared," I said, voice catching, despite trying so hard to keep it together. "Like Frank. And I'm afraid something very bad might have happened to your colleague. Detective Winter is a good man. And I don't have much time."

Gould's mouth formed an O, and she put a hand to her chest.

The stiff line of Thyne's shoulders eased a little, and for one second, I thought the terrible lizard might have been warm-blooded after all. "If a police officer has gone missing—"

"He was kidnapped," I corrected.

"The NYPD must intervene immediately."

"They are."

"Then why are you getting in their way?" Thyne shot back.

I glared behind my sunglasses. "I told you why. He's my—"

"Fiancé, yes, I heard you," Thyne replied. "I do hope the detective comes home safely. But seeing as I have already told the police everything

I know about Dr. Newell, this is not a conversation I need to repeat. Especially with someone who *isn't* a cop."

"Dr. Thyne!" I tried.

"And might I also suggest that you allow the professionals to do their job. That's why we pay city taxes." Thyne sniffed again. "Good day." He began walking away, adding over his shoulder without sparing a glance, "I believe you have work to tend to, Ms. Gould?"

I looked at Gould, still standing in front of me without Thyne to block her, an expression of heartbreak on her face. "Thanks," I said coolly. "For trying. I hope I haven't gotten you into trouble."

"That detective," she began, scratching nervously at the skin below her collarbone, visible from the V-cut of her blouse. "He's really been kidnapped?"

I nodded, silently pocketing my phone.

"He was really nice," Gould murmured. "When he was here to help Dr. Newell." She smiled that cute sunshiny smile from earlier. "My colleagues seem to forget half the time that I have a PhD just like theirs.... That detective used my title, though."

"He's good like that."

"What's his first name?"

"Calvin."

She stepped closer and whispered, "Do you think Dr. Newell is... *dead*?"

"I don't... I don't know," I replied.

"But you don't think it's good." Not a question.

"No."

She pulled back the sleeve of her sweater and glanced at her wristwatch. Gould looked up at me again. "I don't know if I'll be of much help. Your detective spoke with Dr. Thyne and Dr. Newell in private. But I'll tell you what I know."

"Really?"

She nodded. "Meet me outside in about fifteen minutes by the food carts."

"I'LL HAVE a hot dog!" Gould said cheerily to the man operating one of the dozen carts strategically parked outside.

"Pretzel," I said, when he looked to me next.

I took out my wallet and dropped a five on the cart shelf. I knew my street food, and that covered both orders and left a small tip. I wasn't about to get robbed by a shady, dirty-water dog operator thinking I was a tourist. We took our food, thanked the vendor, and sat on the freezing-cold steps outside of the museum.

"Thanks for the early lunch," Gould said before taking a big bite.

"Sure. I'm all about cheap dates."

She chuckled and asked around the dog, "How long have you been engaged?"

"Two months." I broke off a piece of the hot pretzel and forced myself to eat. Despite my stomach growling and hangry tendencies beginning to show, it was hard to get the food down when my guts were in knots.

"How'd you meet?" Gould asked next.

I glanced sideways at her.

"I'm a romantic," she said with a serious expression.

"We met during a homicide investigation."

Her eyes grew. "Oh! Different strokes for different folks. Isn't that the saying?"

Sure. I guessed. I supposed it was better than saying I took out a personal ad to find the love of my life.

M4M.

Turn-on: Victorian America, cake, mystery, handcuffs, men w/ badges.

Turn-off: Decaf coffee, PPE, being arrested.

"So what can you tell me about Frank?" I asked, redirecting the conversation to the matter at hand.

Gould nodded, munched another bite of hot dog, and said, "Assistant curator. He is—er, *was*?—a nice guy. Really smart. Passionate."

"And last Wednesday morning, he received a package with human remains?"

"Toes," Gould confirmed with a shudder. "I deal with bones all day that are millions of years old. Not fresh, still all squishy and bloody."

"And then he got a second one. With an ear inside."

She shot me a quick look, and a passing gust of wind blew the ends of her light-colored hair into the ketchup-and-mustard-splattered hot dog. "He did?"

Oops.

I cleared my throat. "Uh… did Frank ever say who he thought might have sent those packages? Or… who… was *in* them?"

Gould shook her head. "God, no. He didn't say anything to me, at least. It definitely spooked him, though."

"Did Frank have any enemies?"

"No. I mean, I can't imagine he would. He was a really sweet guy. Dr. Thyne squabbled with him a lot, but you met him. He can be a… difficult personality."

"That's diplomatic."

Gould took another bite.

"Were their arguments ever severe?"

"I'm still new. Dr. Newell and Dr. Thyne have been here for a decade at least." Gould finished her hot dog and crumpled the wrapper in her hands. "But Dr. Newell had been working on details for a visiting exhibit. His pet project. Dr. Thyne wasn't impressed with all of the artifacts. They'd been… *discussing* it since the day I was hired."

Discussing. Sure. We'd go with that.

"Did you know Frank's girlfriend?" I continued. "She reported him missing."

"For a few days."

"What do you mean?"

"She used to work here," Gould said, like I should have known that. She leaned close and murmured, "She was let go."

"Really."

Gould nodded. "Angela London."

"Why did she leave the museum?"

"Everything I've heard is hearsay."

"I won't say anything," I promised.

"Well…." Gould was frowning. She shivered a little and admitted, "She might have been stealing."

"Money?"

"Artifacts."

"Stellar," I grumbled.

"You know," she started, "now that I think about it, Dr. Newell might have had an enemy."

"Who?"

"Angela."

"Did he… catch her stealing?" I asked, confused.

"No, no. Again, this is hearsay," she declared. "My second week here, *after* Angela was booted, I heard from down the grapevine that Dr.

Newell had been caught—by Dr. Thyne, no less—fooling around with his intern. If *I* heard about it, Angela *must* have."

Sex, backstabbing, and the pursuit of scientific and artistic truth. Gotta love the academics.

"Can I have her name? The intern?" I asked.

Gould bit her lower lip. "Him. Dr. Newell's intern is a him."

"I see."

"Daniel Howard. He's a student at CUNY."

"And how is he? As an intern, I mean," I said, quickly rewording the question.

"He's a good kid," she said politely.

I looked at my pretzel, tugged another chunk free, and took a bite. "But?" I prompted.

"But… he came as a recommendation by Dr. Hart, a very well-respected field paleontologist. I figured Dr. Newell owed him a favor by taking Daniel when CUNY has more… erm… overachieving students. But he's nice!" she insisted again. "Maybe kind of gaga over Dr. Newell, now that I think about it. I'm of the opinion that an academic should date outside their field. Less controversy."

I kind of understood that, actually.

"Is Daniel working today? I'd like to talk to him if that's possible," I said.

Gould shook her head. "He's got a sporadic work schedule. Dr. Newell was in charge of his attendance. I haven't seen Daniel for a few days, but I think winter break is starting, so maybe he's gone home."

"Where's home?"

"Michigan, I think."

Fuck. That would be extremely problematic, because something smelled off about this internal drama at the museum. With a head curator probably being the individual who fired the assistant curator's criminal girlfriend, then catching said assistant sleeping with a student, there was definitely strife, maybe even motive, to do something potentially fatal to Frank Newell. And considering someone mailed him toes and an ear, only to come to learn his intern hasn't been seen lately?

This didn't sound like it'd be a happy ending.

For Frank *or* Daniel.

The fact that I had zero association or knowledge of either individual prior to today confirmed for me that it was most definitely my reputation that caused the Collector to come rapping on my chamber door. The museum staff had struck out at solving this skull mystery, so the Collector decided upon a different approach. No ifs, ands, or buts about it.

"Thanks for all of this information, Dr. Gould," I said politely as I got to my feet. "It's been… enlightening."

"I hope your fiancé is found."

I swallowed and nodded. "Me too." I started down the steps and then stopped suddenly. "You said the curators had been arguing about an upcoming exhibit?"

Gould paused midmotion in standing. "That's right."

"What's the exhibit?"

She straightened and drew her hair from her face. "It's about the Bone Wars."

"Th-the Bone Wars?"

"Have you heard of it?"

"Marsh and Cope."

"Correct." She smiled with a nod of approval. "Dr. Newell has a fascinating lineup of fossils ready to be loaned to us—many that Marsh and Cope either discovered themselves or were responsible for naming during the height of their intense activity."

"Why is Dr. Thyne against such an exhibit? It's historically relevant to paleontology."

"He feels Dr. Newell is—*was*—focusing too much on the men instead of the dinosaurs."

"Huh."

"But then there was the whole fiasco with the skull. And now that Dr. Newell… well… who knows if this exhibit will ever come to fruition."

There it was.

"Hold on," I said. My heart pounded hard. "What skull?"

"Edward Cope's," Gould stated. "It's gone missing."

CHAPTER NINE

I SAT in a Starbucks about three blocks away from the museum, reluctantly taking up residence in the window seat—back to the simultaneously warm sun gleaming through and the cold air leeching in. I tugged my scarf off and unbuttoned my coat before removing the wedding planner notebook from my shoulder bag. I dropped it on the table and started fishing for a pen.

"Specify the north or south end of the block next time."

I glanced up as Max draped his coat over the back of the second chair. "Are there two Starbucks on this block?"

"As well as a Dunkin' Donuts and three Duane Reades," he teased. He set his hands on the chair back. "Are you okay?" he asked, voice gentle.

I returned to digging through my black hole for the one thing I wanted and couldn't find. "Nope."

"Want a coffee?" Max offered at length.

I finally retrieved the pen, set it on the notebook, and put the bag down by my feet. I slouched my shoulders, staring up at Max.

"What?"

I shook my head. "Nothing."

Max hesitated. "Boss—"

I waved my hand at the counter. "Go. Go, go."

Once Max had turned to fetch a beverage, I opened the notebook. I flipped through the pages and laughed dryly. Two days ago, this fucking wedding had been my only source of pain and displeasure. Two days ago, I had called a few florists for estimates on roses—prices and availability apparently varied by color and species. That had irritated the hell out of me. Not one aspect of the wedding seemed easy to plan.

And Sunday night in bed, Calvin had sleepily reminded me I didn't even *like* roses.

"Why not use carnations, baby?"

I was a smart man. But I lacked common sense. I knew this about myself. I was so preoccupied with the social commentary behind early and morbid Victorian Christmas cards, or the stories of arsenic-laced candies, that I forgot to shave or comb my hair or overlooked that I loved carnations, so *why* wouldn't I use my favorite flower at our wedding instead of one that was cliché and overpriced?

It was sometimes shocking I'd managed to make it to thirty-four.

I flipped to a blank page, took a breath, mentally reminded myself *in and out*, then started writing down everything I knew so far.

Frank had been curating, from what it sounded like, a very impressive exhibit about the history of the Bone Wars and its two leading men: Marsh and Cope. Thyne hadn't been impressed. Gould described him as being upset the focus was on humans, instead of the creatures they had unearthed.

The aggressive hostility Thyne had toward the exhibit didn't paint him in a pretty light.

Angela had recently been fired—possibly for stealing, although I suspected if that were gospel, she'd be in prison. But still. Couple that with the addition of her boyfriend cheating on her with an intern, and that made her one salty individual.

Motive could be professional and personal.

Which brought me to Daniel, the unextraordinary intern. Accepted to work a semester at one of the most prestigious museums in the country, most likely as a favor owed to the renowned Dr. Hart—a modern-day dinosaur hunter who sounded as if he would more often be found in the hills of sedimentary rock than behind a desk. Daniel hadn't been seen or heard from in days, yet no one seemed terribly concerned.

Just a college kid. Probably on vacation.

And then there was the *skull*.

The skull of Edward Drinker Cope himself.

Apparently Frank had wanted to highlight this particular item in his visiting exhibit, which had pissed Thyne off to no end. But Gould hadn't been able to provide me with further details and returned to the museum before Thyne had an opportunity to notice her absence.

This had to be the skull the Collector was alluding to. With the handwritten messages to both me and Frank implying the Bone Wars, and then adding that famous Cope quote, it was a conclusion I felt pretty comfortable making. Although why Cope's skull was, in fact, a museum piece at all, and not attached to the rest of his body, seemed an overlooked detail that needed to be addressed. That, and why did the Collector want the skull in the first place? What about a century-old cranium and mandible was important enough to murder innocent people over?

Was it nothing more than a morbid fascination?

The Collector had already proven to have an affinity for *fresh* body parts…. God… I'd bet antiquated ones totally got their rocks off.

A ripple of discomfort went up my spine and made the hair on my neck stand on end. I tossed the notebook back onto the table as Max returned with two cups.

He sat down and offered one. "House brew," he clarified.

"Thanks."

Max took a sip of his own coffee. "So I found Frank Newell on Twitter. It's not a very active account. Once a month retweet kind of thing, mostly museum stuff. Anyway. His girlfriend is—"

"Angela London."

"Why am I digging into people's social media dirt if you already knew the answer?"

I made a vague motion with one hand. "I found out by chance. One of his coworkers mentioned her."

"Did they mention she's about as toxic as they come?"

"Is she?"

"*Oh yeah*. From what I gathered of her totally unhinged ranting on Twitter, she's recently been fired, has no money, hates Frank—"

"Frank's been sleeping with an intern," I interjected.

"Well, thirty seconds after tweeting about how much she despises him, she follows it up with how much she loves Frank," Max continued. "Really unhealthy personality. She seems like the internet troll who would take it a step too far. Like doxx or stalk kind of too far. I had to scrub myself after going through her timeline." Max inclined his head at my notebook. "What did you find out?"

"Enough to not have an answer."

Max grunted and sipped his coffee.

"Frank had enemies. His girlfriend for sure. And his boss was really against an exhibit he was planning about the Bone Wars."

"The Bone Wars? Did Frank work in the paleontology department?"

"Remind me to double your Christmas bonus."

Max smirked. "Hey, man. Who didn't love dinosaurs growing up?" He leaned forward across the too-small table. "So two people don't like Frank."

"At least."

"But enough to want to kill him?" Max asked before lowering his voice when a woman to my left glanced our way. "This… *Collector* threatens, taunts, then murders people, right?"

I nodded. "I believe the antique I'm supposed to deliver in exchange for Calvin is the skull of Edward Drinker Cope."

"Wait, *what*?"

I explained to Max what the highlighted artifact of Frank's visiting exhibit was supposed to be. I told him about the two other messages I'd received, as well as what I'd pieced together at the hotel when Calvin was still…. *No*. That way madness lay.

"The head curator must be the Collector," Max said with grim satisfaction. "Trying to stop the exhibit from happening because he wants the skull for himself."

"But it's been lost," I answered.

"It still adds up."

"Maybe. But Angela was fired for trying to steal from the museum."

Max drummed his fingertips on the table, sipped more caffeine, then said, "Maybe they're working it together."

"I can't imagine Calvin would willingly get into the car of a stranger or potential suspect," I said, thinking out loud. "I'm under the assumption the Collector is someone who knows him *and* me on some level. It's the only explanation to those text messages."

"Set that thought aside for one minute," Max said. "If this were a team effort, it'd certainly be easier to overpower Calvin."

I frowned at his words. Felt myself deflate a little in the chair.

"I didn't mean… *fuck*." Max seemed to struggle with how to correct himself. "This is difficult to discuss, because it's not a nobody."

"It's Calvin," I said solemnly. I took another one of those deep, soul-cleansing breaths. "You might be onto something. I can't rule out a joint effort yet. There are too many coincidences."

"I bet Calvin thought so too," Max said as he leaned back in his chair.

"He *did* think so."

"Really?"

"Yesterday, after we'd both been sent home, he called to check in with me. He was on his way to the museum for some follow-up interviews. He must have smelled dirt in the department."

"Here's what I don't get, then," Max said. "Why bother coming after *you*? If this is about Calvin."

"Calvin wasn't the target—not in the beginning. We think, after who knows how many failed attempts at procuring the skull through others, the Collector took a different route and went to me because I'm… uh…."

"Well-known," Max supplied tactfully.

"That's it. And when I wouldn't budge, Calvin became incentive. Maybe doubly so, when he started asking more questions. The Collector was able to force my hand and get rid of a nosy cop at the same time."

Max leaned forward once more. "If they were able to get Calvin out of the way… why bother keeping him alive for forty-eight hours?"

The few sips of coffee I'd taken began to bubble and churn acid in my stomach. I said severely, "Because they need me agreeable."

"I HAVE to talk to Angela," I stated.

Max had been performing another social media search on his phone when he raised his head. "Calvin isn't here, so allow me to be your common sense." He kicked me hard under the table.

"Ow! What the hell?" I reached down and rubbed my shin.

"Dude. She might be the killer," he whispered loudly.

I was still massaging my leg. "Did you find the intern anywhere?"

Max reluctantly shook his head before pocketing his cell. "Nothing on Twitter or Facebook that matches the Daniel Howard in question."

"Don't you think that's weird?" I asked. "For someone his age to not have online hangouts?"

"You're not online."

"I'm not a college kid."

Max shrugged. "Maybe he values his privacy."

"Then all the more reason I need to talk to Angela. I've got to find that intern. He hasn't reported to work in days. Think about it. We still have two unidentified bodies—one mailed to Frank and one to me."

Realization softened Max's features. "He might be one of the bodies."

"Right. And I can't be certain if anyone on the museum staff bothered to mention Daniel Howard to Calvin during his interviews."

Truth be told, I was actually a bit scared to meet Angela. From the way Max had described her, I wouldn't be surprised to find out she wasn't playing with a full deck. And even if she wasn't the Collector, that perverse personality still made her dangerous. Anyone willing to steal from a museum had to have unsavory contacts and at least a general understanding of what an item on the black market was worth. Edward Drinker Cope's skull could be worth thousands. Hundreds of thousands. After being involved in three Victorian-themed murder mysteries, nothing surprised me anymore.

Angela had been fired before Daniel vanished on his maybe-college-break and the murders began, that much Dr. Gould had established for me. But I was still uncertain about the possibility of Angela and Thyne working together to obtain the skull. I could hypothesize certain events, but I would need more details to confirm or deny their potential and unsavory business relationship if I was going to make any of the shit I was flinging stick to the target.

Angela *could* have killed Daniel. This whole Collector business might have started as nothing more than a crime of passion. And in order to cover the death up—because she'd have been suspect numero uno otherwise—she fabricated this elaborate... *murder machine.* A bit outrageous, but she could have simultaneously exacted revenge on Frank while getting her hands on serious cash.

I took my sunglasses off and rubbed my eyes. "I don't know why Cope's skull is being punted around museums."

"I hate it when you don't know something."

I snorted. "So do I." I put my shades on again. "It's extremely disorienting."

"It wouldn't have anything to do with mourning rituals?"

"Displaying a skull?" I asked doubtfully.

"They used to display the entire body in parlors."

"Yes, but keepsakes of loved ones after burial were usually something small. A bit of hair preserved in a locket, or a ring made from a glass eye."

"Gross."

"Not by Victorian standards," I chastised. "They had a much more intimate relationship with death than we do today."

Max shrugged. He took out his phone again. "Well, I don't know about the skull, but if you insist on talking to Angela, we have to set some ground rules."

"Ground rules?" I repeated, raising an eyebrow.

He nodded, still studying the screen. "Yeah. Like meet somewhere well-lit and public, for one. Two, don't tell her you suspect she might have offed someone."

"You think so little of me?"

Max glanced up briefly. "You don't have a good track record."

"I feel personally attacked."

He snorted and went back to whatever he was doing. "How are you going to ask her questions without it being suspicious?"

"I'm going to tell her I'm researching the whereabouts of the Cope skull." I snatched my notebook and put it away. "If she's the Collector, she'll know that's the truth but won't realize she's a suspect. If she's innocent, she'll know I'm contacting her because of her recent position in the paleontology division." I grabbed my scarf, paused, and stared at the far wall of the coffee shop. "Except I have no idea how to reach her," I said a bit absently.

"I was hoping you'd realize that before you walked out," Max said with a quiet laugh. "Luckily you have me." He turned his phone around.

I leaned across the table and squinted to read the tiny text. "What am I looking at?"

"Her public Facebook account."

I took his phone. "This is her phone number?"

"Yeah."

"You can do that?"

"Hm-hm."

"For God's sake *why*?"

Max smirked. "I love you, you cantankerous old man."

ANGELA LONDON had been suitably suspicious of me on the phone, which suggested she was not *completely* nuts. She agreed to meet me at Spirits, a bar on St. Marks.

At 2:45 p.m.

On a Tuesday.

During the daylight hours, the cultural hub, famous for its accumulation of individuals on the fringes of society, looked almost lackluster. Several of the storefronts were shuttered until evening hours, while the others that stood open were intended for tourism appeal—shit like sunglasses, funky winter hats, and glass pipes that'd make suburban moms gasp. Once it was dark, the street really came to life.

My taxi drove off, leaving me standing curbside between two massive trees. To the left was a shuttered body-piercing salon and a Japanese restaurant. On the right was some kind of alternative clothing store and a comic shop. Nestled smack between them—Spirits. I crossed the sidewalk and took the steps down into the underground establishment.

Spirits was dim, enough that I was able to change into regular glasses and be comfortable. I shoved my sunglasses into my messenger bag and took a look around. It was very cramped inside—almost no space widthwise, making it impossible to fit more than half a dozen very small standing tables to the right of me. The bar was, at least, quite long, going back the entire length of the room. The walls were painted a dark color, and window décor purposefully blocked out the daylight.

I recognized the musician playing on the overhead speakers—not because I was a fan of Marilyn Manson, but because I'd dated Neil for four years. Despite his uptight, stuffy demeanor, he was a serious hard rock and metal fan. One can imagine that music had been a point of contention in our household. I thought idly, while walking toward the bar, that Manson seemed too mainstream for a place like this, but maybe it was suitable during the slow daytime hours.

A woman sat alone at the bar. She tilted her head and took a shot before wincing and slamming the glass down. She wiped her lips on the back of her hand before noticing me standing several feet away. "The fuck you lookin' at?"

Charming.

"Angela London?"

She started laughing and grabbed for her second shot. "Sebastian?"

"That's right."

She shook her head, muttered, "Fuckin' nerd," then tossed back the next drink.

I took a seat and left an empty stool between us.

The bartender moved to stand in front of me. He was clean-shaven, both face and head, with those big gauged ears like my friend Aubrey Grant had. "Can I get you anything?"

"A club soda." I shifted and looked at Angela. She definitely didn't fit the dark, morbid aesthetic of the bar any more than I did and, until quite recently, had held down a job at a science museum. I wasn't sure why she was judging *my* dress pants and loafers. "Thanks for meeting with me."

"You're researching Edward Cope, huh?"

I nodded. "I own an antique business."

Angela pursed her lips and nodded. "*Wow*." She leaned over the empty barstool and put a hand on my thigh. "That's *so* interesting."

I cleared my throat loudly. "Yeah, I guess so. Cope surfaced during some research I've been conducting on a project."

She kept drunk-nodding her head. "Uh-huh." Angela pushed her hand up higher and very nearly learned I dressed to the right.

I took her wrist, firmly removed her hand, and put it on the bar top. "I'm not interested, Ms. London."

Angela narrowed her eyes and gave me another slow once-over. "Fuckin' queer."

The bartender came back with a club soda and another shot. Before Angela could grab her drink, I quickly took both and reversed their positions.

"Hey—" she protested.

"Why don't you pace yourself. So we can talk."

"Is talking all we're gonna do?"

"Yes."

She rolled her eyes and drunkenly sipped the club soda before sticking her tongue out in disgust. She was pretty trashed, so it was difficult to tell if she knew what I looked like—who to expect when the door had opened—or if my physical appearance was a surprise. There *was* the possibility that even if she were the Collector, she hadn't necessarily ever seen me in person. Reputation and all that. Folks remember my name, not my face. It was also tricky trying to determine if she was aware that I was gay, or if she was simply so sloshed that her knee-jerk reaction to any perceived letdown was to hurl homosexual insults.

Either way. I didn't like her.

"About Edward Cope," I tried once more. "My studies led me to your boyfriend—Dr. Newell? It seems like he's been organizing—"

"My boyfriend," Angela said slowly and methodically, but his name dripped from her tongue like snake venom, "was a sack of shit."

Was.

"Really?" I asked. "Why?"

"Have you ever been cheated on?"

I nodded. "Yeah." I was no saint, but my college boyfriend, Brian, had been a real ass.

Angela pouted and touched my chest. She tried to wriggle her fingers in between the buttons of my winter coat. "You poor thing."

I politely pushed her hand away again. "I'm quite okay, Ms. London."

"Well, I'm not," she clarified before slurping the club soda again. "Frank slept with his intern. *It's so cliché*!" And without warning, she burst into loud, drunken sobs.

Startled, I grabbed a wad of napkins from a nearby dispenser and offered them.

She took the cheap, thin paper and wiped her face. "His *male* intern," she added before looking at me. Her eye makeup wasn't waterproof. "But I'd guess you know what that's like."

"I don't sleep with male interns."

Angela snorted. She scrubbed her cheeks and tossed the napkins to the floor without second thought. "I should have known. They got along so well, after all."

"When you worked at the Museum of Natural History?"

"How'd you know that?"

"Er—I mean, a lot of names and titles and big dinosaur words got hurled at me while I was looking up details on Cope," I said, stumbling to recover.

I'm not sure she bought my attempt at feigning stupidity.

Angela reached over my arm on the counter, picked up her shot, and finished it in a single gulp. "Sure, I worked there," she hissed. "So did Frank. So did *Daniel*."

"Daniel was the intern."

"Hm-hm." Angela licked some spilled drink off her fingertips.

"What can you tell me about the Cope exhibit?" I asked.

"Why aren't you asking *Frank*?" she shot back.

Tread carefully. Shit-faced or not, she might be trying to trap me. I couldn't trust her. For all I knew, those tears had been that of a crocodile.

"I tried," I said, which was sort of the truth. "He wasn't available."

Angela narrowed her eyes. "How'd you say you found my phone number?"

"Ms. London, if I could ask you about Edward Cope."

"Edward Cope is dead," she clarified.

For fuck's sake.

"Yes," I agreed. "He's very dead. About his skull—"

She slid off her barstool, nearly crashing to the floor. I lunged and grabbed her forearms, keeping her standing on heels that were destined to kill her.

"I. Didn't. Take. It." She punctuated each word by drawing closer and closer to my face, until the smell of cheap alcohol wafted from her lips. "Understand?"

"Yes." I looked down, and her pointy, professionally styled nails dug into the sleeves of my coat. "Where is it?" I dared to ask.

The question made her smile.

Wickedly.

Dangerously.

I shouldn't have—

Angela leaned in, pressing her mouth close to my ear. "If I knew…," she said lightly, in an almost singsong voice. It was deranged.

I swallowed and tilted my head to look at her. "Where's Daniel?" I asked very quietly.

"*Daniel.* Daniel is…." Angela considered the question for another moment. "On his back, with a one-inch dick tickling his asshole."

I shook my head and looked away.

She laughed, stepped back, and grabbed the counter to steady herself. "I have to piss," she declared. Angela turned and wobbled from foot to foot as she struggled across the room to the dimly lit sign indicating where the bathrooms were around the corner.

I sat on the barstool as the bathroom door slammed shut behind Angela. I noticed the large purse she'd left on the seat to her right, which had been blocked while she sat at the bar. I stood, moved two seats closer, and opened the purse. Pawing through a drunk woman's bag wasn't my idea of a good time, but I needed *something*.

Anything that would help me connect Angela to past or future events.

Wallet. Spare change. Gum—lots of gum. Half a dozen packages, all cotton-candy flavor. I shoved those back in and tried again. Tampons. *Come on.* I retrieved a ring of keys and nearly put them back before the weight of them gave me pause.

It seemed to be too many keys for one person. There were some charms attached that advertised it as definitely belonging to Angela—a pom-pom, Minnie Mouse, one that said "angel" in glittery, fake diamonds, and a massive *A* in what I suspected was a fake gold polish. But then I realized the excess in keys was due in fact to the second ring attached. Four additional keys. No charms but for an *F* that matched the *A*.

Why did Angela have Frank's key-ring?

I looked up, intending to watch the bathroom door, but made eye contact with the bartender by mistake. Caught red-handed.

"She's too drunk to drive," I blurted out, holding up the keys. "I'm holding on to these so she doesn't get any ideas."

If he was suspicious, I must have come across sincere enough. "Good call. She's been pounding whiskeys for a while. I was about to cut her off."

When the bartender turned his back, I got to my feet, quickly unhooked Frank's keys, and shoved Angela's ring back into her purse. I pocketed his, dropped some cash on the counter for the soda water, and slipped out the front door as Marilyn Manson asked if I was willing to kill for him.

Chapter Ten

I LEFT St. Marks in a hurry, crossed Third Avenue where the street morphed into East Eighth, and didn't stop until I'd reached the famous Cube at Astor Place. I moved around the massive, ugly sculpture and let it block me from view so I could take a moment to catch my breath and check the timer app.

Forty-two hours remained.

I was glad to be away from Angela London. Not least because I was spoken for and didn't enjoy being pawed at. But mostly, she was… *unnerving*. Of course she'd also been so falling-down drunk that it'd made any sort of serious discussion a lost cause. Except for the acknowledgment of the Cope skull. Angela had said she didn't take it. That didn't mean she didn't at least *want* it.

I stared at my phone's screen as I recounted that haphazard dialogue. Automatically, I found myself pressing the text icon and choosing Calvin's name out of the list of ongoing messages. It was an involuntary motion—to check in, to say hello. I scrolled through older conversations and smiled. A lot of I-like-yous and see-you-tonights. Written promises. Vows of safety. Assurances of dinner dates and errands run. Everything I could ever wish for—*hope for*—in a lifelong partner.

I dipped my chin and pressed my scarf to my nose as it started to run with the threat of tears.

"Come on," I said to myself in a firm voice, forcing the tightness in my throat to ease. "*Stop*." I clicked off the screen, but then it lit up and started vibrating with an incoming call. No one I knew, but the area code was local. A startling fear punched me right in the chest. What if this was the Collector? I answered with a rushed "Hello?"

"Sebastian Snow?"

"Yes?"

"This is Detective Alex Wainwright. I work in Major Cases for the NYPD."

"O-oh. Uhm, hi."

"I'd like to meet with you and discuss your fiancé, Detective Calvin Winter."

"What? Why?"

"Are you busy?" he asked with a bit of an accusatory tone.

Yes, technically. I had the keys to Frank Newell's apartment and was going to… uh, well, what, exactly? Let myself in and poke about? Hope to uncover a clue Calvin overlooked after Frank had been reported missing, when Calvin would have already thoroughly scoped out the paleontologist's home first and foremost? I needed to speak with Neil. And Quinn. I had to know if the intern had come up in their initial investigation. Daniel was my next stop in the ongoing adventure of Where in the World is Edward Cope? I *knew* it.

"I'm not—no. But this morning the NYPD told me to get lost."

"And now I'm telling you to *un*lose yourself," Wainwright replied, firm but polite. "Why don't you come downtown to 1PP?"

One Police Plaza.

"Or should I send a car?" he asked.

I craned my head and could barely make out stairs to the Downtown 6 across the street. "No," I answered. "I'm only a few subway stops away."

I WAS put in a room for questioning. As if I was a suspect.

I mean, look to the spouse. That was policing 101. And being gay didn't seem to make a difference in that angle of approach.

But Calvin *wasn't* dead.

So I was pretty goddamn offended. Not that anyone bothered to ask me.

"I was under the assumption these rooms had more space to stretch out," I said as the door opened and a well-built middle-aged man with what I guessed was salt-and-pepper hair stepped inside. He pulled it off well. In fact, he probably looked sexier now than he did at twenty-five.

He smiled, bemused. "You must be Sebastian Snow." He sat at the table with me. "Detective Wainwright."

"The production value of real life is always a bit of a letdown after comparing it to the movies," I continued.

Wainwright opened the file he slapped down on the tabletop. "What do you say we skip the bullshit, hmm?"

"That'd be preferable," I said.

Wainwright motioned to his own face, as if he were wearing glasses. "Take them off."

"No."

"Excuse me?"

"I have a light sensitivity." I motioned upward. "And fluorescents give me headaches without sunglasses."

Wainwright was quiet for a moment. He leaned back in his chair, rested an ankle on his knee, and folded his hands into his lap. "You met Detective Winter last year during the Nevermore murders."

"Is that in your file?"

He smiled.

"That's private," I added.

"It's not really a secret," Wainwright countered. "Not anymore." He looked at the papers. "How would you describe your relationship with Detective Winter?"

"Well, I can't be certain, but I think he likes me," I replied, holding up my left hand to show off the band on one finger. "Why am I being interrogated?"

"You're not. We're talking."

"I wasn't born yesterday."

Wainwright let out a breath through his nose. He shut the file. "You're agitated."

"You're damn right I am."

"Why?"

"I know that's a rhetorical question—you're hoping to glean some sort of proof I'm responsible for Calvin's disappearance and make this an open-and-shut case. Poke and prod all you want. It's not going to prove anything more than I love Calvin. And with every single second that ticktocks by, my very foundation is falling out from under me."

Wainwright considered my response.

I gave him nothing but the sincere upset that'd been festering inside me since this morning.

Straightening, Wainwright leaned over the table, elbows resting on the folder. "Tell me what happened."

"You're the cop. I think you have access to the investigation Calvin was working."

"No. This morning. Tell me what happened."

I turned my head and studied the large, public-school-style clock on the wall. "We don't have time for this. Calvin is going to be dead in forty-one hours."

"Says who?" Wainwright asked, his voice still neutral.

"I sure as hell hope you're not serious," I replied. "The person who abducted him. The Collector. My final note said I had forty-eight hours before my reward—Party C—*Calvin*—would be forfeited."

Wainwright removed a pen from his suit coat pocket. He clicked the top absently.

My eye twitched.

"I read the note," he confirmed. "It doesn't say he'll be dead. Why do you believe the wordage implies this outcome?"

"Uh. There are two unidentified chopped-up bodies and a third person has been missing for five days. Call me melodramatic, but I'm pretty sure Frank Newell is dead somewhere. Maybe in pieces. I'm not willing to take any chances. I refuse to be called in to identify *parts of Calvin*."

Wainwright *click*, *click*, *click*ed the fucking pen some more. "How do you know about Mr. Newell?"

"Calvin told me."

"He told you details about an ongoing investigation?" Wainwright confirmed, raising an eyebrow.

"We tell each other all sorts of secrets," I said, deadpan. "Sometimes we even stay up late, write in our diaries, talk about boys."

"I'd appreciate honesty without the sarcasm, if you don't mind."

"Why am I being questioned?" I protested. "This is harassment."

"No, this is protocol."

I stood up.

"Sit *down*," Wainwright said, raising his voice.

I did not.

I never was good at taking direction. Sue me.

"We spent the night at a hotel near Times Square. We woke up at seven o'clock," I said. "Calvin took the dog out. I lay in bed."

Wainwright opened the folder again. "What else?"

"*What else*," I echoed mockingly. "Let's see. We took a shower together, jerked off… oh, was that not the detail you were looking for?"

"Mr. Snow—" Wainwright started, and now he was frustrated again.

"I *love* Calvin," I said over him, thumping my own chest hard with each word spoken. "I wouldn't ever raise a hand to him. I get down on my knees."

"Just walk me through the rest of the morning," Wainwright replied tightly.

"There's nothing else to tell," I argued. "Officer Rossi came to the hotel—he was assigned as police protection for me, when the assumption had been that *I* was the Collector's next target. Calvin left first, and I went to work maybe… fifteen minutes after."

Oh.

"Calvin's brother called," I added.

Wainwright waited.

"When Calvin had gone downstairs to meet Rossi. I talked to Marc."

"Go on."

I slowly, reluctantly, slid back into my chair. "Marc's in the city on business. He's an architect. He wanted to speak with Calvin, but I didn't think it was a good idea."

"You told him as much?"

I considered my *shortness* with Marc at the Emporium. "Sort of. Over the phone I asked him to meet me at my antique store. I didn't want Calvin to stress over family matters while he was so wrapped up in this case. They have an… estranged relationship."

"Why?"

"Why do you think?" I shot back.

"You?"

"By proxy, yeah. I'm a threat to the picture-perfect all-American 1950s lifestyle the Winters try to present their family as being." I shut up suddenly and stared at the dent in the middle of the metal tabletop. I hadn't given Marc even a nanosecond of my time since I'd left the Emporium that morning. But wasn't it odd… very odd… that after a year, he suddenly walked back into Calvin's life within an hour of his disappearance?

If I hadn't answered the phone, Calvin might have been missing now with no one the wiser. He'd have almost certainly met with Marc, if even for a few moments. Because Marc was his brother. Despite the emotional distance between them akin to that of a canyon, Calvin wouldn't hesitate to get into a car with Marc. Except Marc had been with me at the time of those text messages and phone call from the Collector.

Another consideration. Calvin had a younger sister. Ellen. I think she was a CPA or whatnot at an international tax firm. Hirth & Lock—Hirth & Stock? Lock, Stock & Barrel? Something like that. Point was, she too had a sufficiently high-paying, impressive-sounding, and extremely white-collar career. She and Marc wouldn't have callused hands like Calvin. Wouldn't have bullet scars like Calvin.

Calvin, hero or not, stood out like a sore thumb in that family. He was the stereotypical middle child who couldn't be as impressive as the firstborn, and who would never be as innocent as the baby. He was forever overlooked and underappreciated until he somehow let down the Winter name.

I wondered where Ellen was today.... Pennsylvania with the rest of the family? Or perhaps... did CPAs travel?

Was I really considering the possibility of Calvin's siblings conspiring to kidnap him? Okay, maybe not *kidnap* him. Take him back to Pennsylvania—to his parents. To be talked straight, so to speak. Especially now that Marc knew we were engaged. The mere notion of Calvin being forced into some backward-ass therapy—to be conditioned to hate me, or hate himself—was enough to make me want to vomit. And I'd done that one too many times this week already.

My face must have blanched considerably while I worked through this possible motive, because Wainwright paused whatever line of inquiry he was on that I was ignoring to ask, "Are you all right?"

"Have you spoken to Marc?"

"No." Wainwright stared at me for a beat, then added, "Not yet."

Good. So he had plans to.

"Calvin also has a younger sister. Ellen. Except her last name is hyphenated. Winter-Brown."

"Is she in the city too?"

"I don't know. You should find out," I answered.

"Why?" Wainwright asked. It wasn't a simple inquiry. He was digging deep into human connections—untangling and interpreting motivation, reasoning, witnesses, clues—all from the words I said. Or didn't say.

"Because I find it very strange that his brother, who hasn't once picked up the phone to ask Calvin how he's been in twelve months, is suddenly ready to make amends the same morning he goes missing. That's why."

Wainwright nodded, made a note on one of the sheets of paper, then asked, "How's business?"

"Sorry?"

"You mentioned you had a shop."

"It's been fine," I said warily, sensing a trap.

Wainwright clicked the pen again. "Victorian curiosities and oddities, is that right?"

"Do you have my tax returns in that folder too, chief?"

Wainwright chuckled. I was glad someone was getting a kick out of this waste of time. "You've been involved with the NYPD a few times, Mr. Snow. We notice things like that."

"Even here, all the way downtown?"

"Even all the way down here, inside this ugly-as-hell Brutalist building," he agreed, smiling. "For example, I noticed during your last three run-ins—"

"I've only *had* three run-ins," I corrected.

Wainwright continued without amendment. "There were a number of extremely rare, highly valuable artifacts involved." He regarded me with a very stern, cop-like expression. Calvin had used that same stare on me when he once upon a time didn't like me so much.

I waited for Wainwright to continue.

"Detective Winter's investigation notes suggest we ought to expect a similar occurrence again."

"You mean, stumbling across a valuable artifact of American origin, circa 1837 to 1901?" I asked, feigning clarification.

"That's right."

I snorted, laughed dryly, and leaned back in the chair. "Unbelievable."

"Something funny?"

"No, actually. It's so far from funny that I want to smack you," I said automatically and without consideration of the consequences. "I didn't abduct Calvin. I didn't kill anyone. And I certainly didn't threaten *myself* in order to have a viable excuse to steal and profit off some long-lost artifact like it's found pirate booty. Your little black book should be able to tell you that never once have I profited from these events I've gotten caught up in."

"That's true," Wainwright said calmly and with a nod of his head. "But the last one put you in the hospital for an extended period of time. I imagine that was a rough financial burden."

"You know what else was a financial burden? *College*. One more implication like that and I'm out the door and hiring a lawyer."

He held his hands up in an act of surrender. "My apologies. Let's move on."

Detective Wainwright asked me more questions. He went over my statement with a fine-tooth comb, sometimes backtracking on my answers to see if I'd answer them the same as before or get caught up in a lie of my own making. If the circumstances were different, if this were a run-of-the-mill murder, maybe I'd have found it amusing, being investigated again. A Snow and Winter Christmas tradition.

But it wasn't funny.

Not this time.

On the plus side, Wainwright seemed to be more focused on the details of that Tuesday's early morning than how I'd been spending the afternoon. If he'd pressed a bit more, I would have been honest. I would have told him about the conversations at the museum, tracking down Angela. I might have even told him I stole her missing beau's keys. But he didn't ask. And that was fine. Because unlike the cops, I was taking the Collector's warning seriously.

No LEO help.

I stood, gathered my shoulder bag, and walked to the door when Wainwright deemed our conversation complete.

"Oh, one last thing, Mr. Snow."

Hand on the doorknob, I turned.

"Out of curiosity…." Wainwright looked up from his papers and clicked that dumb pen again. "What would Detective Winter's siblings know about this investigation?"

I had no idea.

I couldn't be sure how much an architect and CPA knew about Edward Drinker Cope and his mysterious, misplaced skull. Or why they'd even care. But they did have the personal relationship and motive angle to seriously consider. Maybe even greater motive than Dr. Thyne and Angela London, although in comparison, those two knew more about Cope and his involvement in the Bone Wars.

And yes, *this* fact was most likely coincidence, but it was worth noting that both Marc and Ellen lived in Philadelphia, and that later in his life, Cope had lived and curated in Philadelphia.

I opened the door and said, "I'm not sure. But isn't that why you're the detective?"

"Stay in the city," Wainwright responded.

"I know the routine." I shut the door behind me, started down the hallway toward the elevators, and collided with an officer as I rounded the corner. "I'm sorry," I proclaimed, stepping backward and pushing my sunglasses up the bridge of my nose. "Bad eye—Rossi?"

Nico Rossi drew his thick eyebrows together and crossed his arms. "What're you doing here?"

"I'm on tour. 1PP was listed in *Out* magazine as one of the Top Ten Must-See Attractions of New York."

Rossi rolled his eyes.

"This isn't your precinct," I stated.

"I have a meeting with Major Cases," he said, trying to make it sound more impressive than it actually was. And maybe that would have worked, if I hadn't just concluded the same appointment.

"Oh, you mean the interview with Wainwright?"

Rossi narrowed his eyes.

"Second door down."

"What did you tell him?"

Odd tone. Odder question.

"The truth."

Was he concerned about how I might have painted his personality, knowing full well how desperate Rossi was for a promotion? But he didn't matter. The truth had been, Rossi was an afterthought in this crime. And inconsequential to the timeline. I'd only mentioned his name to Wainwright once. Because as soon as Rossi had shown up, Calvin disappeared.

I guessed the egotistical prick had made this all about himself in his head. "You're going to be arrested if you keep interfering," Rossi said.

"I'm not interfering. In fact, the minute you arrived, nipping at the heels of your sergeant, you watched me get booted from the scene."

Rossi broke the stare-down first. He purposefully shoved my shoulder as he rounded the corner, walking down the hall I'd come from. I didn't move, but cast my eyes down and titled my head a bit in order to listen to his retreating footsteps. There was an itch between my shoulder blades. A prickle of discomfort. A sort of sixth sense warning that I was being watched.

Chapter Eleven

I NEEDED a minute.

A moment to collect my thoughts and soothe my hackles and plan my next line of attack. And the only place I could be alone, not freezing my nuts off, and without being watched by dozens of uniformed officers, plainclothes detectives, or security cameras, was the bathroom on the ground floor. I put the lid down on the toilet and sat on top in one of the two stalls in the men's room. My messenger bag toppled over on the floor, and I rested my elbows on my knees. I stared at the dirty grout between tiles.

The door opened and someone stepped into the room, disrupting the stillness. The echo of voices, ringing phones, and pings of the elevator bay slipped inside before the door fell shut. A man walked to the row of sinks, ran water, and then grabbed a paper towel.

I squeezed my eyes shut.

"Seb…?"

Neil?

I opened my eyes, stood, and unlatched the stall door. I poked my head out and saw Neil standing at the sink, studying the stalls and urinals in the mirror's reflection. "What gave it away? My loafers?"

His mouth quirked a little. "Your bag." He leaned to one side, tossed the wadded-up towel into the trash, and turned around.

I looked down at the bag between my feet. Max had bought me a pin for my last birthday—it read *SUPER SLEUTH* under the lens of a magnifying glass. It'd been attached to the front pocket for months.

"Oh." I stepped out of the stall, hoisting the bag onto my shoulder. "What're you doing here?"

"Washing my hands."

"Smartass."

"Who do you think I picked it up from?"

"If it walks like a duck, quacks like a duck…"

"It must be Sebastian," Neil concluded, smiling again. "I'm a cop. My presence here isn't really a matter of conjecture."

"Except that you don't work out of the police headquarters."

"No." He slid his hands into his trouser pockets. "Why are *you* here, Seb?"

"I got out of an interview that bordered on an interrogation."

"What?"

I pointed at the ceiling. "With a Major Cases detective."

"Alex Wainwright?"

"Okay, you need to stop doing that."

Neil shook his head. "I'm on my way up there to talk with him too. He's one of the detectives assigned by the chief to investigate Calvin's disappearance. I'm assuming he's constructing a timeline of everyone who's seen or worked with Calvin in the last few days."

"Do you have to go now?"

Neil removed his hand to check his watch. "I have a few minutes."

"Can we talk?"

"Do you want to get a coffee or something?" Neil asked, starting for the door.

I grabbed the sleeve of his winter coat, stopping him. "No." I looked up at his face. "Those texts said *no cops*, Neil. This is getting dangerous for Calvin."

"You sound paranoid," he answered, but Neil's voice was quiet. Subdued. There was no malice in that statement, because he knew as much as I did that this was not the time—not the victim—to challenge the rules set forth by the Collector.

"I think I have good reason to be," I replied.

Neil put a hand up as if to say *hold that thought*. He walked to the main door of the bathroom, opened it, made a come-hither motion, then stepped back as Quinn walked inside. Neil threw the dead bolt, securing us in the men's room and keeping out any prying eyes or ears.

Quinn gave me one look and shook her head. She held her winter coat in one hand, the other resting on her hip. "Your ability to show up in all the wrong places should be considered an Olympic sport."

"Sebastian was called in by Wainwright too," Neil supplied.

"It's protocol," she said. "You're not a suspect."

"But I *am* a person of interest," I said. "Wainwright suggested my hospital bills are a financial strain I can't handle. He not-so-tactfully suggested I could have easily set this dumpster fire myself in order to have a viable outlet in which to steal an expensive artifact."

Quinn scrunched up her face. "Let me see if I understand. In Wainwright's version of the story, you're the Collector. And you exchange an artifact with yourself for Calvin's safe return?"

"Basically," I answered. "I'm an antique dealer, so I can find the item of interest, Calvin will miraculously come back safe, and then I'll fucking sell it on the black market for cash."

Neil shook his head. "He was trying to get a rise out of you."

"Well, it worked!" I snapped. Before Neil could get his next word out, I added, "Don't tell me to calm down. It's bad enough he's suggesting I'd hurt Calvin. But being accused of dirty business practices is like being punched in the dick after I'm already on the floor." I took my sunglasses off, closed my eyes, and pinched the bridge of my nose. "No one is *listening* to me."

Neil said, quite low, "We are."

I hadn't realized how badly I'd needed those words said to me.

My eyes still closed and head down, I muttered, "This is usually when Calvin lets me bounce ideas off him. Where he gives in to my sleuthing enough for it to be of some use to him."

"So start bouncing," Neil replied. I heard him pull the sleeve of his coat back to check his watch again. "You've got three minutes."

"Any additional factoids will need to be the abridged version," Quinn added.

"I have three sets of suspects," I said.

"Three?" Quinn repeated warily.

I put my sunglasses on and looked at her. "First—Dr. Logan Thyne, head curator of the paleontology department at the Museum of Natural History, and accomplice, Angela London, who was recently fired from said division."

"Reasoning?" Quinn asked. She was all business now.

"Frank Newell's upcoming exhibit on the Bone Wars was set to feature the actual skull of famed paleontologist Edward Drinker Cope. Thyne was against the skull being on display, and Angela was let go for possibly attempting to steal? The details are a bit murky."

"Is that the skull referenced in the Collector's notes?" Quinn asked.

I made a shaking motion with my hands. "The Magic 8 Ball says… all signs point to yes."

"What's the skull worth?" Neil asked.

"See, you always ask me that," I replied, indicating toward him, "when I'm *not* holding an antique in my hands to appraise."

"Ballpark it," he growled.

"Zero dollars. *A million dollars*. It's a human skull, Neil. It'll go for whatever someone is willing to pay." I held up two fingers. "Second—Marc and Ellen."

"Who?" That was Neil.

"Calvin's brother and sister?" Quinn spoke over him.

They both looked at each other.

"It's a bit of a long shot—" I started.

"It's a fucking tinfoil-hat theory," Quinn corrected.

I put my hands on my hips. "I think Marc's sudden appearance, of all possible dates in the calendar year, should be an itsy bit suspect. He'd originally called Calvin, but I answered. I don't know how either of the siblings tie in with the Cope skull, but the personal motive to get rid of me or to take Calvin out of this life he's carved for himself is—it's there. For sure. Marc said he wanted to 'fix this.' I'm not so convinced that meant sharing a glass of eggnog with his brother over the holidays."

Neil shifted from foot to foot. I could feel his sudden anxiety ripple off him like spikes on a Richter scale. He was, after all, pushing forty and still hadn't come out to his own brother. Although whether Chester Millett believed Neil's insistence of bachelorhood all these years remained to be seen.

"Third—Nico Rossi."

That made Quinn snort. "Mr. Kiss-ass doesn't exactly strike me as the sort who turns to cold-blooded murder in order to land himself a promotion."

"But think about it," I said. "Rossi doesn't like Calvin. He most *definitely* doesn't like me. And yet, when Calvin requested police protection, we got Rossi—who told me he volunteered for the opportunity. Why would he do that?"

"Go on," she instructed, her expression hard and drawn.

"One of the first things he said to me yesterday was that my reputation preceded me. And he knew Calvin and I are engaged. What a perfect way to end up the new face of the NYPD than to be the one who arrests that busybody sleuth half of the force doesn't like, while simultaneously rescuing Homicide's golden goose."

Neil was shaking his head. "No. At least, it couldn't be Rossi working alone. He was with you at the time of Calvin's disappearance."

"So he's got an as of yet unknown accomplice," I agreed. "My other theories all involved two people."

Quinn interrupted us. "How could Rossi know about anything related to the dinosaurs and whatnot?" I could tell from her forced civil tone and the stern lines around her mouth that this was the theory she not only agreed with most, but the one that was downright pissing her off.

I shrugged. "I don't know. There's a hole in each suspect theory, but I know I can figure this out. So long as Wainwright doesn't arrest me first, or the NYPD doesn't piss off the Collector and Calvin gets—" I stopped and shook my head. I couldn't say the thought out loud.

"What do you need from us?" Neil asked. "We've got to go before we keep Wainwright waiting."

I said, "I need you both to hold the line. Give me the head start to find Calvin. Also." I reached into my messenger bag, retrieved Frank's key-ring, and held it up. "Did Daniel the Intern come up in your initial interviews? I need his address."

Quinn was reaching into her coat for her notepad even as she asked, "I don't want to know how you got his name, do I?"

"Probably not."

"What's with the keys?" she asked, flipping pages.

"I stole them," I stated. "They're Frank Newell's."

"Where the fuck did you steal them from?" Neil objected.

"Angela London's purse."

"I didn't hear any of that," Quinn said to herself.

"He was meticulous—*Frank*," I said, watching Quinn rip a page from her notepad. "I mean, he *labeled* his keys, so I can only imagine what his toiletries are like." I jingled the ring. "These two are his apartment building, and another for his mailbox. But this?" I held up the last key. "No label. Why wouldn't he mark this one? I think it's a copy Daniel gave him. There's no label, because why advertise you're cheating?"

Neil frowned.

Quinn gave me the paper. "Calvin and I went by Daniel's place last Sunday," she said, indicating the address she'd written. "No one was home. We didn't have a warrant to enter, nor was there any probable cause. Neighbors said he was a quiet kid. They couldn't remember the last time they'd seen him."

I shoved the paper and keys back into my bag. "Thanks." I started for the door.

"How's finding Daniel going to help?" Neil called.

"At the end of the day, this is about that stupid skull. With Frank gone, Daniel might be the only person left who knows of its whereabouts."

"He might be dead," Neil said solemnly.

I twisted the dead bolt and looked over my shoulder. "Yeah. He probably is."

I SWAYED with the motion of the Uptown C coming to a stop at 135th Street. The doors opened, and more folks shuffled off than entered. I leaned over in my seat, spinning my cane impatiently between the palms of my hands. I'd started the trek to Daniel's apartment at Chambers Street—way the fuck downtown, only a few blocks from the Police Plaza. My options for travel had been either subway or taxi. And at about five in the evening, traveling over 155 blocks in a car, during rush hour? I'd have reached Daniel's by… oh… next week.

So I sucked up my dislike of the subway, hopped on the A, and made a straight shot on the express all the way to 125th Street. I transferred to a local train and was now willing the conductor to close the doors and pull out of the station. As if reading my mind, the doors slid shut and the train lurched ahead. A kid stared at me from across the aisle—the cane and sunglasses tended to have that effect—and a few seats away, a teenager was trying to push candy bar sales on disinterested riders. Other than the addition of a dank atmosphere due to melted snow and blasting floor heaters, the remaining ride was uneventful.

The muffled, static voice of the conductor announced 155th Street, and I jumped out of my seat. The doors had barely opened before I shouldered my way out, went through the turnstiles, and hiked the stairs up to the street. I collapsed my cane, shoved it into my bag, and took a moment to gather my bearings. Mid-December meant the sun was already gone…. Which, despite a drop in the temperature, wasn't really a matter of contention with me.

As I started uptown on St. Nicholas Avenue, I decided it'd be a good idea to do some multitasking. Detective Wainwright's favorite suspect was me, for no other reason than being the person closest to Calvin. I'd tried to impress upon him to at least do his due diligence on Marc and Ellen, but I wasn't holding my breath. Myself, on the other hand—I had too many suspects to consider. If I could confirm alibis and knock some names off the list, I would be better prepared to defend myself against Wainwright's inevitable return. So I took out my phone, did a brief Google search to procure the phone number of A & F Designs out of Philadelphia, and called their office.

"A & F Designs, how may I direct your call?" asked a very professional, borderline robotic female voice.

"May I speak with Marc Winter please?"

"I'm sorry, Mr. Winter is out of the office this week. Is there another senior architect I can connect you to?"

"Oh, that's right!" I answered cheerfully, ignoring her question. "He mentioned that the other day. New York City."

"That's right," she said, and I could hear her smile.

"You don't happen to have the number for the office I can reach him at in New York, do you? I've been working on a project proposal with him…." I feigned hesitation. "No, I suppose I can put it in writing. It'll take a while, though. I'm a finger-pecker with keyboards."

She chuckled. Nothing like a bit of self-deprecating humor to lower a stranger's defenses. "He won't mind being interrupted if it's regarding an ongoing proposal. May I have your name, and I'll transfer you directly?"

"Huh. You can do that? Across states?"

"Technology is a wonderful thing," she said lightly.

I needed confirmation that Marc Winter had really coordinated this business trip with his office and his ass was planted at a desk in the city. I wanted to be certain, beyond a shadow of a doubt, that Marc had contacted Calvin when he did because he was nothing more than a selfish prick. That he didn't want to start another new year with this unease between them. And his company's need to have him in the city right before the holidays was the final push Marc needed to pick up that damn phone and call.

Basically, I didn't want to believe my in-laws were murderers.

"Er—tell him it's Sebastian Snow," I answered.

"Thank you. Please hold."

Mello guitar music started playing in my ear as I passed the playground of a public elementary school. I'd walked by a few brownstones and reached the end of the block when a familiar voice spoke.

"Mr. Snow?" Marc answered, an impressive combination of both wariness and annoyance in his voice.

"Mr. Snow is my father," I replied, coming to a stop after crossing the street. "I'm only thirty-four. *And*, like it or not, we're going to be legally related soon. Why not give *Sebastian* a try?"

Was that too bitchy?

"Sebastian," Marc woodenly stated. "Why are you calling me at the office? Unless it's to apologize and explain what the—" He paused and then murmured into the phone, as if to keep from being overheard. "What is going on with my brother?"

"Apologize?"

"Yes," Marc retorted.

"No," I said simply.

"No… *what*?"

"I have no intention of apologizing to you. If Calvin asks me to exchange polite small talk with you over dinner, sure. I'll pass you the salt and pepper with an award-winning smile and even pretend I mean it when I tell you I can't wait to 'do this again.' But I don't make it a habit of apologizing to bullies."

"Are you *quite* finished?" Marc asked.

"When you're done making demands, I'll stop telling you to go fuck yourself."

Marc was silent.

I stamped my feet a few times and the wind rustled my hair. "I called to see if you were the sort who actually works on business trips, or the one who holds meetings at the hotel bar."

"Of course I'm working. You know, *Sebastian*, I really tried giving you the benefit of the doubt. I wanted to do that for Calvin. But you are an obnoxious sonofabitch."

"I've had a long day."

"Where the hell is my brother?" Marc asked.

"It's… an overwhelming story. I can't really explain on the phone."

"Then it'll be convenient for *Calvin* to explain it to me in person. I'm staying at The Bellows on East Forty-Ninth. He can meet me there. I'll even send a car."

"Calvin is busy—"

"Bullshit," Marc said, cutting off my lie. "I was there for that phone call before cops swarmed your cheap spook store and threw me out."

"Let's keep the blows above the belt."

"Tell me the truth. Tell me where Calvin is or I'm hanging up," Marc threatened.

I pulled my cell back and hit End. "Beat you to it, asshole," I muttered.

Okay, so… that hadn't gone according to plan.

Not entirely, anyway.

Marc was for sure in New York on business. That much the receptionist had confirmed by internally transferring me to his desk in Manhattan. But he didn't like me. I daresay Marc might have even hated me, although so long as it was because I was an unapproachable ass and nothing more—fine. No love lost.

But despite his animosity toward me, his concern regarding Calvin's radio silence had seemed sincere. Of course, a psychopath would fake genuine human emotion in order to better blend into society.... And a psychopath with a murderous streak—*no*. I was letting my personal opinion and flair for the occasional dramatic conclusion color Marc in a light that was simply not true.

I was certain he wasn't working a side hustle after the closing of Architect Business Hours, which included lopping off body parts and mailing them to guys like me as a not-so-veiled threat to find him the skull of Edward Cope *or else*! I mean, what would a paper-pushing guy like Marc even *do* with the skull of a once-infamous man, now barely recognized outside of his extremely specific scientific focus? Senior architects made good money, so I couldn't imagine him wanting to sell it. And unless Marc's suburban lifestyle included an impressive collection of human skulls that he kept in his basement man cave....

I started walking again.

I supposed anything was possible. But to be honest, I was no longer convinced of Marc's involvement. Maybe I never had been. Not really. The problem was, he and Ellen were the only "suspects" who had the personal connection that could have possibly explained the text messages to our friends and family. Without them, I had to consider Dr. Thyne and Angela London to be a hell of a lot more dangerous than I'd initially given them credit for.

Or perhaps Rossi knew us a lot better than I'd realized.

A residential building up ahead advertised its street address in big impossible-to-miss numbers above the arched doorway: 637. I took out Quinn's note, confirmed this was the address I was hunting for, and went to the front door as I fished out the keys. I chose the one without a label and tried the lock.

Schiiick.

I smiled and slipped inside. I eased the door shut behind me and immediately checked the half a dozen mailboxes on the wall to the right.

I scanned the handwritten names and then stopped on 3B. It was left unlocked by the carrier, due to an overflow of mail. I nudged the box open and scanned the dates of D. Howard's post.

Huh. The oldest envelope seemed to have been stamped and delivered on Saturday. Considering the pileup, it was likely Daniel hadn't been home since then. Only three days and there'd been enough deliveries to stoke a cozy fire for some time. Kid needed to lay off the subscription services.

I shoved the magazines and other junk back into the mailbox and took the stairs to the third floor, holding on to the handrail as a guide through the unfamiliar building. I opened the door that separated the stairwell from actual apartments and tiptoed in salt-encrusted loafers to 3B. I tried the doorknob. It was old and shitty, definitely not something that'd been replaced by the landlord in my lifetime, but it was locked all the same. I tried each of the keys on Frank's ring just in case, but it seemed like Daniel had only provided Frank with a copy of the key to the *outer* door. I guess he assumed he'd be home to let Frank into his actual apartment when the other man stopped by for a midnight tumble.

I swore under my breath and turned to 3A. It appeared dark under the door. I creeped close, pressed my ear to the wood, and listened. It was quiet. And not the sort of quiet where you can still hear a human *existing*. Maybe—hopefully—they were at work.

I straightened and returned to 3B. I turned sideways, gripped the doorknob in one hand, and without giving myself the opportunity to second-guess this potentially awful plan, slammed my shoulder *hard* into the door. It splintered and flew open with me following suit, shouting expletives the whole way down. I crashed to the floor as the broken door knocked hard against the wall.

I rolled onto my back and looked up at the threshold. If I'd had a gun and badge, that would have come off as a really cool action-movie entrance. But seeing how I was me… I sat up and staggered to my feet, winced, and rubbed my shoulder.

"God," I said through gritted teeth. "That's gonna leave a mark." I flipped a light switch above an end table near the door and took a step into the studio apartment. The very first thing I noticed was…. "Decomp."

Things were not looking up for Daniel.

I put my sleeve to my face, trying to mask the stench as I poked about the home. There was no body in the neatly made bed. Or underneath.

No one lay across the floor like a broken doll, and no goodbye messages were written in blood on the walls. The studio was quite orderly, in fact. A bookshelf housed mostly nonfiction, likely titles assigned throughout Daniel's college experience.

On the desk at the foot of the bed was a neat pile of spiral-bound notebooks and a day planner. I flipped through a few recent pages. No personal memos. It was all school-related. A space in the middle of the table suggested a laptop usually sat there but was suspiciously absent now. A single picture—a retro Polaroid—was propped against the desk lamp. I picked it up by the corner, brought it closer, and fished out my magnifying glass from my bag. I studied the photo, and my stomach dropped like a rock sinking in water.

It was my Head-in-the-Box. Daniel. *Daniel* was the victim couriered to the Emporium!

The kid was smiling for the camera and standing close—closer than *just colleagues* would—beside another man with several years on him. Frank Newell, I presumed. He had an arm over Daniel's shoulders. A hefty college ring was on one finger. Fuzzy out-of-focus dinosaur displays filled the backdrop of the picture.

"Jesus." I frowned and gently set the photo back where I'd found it. "Poor kid."

I'd honestly agreed with Neil that Daniel was likely dead, that the reality of our situation didn't leave room for the possibility of him being on winter break in Michigan… but still….

I took a step back and opened the closet door. Half a dozen hangers were empty, but I couldn't find a laundry basket to suggest they were simply in need of a wash. Absent clothes, missing computer, uncollected mail—why had Daniel tried to run?

The house still stank of death. I checked the bathroom last, half expecting a chemical soup in the tub eating away at human remains. But no. It even appeared as if Daniel had recently scrubbed the porcelain. I walked out of the room, down the short hall, and toward the refrigerator. I tugged the door open and studied the contents. Take-out containers, soda and cheap beer in cans, and a whole pot of macaroni and cheese.

A fly buzzed in front of me as I shut the door. I swatted it away.

Another flew past.

Then a third.

What the…?

I looked to the right. A cardboard box with the top open sat on the table. More flies buzzed around the contents. I walked forward, tilted the box to look inside, and a cloud of insects vacated. What remained were two rotting human hands, cut at the wrist. One of the fingers wore a gaudy class ring.

Well… now I knew why the kid attempted hightailing it out of New York. I wasn't sure where Daniel's second package would be, but it didn't really matter. He hadn't tried to find and deliver the Cope skull in return for his life. He'd run instead. Tried, anyway. Tried and failed.

The first victim—the one sent to Frank—was still an unknown. But otherwise, the routine Calvin had initially established was adding up. Frank was likely dead by Friday night and used as a threat to Daniel. Daniel was dead by Sunday night, and delivered to me bright and early Monday morning. I'm sure if I cared to look a bit longer, I'd have found the note that accompanied his lover's severed hands. The only variation in this gruesome game was that I'd received three packages and messages, when the others had only gotten two. And that was because of the sudden change in the Collector's plan—which assured me I had until Thursday morning.

Roughly thirty-nine hours to go.

I raised my arm, coughing and breathing into the fabric of my coat when the odor of decay became too much. With my other hand, I folded the tops of the box down to study the postage. Or lack thereof. I wondered if this, like Frank's first package, and mine, had been delivered by courier.

I stepped away and took out my phone. I opened a text with Quinn and sent: *MAybe 4th suspct is courier. Confirm DH is ded head at Emporium.*

She answered almost immediately. *Copy. I will follow up.*

I added: *Confirm Frank dead too.*

Understood.

Dnt enrage courier. No cops.

I rolled my eyes and corrected the last message with: *engage.*

The assortment of items kept on the funky, old-world-charm, bronze end table near the door fell to the floor. I quickly spun on one heel—in time to see a stranger grip the stand like a baseball bat and take a swing at me. The side of the rounded tabletop grazed my face, enough to throw me to the floor, but not enough to knock the teeth from my mouth, which told me it was a cheap, aluminum metal, probably fabricated in China. I'd never been more thankful for crappy student-affordable décor in all my life.

"W-wait!" I protested, looking up and rolling to the side when the stranger brought the table down.

The metal dented inward upon kitting the floor, and the sound reverberated off the walls.

"What'd you do to Dan?" the stranger shouted.

"Hold on! Put that down!" I scrambled backward like a crab, managed to stand, and skidded down the hall when the table came at my head again, only to hit the wall directly where I'd been standing half a second prior.

"Where's Dan?" the man shouted again.

I grabbed the wooden chair at the desk and used it as if I were an animal tamer trying to keep back a wild tiger or lion. "Stop!" I protested. "Or I'm calling the cops!"

"*You're* calling the cops?" he said. "You're the one fuckin' breakin' and enterin'!"

The guy was actually a kid—a college student. I'd guess the same age as Daniel. Probably a classmate, although he was a lot less put-together-looking in a pair of Levi's, a baggy sweatshirt with the hood pulled up around his face, and hair hanging nearly to his shoulders in limp, stringy strands.

I held a hand out, slowly lowering the chair with the other. "I came looking for Daniel," I said carefully. "I know he's been missing."

The kid narrowed his eyes, tightened his grip on the impromptu weapon.

"Probably since Friday night, right?" I asked. "His boyfriend is missing too."

That got the guy's attention. "You know Frank?"

I nodded. "I know Frank. I know Angela too."

Wrong answer. The kid raised the table again, ready to strike.

"Whoa, whoa! *Hey*!" I shouted.

"That bitch is psycho!"

"Listen…." I held my hands out, moving slowly. "I know how this looks, but I swear I'm here to help. What's your name?"

"Jason," he answered with a touch of reluctance. Jason lowered the table, then awkwardly crouched to set it on the floor. "Who're you?"

"My name's Sebastian. Are you a classmate of Daniel's?"

Jason stiffly nodded. "Yeah, man. Dan's been gone for days."

"Have you notified the police?"

He snorted. "Nah."

"Uh… why not? You seem concerned."

"I am! But you smoke a little weed and suddenly no cop takes you seriously."

I rolled my eyes and realized belatedly, as my adrenaline began to wane, that my jaw was *throbbing*. I gave it a gentle rub.

Jason pulled back the hood on his head. "You really lookin' for Dan?"

"Really."

"Do… do you think he's dead?"

JASON DUMPED copious amounts of crushed red pepper all over the slice of pizza I bought him. "I knew it," he said. He set the shaker aside, folded the pizza, and took a massive bite like he hadn't eaten all day. And considering he was a grad student, that might have very well been the truth.

"You knew Daniel was dead?" I asked gently.

We stood at a tall table in a corner joint simply called Grandma's Pizza. The overhead lights were twitchy fluorescents, and the wobbly table was still messy with a previous customer's sprinkled parmesan cheese. But it was warm inside—the giant pizza ovens spitting out pie after pie—and the employees were doing a brisk trade like any good cheap-slice shop should.

Jason guzzled his can of Coke before saying, "Yeah. I mean, I guess I'm not surprised. You know?"

"No, I don't know," I said. A slice of pizza sat untouched on a paper plate in front of me.

Jason took another huge bite, grease dripping down his fingers. "Angela. You said you knew her."

"Yes, but I only met her today."

"She killed Dan." He shook his head forlornly. "I know it," he said for a second time.

"Why do you think so?"

Jason was already chewing on the crust. "She's crazy. Dan said Frank was afraid of breakin' up with her. Like, she'd threatened to kill herself. *That* kinda nuts."

"I see."

"But Dan. I dunno…." Jason looked up as he finished the crust, staring thoughtfully at the far wall. "I guess he didn't date much in Michigan. He was just so in love with Frank. Like a puppy dog. Frank was all he fuckin' talked about. I warned him shit would get bad if someone like Angela found out...." Jason smiled a little and finally looked at me.

I pushed my slice of pizza toward him. "What do you know about the work Daniel did at the Museum of Natural History?"

Jason again shook a mountain of peppers onto his pizza. "He helps Frank with exhibits. He wants—*wanted* to be a curator."

"Did you intern there as well?"

"Nah." Jason folded the slice. "I'm scheduled to go on a dig with Dr. Hart in a few months. I like playin' in the dirt." He took a bite and said around the mouthful, "Museums got too much politics. Dan liked it, though. Or liked it 'cuz Frank did. Whichever." Jason looked down and dragged the slice through the blobs of grease drip-dropping onto his plate.

I opened my mouth to speak, but Jason continued.

"Dan thought Angela was gettin' suspicious. I told him to drop the internship."

"You seriously thought she would kill him?"

"Yeah! What's that shit called—crime of passion or something? But Dan said no. He had to help Frank with some issue regardin' an upcoming exhibit—"

"I heard," I answered. "Dr. Thyne thought it was unnecessary to focus on Edward Drinker Cope more so than the fossils discovered during the Bone Wars."

Jason didn't seem convinced on the matter. "That's what Thyne says. I think that buttoned-up fossil is full of shit. AMNH accused the University of Pennsylvania of sending a box with no skull inside. UPenn accused them of losing Cope's skull. Dan said the drama's been fuckin' wild." He finished the slice, downed the last of his soda, and wiped his mouth on a napkin. "Frank fired his own girlfriend. He thought she'd stolen the skull."

"But the skull," I continued quickly, "has it been found?"

Jason shrugged. "I dunno. And Dan told me Frank got a package at the museum—fuckin' human toes or some shit. Frank got real squirrelly. Dan was scared. Last time I heard from him was Friday night." Jason stopped, apologized under his breath, and wiped his face with the sleeve of his sweatshirt. "He was cryin', said Angela killed Frank—he was going back to Michigan. Never saw him again. I've gone by every day to check." He tapped the tabletop with an index finger. "Thanks for dinner, man. I gotta go, though."

"Sure." I nodded. "I'm sorry about your friend."

Jason's mouth worked, but he shook his head and started for the door. "You know," he said with a glance back at me, "if that cop had done his fuckin' job, Dan might still be alive."

I bristled a little. "What cop?" I couldn't imagine a situation in which Calvin and Quinn would have met Jason, since he didn't work with all the other monkeys at the circus.

"Dan said the new doc at the museum had a boyfriend on the force. Dan told the guy what was going on. Like I said, he was afraid. *And* naïve enough to think all cops are good cops."

I scowled a little at that last comment. Sure, dirty cops were a thing, this much was true. But I didn't like or appreciate the negative attitude on principle. This was news, though—so I reined myself in. Dr. Gould was new to the museum. And she knew and worked with Daniel the Intern. It didn't seem too outrageous to suspect the poor kid had reached out to her Main Squeeze for help. Possibly with Gould none the wiser. If she'd known Daniel sought out help, I felt like that bubbly young woman would have been honest to a fault with me during our chat earlier.

"Did Daniel tell you the cop's name?" I asked.

Jason ran a hand through his grubby hair. "He might've. I don't remember. I got a Snapchat, though."

"What's a Snapchat?"

Jason gave me a skeptical look but kept talking. "Dan thought he was cute. I ain't into dudes, but I've no problem appreciatin' them." Jason was digging his phone out of his jeans pocket.

I stepped away from the table and squinted at the screen he held out. It was a discreetly taken photo, like Daniel didn't want to be caught creeping on a hottie. Some kind of text flashed over the picture, and little hearts bounced up and down, nearly distracting me from the face of Officer Nico Rossi waiting on the steps of the Museum of Natural History.

What a small world, after all.

Chapter Twelve

POP OPENED his apartment door. His face was solemn. "*Kiddo.*" He reached a hand out and pulled me inside.

I let my messenger bag slide off my shoulder and hit the floor with a loud thud, and I wrapped my arms around Pop's neck. "Dad," I choked out.

Pop hugged me hard, and that made it all the more difficult to keep from crying. It was after eight at night by the time I returned from the Daniel Debacle. And if there was ever a moment in my life that I *needed* my father, it was now. Now that my shoulder hurt, my face hurt, my soul hurt.

And he knew. He knew everything. I didn't care how.

Pop patted my back firmly and stepped away. He reached under my sunglasses with his thumbs and discreetly wiped my face. "Neil told me," he murmured.

"*Neil* did?"

Pop nodded and pointed across the room. I followed his line of direction and was surprised to see said man sitting at the dining table. He and my dad hadn't gotten along well when we'd been dating. At least, nothing like how Pop was with Calvin. I realized afterward it was because even from the start, Pop hadn't approved of Neil. He knew four years before I did that we were far too different for each other. And not the sort of different that had two people complementing each other's strengths and weaknesses. We were the kind of different that made us simply want to punch each other.

But that was in the past. And it'd stay there forever. Neil and I, I think it was safe to say, were finally friends. He'd more than proven his commitment to our new relationship while I was in the hospital after being shot. In fact, he'd been the bigger man in working to establish this new closeness from the get-go. I accepted equal fault for our breakup, and maybe I'd come to terms with it sooner than Neil had, but he'd been the first to show his apology through action.

Neil stood from the table, absently picking up his coat from the back of the chair. "I thought your dad should know what's going on."

I nodded. "Thanks." What I meant was *thank you for being a cop and knowing* how *to tell him and* what *to tell him because I'm too close and too committed to the outcome of this case and... I can't.*

"Sure," Neil said simply.

Pop left my side and walked to the freezer in the kitchen.

Dillon trotted across the room and stopped in front of me to lick my hand.

"How'd Dillon get here?" I asked.

"Ms. Harrison gave me a ring earlier this afternoon. I picked him up from Good Books," Pop explained.

I gave Dillon a good scratch behind his ears.

Pop returned and held out a bag of frozen peas.

I straightened, took the offering, then smiled wryly. "I was going to ask Santa for one of these."

"It's for your face, troublemaker," Pop answered with a forced smile.

I put the bag against my bruised jaw and swollen lip, meeting my dad's gaze.

"Sebastian," he murmured with a simple shake of his head.

"Dad—no. Don't tell me to stop. Don't tell me I can't do this."

Pop's jaw tensed, and he crossed his arms. "You're not a cop, kiddo."

"Good. That's the only reason Calvin is still alive."

"Whoever is behind this," he began, severe upset barely contained beneath a calm tone and precise speech, "is not a person. They are a *monster*. And I'll be damned, Sebastian, if I see you in one more hospital bed. If I—" He stopped.

Bury my son.

I lowered the bag of peas, started to speak.

"William?" Neil interrupted. "Major Cases is investigating Calvin's disappearance. And they're good detectives."

I snorted.

"But they aren't your son," Neil continued. "Sebastian has the intelligence, persistence, curiosity, and dumb luck that without, I'm confident we won't find Calvin in time." He looked directly at me. "I've had every opportunity afforded to me to do right by you, and I never have. Not once. I told you I'd have your back on this. And I meant it." Neil turned his head to look at my father again. "Even if it costs my badge and my career, I won't let anything happen to your son that a bag of frozen peas can't fix."

Pop took a deep breath. "I have your word?"

"You do, sir." Neil stepped closer, reached his hand out, and shook Pop's.

I looked down at the bag, now beginning to sweat in my hands as it thawed. I really hoped, for everyone's sake, I wasn't the cause of Neil losing his only real sense of purpose in life.

IT TOOK further convincing before Pop was okay. Not that he was actually *okay*. But… until he was at least agreeable to me forgoing the safety of his nest for the big bad world. I didn't want to leave my dad alone, not with everything going on, but I also didn't want my mere presence to rain shit down on his parade. He promised to check in with me, had never removed Neil from his cell phone contacts, and had both Maggie and Dillon as frontline home defense. So I hugged and kissed Pop before absconding to the Times Square hotel with Neil and a bag of mushy peas.

I think what also helped—believe it or not—was Neil suggesting to my dad that he'd stay the night with me, and me actually not bitching about police protection. Not that I'd turn my nose up at Neil's aid. Not anymore. Not after he put himself in the line of fire on both the Curiosities and Moving Image cases when any other man could have and *should have*, despised me.

"I still smell like that basin," Neil said upon closing the door to the hotel room.

"A bit, yeah," I replied. I shed my coat and scarf, changed into my glasses, and cast my bag aside. "You might want to get one of those little pine trees for your car."

Neil gave me side-eye before hanging his winter clothing in the closet. "Can I use your shower?"

"Sure." I sat down on the bed. "Do you still carry a change of clothes in your car?"

Neil held up a small bag he'd brought inside with him. "Always." He went into the bathroom and shut the door. The shower turned on a moment later.

From the day he'd gotten that swanky BMW, Neil had always kept a change of clothes in the trunk. Apparently you could only work so long at a job that dealt with as much human excrement, fluids, and remains as

Neil's before you just *needed* a spare change of socks and maybe a fresh shirt to get you through the rest of the workday.

I stood again, walked to the duffel still beside the desk from that morning, and bent down to paw through the contents. I pulled free one of Calvin's ties in my quest for wherever I'd shoved my pajamas. I smoothed the silky material and slowly rose. There were a few creases from being carelessly shoved into the bag. God. It'd been so long since I'd worn a tie, I didn't really take care of them the way I should.

Would I wear one at our wedding?

Would I even have—

The bathroom door opened to my right.

"Is it silk?"

I startled and looked up. Neil stood in the doorway—jeans, no shirt, wet hair. I glanced down at the fabric I was still trying to rub the wrinkles from. "Oh. Yeah. It's Calvin's."

He took a spare hanger from the closet, walked toward me, and took the tie. He brought it into the bathroom, hung it on the back of the door, then exited. "The steam from the shower should fix it."

"Thanks."

Neil shrugged and sat down on the opposite bed. He ruffled his hair with one hand.

"I mean, for—a lot," I stated. "What you said to my dad. And—other stuff."

"I don't like you speechless. It makes me uncomfortable."

I laughed. "Asshole."

"There you go." I felt Neil watching me as I returned to rummaging through the duffel bag before finding my pajamas shoved into the outer pocket. "How's your face?"

"It's been better. I was hit with a table." I unbuttoned my shirt and tossed it aside.

"*Jesus Christ*." Neil stood. "What happened to your shoulder?"

I put a hand on the bruise and suppressed a wince. "I had to open the door somehow." With a bit of a struggle, I pulled the T-shirt over my head.

"Quinn says you confirmed the identity of the victim delivered to you as Daniel Howard." Neil pulled the covers back on his bed and let me finish stripping without an audience. "And that Frank is dead."

"Frank's hands were delivered to Daniel's apartment. They're decomposing in a box on his kitchen table."

Neil shook his head. "Cleaning up after your adventuring is going to require cashing in every favor I've been saving for a decade." He sat. "And I might still owe a hand job afterward."

"You're good for those."

He grunted. "What else?"

I walked across the room and went into the still-warm, damp bathroom. I explained what I'd gleaned from my afternoon of breaking and entering as I washed up and removed my red-tinted contacts. From confirming Frank's identity via his college ring, to my gladiator battle with cheap furniture against Jason, and all of the disheveled student's damning evidence against Angela London and my Brooklynite buddy Rossi. I even begrudgingly mentioned my call to Marc Winter.

"Calvin's brother did *not* do this," Neil called from his bed. "I'm in full agreement with Quinn on that."

"Yeah. He probably didn't," I agreed. I turned off the lights and walked carefully through the dark. "But I also don't think Angela killed anyone." I set my glasses on the nightstand and climbed into my bed.

"No?" Neil asked quietly.

"She doesn't seem like the kind of person who could do that—take a life. Let alone several. Maybe in the heat of the moment, something awful could happen, but it'd definitely be directed at Frank. As far as she's concerned, he's the enemy, the one who broke her heart."

"Hmm."

I rolled onto my side and studied the blurry outline of Neil a few feet away. "But chopping off a man's hands at the wrists requires a certain kind of steel stomach. I don't think hers can handle much more than cheap whiskey."

Neil was quiet. A thinking quiet. He shifted to cross his arms under his head.

"Rossi has the motive," I stated into the dark.

"You said that before."

"Well, if he's really dating one of the staff members in the paleontology division.... *You* know how easy it is to learn a thing or two about someone else's profession when sharing an intimate relationship."

"Do I?"

"Hi, honey. How was your day," I said teasingly.

"Yeah, that sounds familiar," he agreed. "But do you think enough honey-how-are-yous would give Rossi all the information he needs on the Bone Wars in order to plug those minute details into the messages?" Neil turned his head to look my direction. "He managed to stump *you*, if that's the case."

"Ouch. Now I've got a bruised ego to go with the rest of my boo-boos," I answered. "Maybe his girlfriend is his partner."

"In crime?"

"It's possible. Dr. Gould met with Calvin in his initial interviews. She's got a really sweet personality. And if it's a ploy—it's a believable one. She wouldn't have necessarily had to overpower Calvin. A few sweet words may have been all it took."

"I suppose it's the most we've got to work with," Neil replied.

The central heat kicked on.

"I learned that the Cope skull was originally an artifact housed at UPenn."

"Does the backstory matter in this instance?"

"You're asking *me* if history matters?" I said mockingly.

Neil looked at the ceiling again. "You're right."

There didn't seem to be anything else to say after that. To do—sure. There was plenty I could be doing. I didn't want to stop moving, not until my redhead was in bed again, his legs twined around mine and his head on my chest. But as it stood, I was already operating on too little rest, not enough food, and I could confirm from experience that multiple adrenaline spikes could wreak havoc on the human body. I was on a crash course toward making mistakes. Maybe critical, life-threatening mistakes.

I yawned so deeply, my jaw cracked. My eyelids drooped. "Neil?" I murmured. "You awake?"

"No," he responded.

"Last night, at my place," I continued, "you said I'd interrupted your night."

Neil was silent.

"Was it a date?" I could feel, rather than see, his surprise. "It was your clothes," I told him.

"What about them?"

"You were wearing your it's-not-a-date date clothes." I was well acquainted with that particular portion of Neil's wardrobe.

"All right, Miss Marple. Calm down."

"Where'd you meet him?" I asked.

Neil let out a long pent-up breath. "I swiped right," he said, before adding, "Pretend you know what that means."

"How'd it go? Before you got called in."

"It didn't."

"I've clearly assigned a value to 'swipe right' that's nowhere close to accurate," I muttered.

"I was stood up," Neil answered with a tinge of embarrassment.

I propped myself up on one elbow. "Why?"

"I can only presume that if I knew *why*, I would have been able to avoid waiting at the bar for over an hour." Neil rubbed his face. "Sorry. I should listen to a few angsty Depeche Mode songs and get on with my life."

After a moment of consideration, I said, "You'll find someone."

"That no-sympathy thing works both ways, just so you know."

"It's not sympathy," I answered, getting comfortable once more. "Trust me on this: stop being afraid."

"Of what?"

"You."

MY STOMACH woke me from a deep sleep. I sat up and rubbed my tired eyes. Anemic light crept in between the not-entirely closed curtains, and the room had that briskness unique to winter mornings. I grabbed my glasses off the nightstand. Neil wasn't in his bed, but a piece of paper with the hotel logo lay on the comforter. I crawled out of the warm nest of blankets, reached across, and snatched the note. In Neil's clean handwriting was a notice that he'd gone downstairs to grab us breakfast.

I stood and carefully stretched, testing the aches of various body parts, then started toward the bathroom.

My cell rang.

The biggest coffee they offer, I thought, mentally answering Neil's inevitable question on the other end of the call. I returned to the beds and picked it up from the nightstand.

Not Neil.

Not a number I recognized, in fact.

My underarms immediately began to sweat as I hit Accept and brought the phone to my ear. "H-hello?"

I was greeted by living silence. I nearly spoke again but caught myself at the subtle sound of rubbing or scratching against the microphone.

Then it grew louder.

A huff of air—of breath.

"B-baby?"

One word. My *favorite* word. That's all it took to fill me with hope again. My knees buckled, and I dropped to the floor like a sack of potatoes. "Calvin? Oh—God—where are… are you okay?"

Calvin grunted again. "Machinery," he murmured before there was more friction over the line.

Machinery?

"Calvin?" I asked more insistently.

"Old machinery," he clarified, voice gruff and thick, as if every word was a struggle to pronounce correctly.

He sounded out of breath. In pain. He must have been disoriented, because what the fuck was he talking about? And *why* was he dragging the phone across what sounded like a wooden floor?

"Gray… *ngh*… skyline. Rooftops. It's—" Calvin stopped. His breathing was erratic. "P-probably five… seven… stories."

"I don't understand," I answered.

Why wasn't he—wait.

Stop.

Think.

Calvin was a soldier. He had a decade of experience working overseas in hostile situations. He would have been trained to survive dangerous encounters. To document the details of his environment. And in the worst scenario imaginable, he would be able to assess whether escape would be possible. Belatedly I realized he wasn't wasting his time or sparse energy on sweet nothings, nor was he confused and babbling incoherently. He was telling me everything he could about his location. Calvin had already determined he couldn't escape without intervention.

I jumped to my feet, ran to the desk, and started writing down everything he said on the complimentary notepad. "You can see the sky," I said, clarifying that I now understood. "You're high up—higher than the surrounding buildings. There's old machines. What else?"

Calvin cleared his throat as he tried to speak again. Every unsteady breath he took sent me into a near tailspin, but I had to keep my shit together. If I lost it now, Calvin had zero chance.

"Calvin?" I pressed. "Can you hear anything?"

"Hum," he murmured.

"Like… like a person humming?"

"*Ngh*… steady hum." The phone clattered like it'd been dropped. I could hear Calvin swear from the distance. "Baby."

"I'm here."

"It was bumpy." He sounded as if he'd fallen and was on the floor, close to the phone. Calvin made another pained sound. "Can't… *remember*."

"You're doing great," I insisted.

"Bare brick."

Brick?

Brick helped, actually.

"Calvin—the floors. What do the floors look like?"

He made a sound, as if consciousness was becoming more difficult to hold on to by the second. "Wood. Dusty. Broken."

Without warning, Calvin gave an unintelligible shout into the phone. There was a struggle, like someone had joined him in an unfair match of human strength—and Calvin was on the losing side. And all at once, the distorted sounds silenced.

"Calvin?" I called. "*Calvin*?"

An inhumanly deep and robotic voice spoke suddenly—one of those voice distorters. Stereotypical in all the worst ways. "Party C's behavior is somewhat remiss. You have twelve hours to collect your reward."

"T-twelve? *No*!" I shot a look back at the alarm clock. "I still have twenty-four hours. I know what you want—the skull of Edward Drinker Cope. I'll find it. But I need the full forty-eight hours you promised!"

"Should Party B fail to collect on his sum, will he wage a bitter war against Party A?"

"I won't fail!"

"It would be such a sensational scandal. Until the very end."

"Tell me where Calvin is," I demanded. "I'll get the skull. I'll meet you there."

The robotic voice laughed.

Beep.

Beep.

Beep.

"CALVIN'S IN Brooklyn!" I all but shouted at Neil.

"You don't *know* that, Seb! Yes, sorry, I'm here," Neil said into his phone, essentially putting his argument with me on hold.

"You say that like I wasn't born and raised here—like I wouldn't be able to put these clues together," I continued without a breath, waving my piece of paper in his face.

Neil grabbed my wrist, pulled my hand out of his line of vision, and strained to listen to the voice on the other end of the call. "Ben Dover." Neil looked at me. "What does that name mean to you?"

"That he should have gone by Benjamin," I retorted, yanking free from Neil's vise grip.

Neil rolled his eyes, thanked the caller, and hung up. "That was the lab. DNA came back on the first victim—the one who was mailed to Frank last week. Ben Dover. He was reported missing last Wednesday when he didn't show up to work and wasn't returning calls."

"Where'd he work?"

"NYU. He was a professor of photography. How's that tie in with your Cope skull history lesson?" Neil questioned. He typed out a text message at the speed of light before looking up at me.

"Who gives a fuck?"

"*You* gave many fucks last night."

"The Collector has taken twelve hours off the clock, Neil. We don't have time to play their game. Calvin needs help *now*!" I held up the paper again. "He thinks the building is five to seven stories. He can see over roofs, so he must be near the top, and it's definitely turn-of-the-century. Exposed-brick walls, what sounds like original wood flooring—he said there's machinery in the room. I suspect it's an old warehouse or factory that hasn't been converted into some swanky hipster joint. That fits into the search radius Quinn and I discussed yesterday."

"Sure it does," Neil agreed. "But that description alone covers Dumbo, Vinegar Hill—hell, even the Navy Yard could be a possibility. I can't set you loose on Brooklyn, shouldering down more doors, without at least narrowing that radius to a single neighborhood." He dialed another number on his cell. "I'll put in a request to have that number Calvin phoned from get tracked by cell towers, but I'm going to guess it was a burner. We might not get much."

"You know who else is from Brooklyn? *Rossi*."

"Please stop talking, Seb. For thirty seconds." Neil stared at me hard before a static voice over the phone captured his attention.

"I'll stop talking when I'm dead," I muttered. I moved away from Neil as I chose Pop's number from my contacts and gave him a ring.

He answered immediately, as if he'd been staring at his phone, waiting for me to call. "Sebastian?"

"I need your help, Pop."

"What's wrong?" he asked with alarm.

"Did you know a professor at NYU named Benjamin Dover?"

I could practically hear Pop's struggle to calm himself upon realizing I wasn't asking for him to come bail me out of jail or informing him I was in the ER. "Ah… no. No, I don't think so. Why?"

"He taught photography up until last week," I explained.

"Photography? Definitely not, then. You know how little overlap—what happened last week?"

"He was murdered."

"Good God," Pop murmured.

"Do you think you can do a little recon on him?"

"What kind of information are you looking for?"

"I'm not sure. But these murders and word games, the nonsense surrounding Edward Cope—it's all connected to the Museum of Natural History. And yet Benjamin Dover, working in a completely unrelated field, at an unrelated location, was Patient Zero. I need to know why."

"What if it's nothing more than his reputation, Sebastian?" Pop asked. "Like you. You, too, work an unrelated field, and yet you've been pulled into this."

I thought of Rossi, of how he was a perfect example of six degrees of separation, and said, "No. I kind of… figured out my connection to the museum."

Pop took a breath.

"Start with the obvious," I instructed. "See if his curriculum somehow involves fossils or dinosaurs or that sort of thinking. Check to see if he has any personal exhibits currently open somewhere in the city."

"I'll talk to a few colleagues," Pop agreed. "But, kiddo, I'm no detective. I can't promise I'll find anything more than dead ends."

I glanced up to see Neil had finished his phone call and was watching me. "I know, Dad. But I've only got twelve hours, and I need all the help I can get."

CHAPTER THIRTEEN

"I WANT you to go with Quinn," Neil said as we exited the hotel. "Check out Benjamin Dover's apartment and see what you can find."

"It's a waste of time," I said. "My dad's making some calls about this guy. We don't need to go looking in his underwear drawer in the meantime. Let's go to Brooklyn and—"

Neil stopped buttoning his jacket and took my shoulders with both hands. "In every you-can't-make-this-shit-up mystery you've been involved in, the history has mattered. The murders have always been traced back to a thing—*an artifact*—with some kind of ridiculous significance." He let go with a bit more care before adding, "Don't forget you're smart and history is what you do best."

"But if we know—"

"We *don't* know where Calvin is," Neil retorted. "And we can't have the entirety of the NYPD running to the rescue, right? Calvin managed to make a phone call and pissed this guy off enough to cut our remaining time in half. *And*," Neil continued, leaning closer, "if it is Rossi, the moment he sees uniformed officers or even me or Quinn, he might go to extremes. These remaining hours—these are the most dangerous for Calvin. We can't get sloppy now."

"I hate you."

"You like me," Neil corrected. "And you hate *that*."

After we spent a few minutes shivering in the morning cold on the side of the road, a light-colored car pulled to the curb in front of us.

The passenger window was rolled down, and from behind the wheel, Quinn called, "Get in. We're going to solve a murder."

"Seb," Neil said, stopping me as I walked toward the edge of the sidewalk.

"What?" I looked over my shoulder, hand on the car door. "*Be good*?"

Neil smiled a little. "Be careful." Both of our names were called from down the block, and Neil quickly looked to the left. I couldn't make out the figure's details, but I did recognize the voice.

Detective Wainwright.

Surprise, surprise.

Neil motioned discreetly for me to get going, walked toward Wainwright, and cut the officer off from approaching me.

"Sebastian," Quinn snapped.

I opened the door and slid into the passenger seat. I'd barely shut it behind me when Quinn pulled onto the road again and shot off toward Ninth Avenue. "Jesus, Quinn!"

"Buckle up," she said around the end of her cigarillo.

I didn't have to be told twice. Hell, I didn't even need to be told once. I shoved my bag down onto the floor between my feet and quickly pulled the seat belt on. "That was Wainwright."

Quinn gave her rearview mirror a quick look, removed her cigarillo to tap ash out her partially open window, then nodded. "Yeah."

"*Why* was it Wainwright?"

"Because Wainwright smells shit in the ranks."

"Rossi."

She snorted and took a puff of the vanilla-flavored tobacco. "Close."

I furrowed my brow and looked at her. "What do you mean?"

Quinn shook her head a little and leaned one arm on the door. "Trying to convince Major Cases that you're a harmless pain in the ass is easier said than done. I've been suspended without pay."

"*What*?" I protested. "Why?"

"Wainwright thinks I'm suspicious." She took another puff. "Can't blame him, under the circumstances. Why is Calvin's partner trying to hold the NYPD back from rescuing him, you know?"

"Because Rossi took him, and if any cops see him, then his whole plan blows up in his face."

"Yup."

"And Rossi's already panicking," I explained. "Calvin called me this morning."

Quinn shot me a look. Half a dozen different expressions seemed to dance across her face. She turned to the road again, grip tightening on the steering wheel. "*And*?"

"He's alive."

"Well, he sure as shit wasn't calling from beyond the grave."

"He sounded drugged. He could barely form coherent sentences."

She swore.

"He gave me details about his location. Neil's trying to reduce the search radius. He's somewhere in Brooklyn. You were right about that."

"Ever the soldier," she said, mostly to herself.

"The Collector—you know, fuck it. *Rossi* caught him. I think he gave Calvin more drugs to knock him out. Then he told me I only had twelve hours left instead of twenty-four."

Quinn made a sharp turn downtown, and the traffic she cut off honked noisily.

I grabbed the dash. "Could you stick to the road and not the sidewalk?"

"You heard his voice?"

"He used one of those modifiers." I looked in the side mirror, although the hotel was long behind us. "What's going to happen to Neil?"

"Wainwright's probably seeing to his suspension too."

ACCORDING TO the missing persons' report Neil had obtained that morning, Benjamin Dover was fifty years old, six feet tall, an estimated 170 pounds, with brown and gray hair. He'd last been seen leaving a bar at 2:00 a.m. in Greenwich Village and walking home a week ago last Sunday. He had not been heard from since. He was unmarried and had no known significant other, so a wellness check wasn't performed until Wednesday when a colleague called the police. The responding officers noted that the apartment was orderly, nothing appeared missing or out of place, but that there was also no indication Dover had gone on any sort of impromptu trip.

Despite her suspension status, Quinn had been able to gather a few additional details on Dover while driving to the hotel to grab me before Wainwright did. Dover had been an instructor at New York University for eighteen years, with the occasional freelance gig or personal art show on the side. Before he'd landed his position of teaching the next up-and-coming Robert Corneliuses of our time, Dover had been pursuing a career in photojournalism.

"I don't understand the connection Dover has to the museum." I shut the passenger door and slung my bag over one shoulder.

I hurried across Sullivan Street with Quinn to a multiuse building. The ground floor storefront was under construction, despite the freezing-cold weather. Guys in hard-hats and reflective vests moved in and out of what was technically the window display. Hammers banged, electric saws deafened the city ambiance, and the side door leading to the apartments above had been left propped open from all the comings and goings.

My stomach growled noisily as I caught a whiff from the dumpling store to the left. I hadn't partaken in the pastries or coffee Neil had brought up from the hotel's morning buffet, because Calvin had phoned and I was, rightfully so, in a tizzy at the time. Now that I hadn't had more than half a pretzel since around noon yesterday, I was getting pretty terrible hunger pains. But worse was the guilt over even wanting to take a breath and eat something. Because how was it fair—going into a warm restaurant, sitting down, and filling my belly—while Calvin was cold, drugged, and in imminent danger?

"I didn't think college professors made such good money," Quinn said, ignoring my statement.

"What?" I looked away from Divine Dumplings' window decal and down at her.

"Didn't your father teach at NYU?"

"Sure. I mean, Pop has a nice place too, although he's been there most of his life. It's rent-controlled."

"This is an expensive neighborhood." Quinn made a motion to her left and right. "Plus he's got a view of the Empire on one end, and One World Trade on the other."

I glanced either direction, and sure enough, I could barely make out the blurry, gray shape of spires on the horizons. "The report did say he freelanced," I suggested.

"Must be an *artiste*."

I spared her a small smile. "You mean, he must sell pretentious collections for a cool mil that can only be described as 'the communal sense of self is a wasteland,' or 'the absence of objectivity represents the performance of my manhood.'"

Quinn took a final puff from the butt of her cigarillo, dropped it to the ground, stomped it out with her heel, and muttered under her breath. She went to the side door and strolled in with the confidence of someone who lived in the building. I followed, the two of us quickly taking the stairs to the second floor. Quinn unbuttoned her coat as she reached the landing. Her steps slowed as she removed a pistol from her shoulder holster and approached the lone apartment door.

"I thought you were on suspension," I whispered.

She glanced at me and raised the gun. "My off-duty weapon," she said nonchalantly.

I stopped walking when Quinn held her hand back to put distance between us.

Her pistol held at low ready, Quinn knocked loudly on the door. "Mr. Dover!"

With the exception of what sounded like a jackhammer being added to the magnum opus downstairs, silence was her only response.

Quinn put both hands on her weapon. "NYPD!" she called next.

"We've already established he's dead, Quinn," I said from the stairs.

She ignored me, stepped to the side, and kicked the door with her boot. The lock broke, wood splintered, and the door flew back.

"*Holy shit*!" I shouted.

She pointed at the mess and glanced at me. "That door was already open. Right?"

"R-right," I agreed, offering a quick nod before joining her. "I knew the door thing was cooler when cops did it."

Quinn gave me a dubious expression, which I'd been on the receiving end of on more than one occasion, before walking into the apartment. She kept her pistol out, methodically checked each room, then motioned for me to enter. "All right, genius."

"Do *the thing*?" I asked, walking over bits of shattered wood on the kitchen floor.

"You got it."

Moving past the spacious countertops and fancy fridge, I stepped by Quinn and into the main living room on the right. Expensive leather furniture. Big-screen television. Large windows overlooking the street. A few potted orchids were dead on the sill. It was a pretty generic pad for a middle-aged bachelor, although a few framed prints—black-and-white photographs, judging by the density of the shades—hung on the walls to break up the monotony. They were pleasant enough, but contemporary art was not my forte.

Quinn whistled from behind me like she'd found something interesting.

I left the living room, walked past the kitchen doorway again, and turned into a weird alcove nestled in the back of the apartment. This was much more in tune with what I expected from a professional artist—an at-home studio. Lots of frames and samples, mounting tools, a laptop, camera collection on a nearby shelf, and laid out on a worktable, various prints that never reached the final stage of "gallery-ready."

"Find something?" I asked.

"These, for one." Quinn motioned to the enlarged photographs carefully set out on the table.

I hastily took my magnifying glass out and leaned over to inspect the pictures. They were dated. Nothing antique or even retro about them, but for the fact they'd been taken on physical film. The quality of the photos had an *alive* sensation to them that digital pixels always seemed to lack. Further examination of the unfortunate wardrobes worn by the subjects placed these pictures sometime in the '90s.

The locations and faces were different in nearly every frame. The one constant—a human skull. Pictured alongside dusty, smiling men in a desert, on the cluttered desk in an office, in its own chair beside a sleeping woman at an airport gate, even settled in between two sweating cans of beer on what looked like someone's back porch.

"Huh" was all I got out.

"Edward Cope," Quinn stated.

"We don't know that," I warned. "It could be the skull of Henry IV."

Quinn picked up a sheet from the table. "The Cope Chronicles," she read aloud.

I raised my head, studied the printed title with Dover's name underneath, looked at the photographs again, and swore. "UPenn accused the Museum of Natural History of losing their Cope skull after shipping artifacts for the upcoming exhibit, and AMNH insisted UPenn never even sent the skull."

"The museum was right," Quinn said.

"No shit… but I don't think it was anything more sinister than a simple cataloging error. Edward Cope has probably been missing from UPenn ever since Beanie Babies and fanny packs were cool. Which means he wasn't on display. Storage, most likely. Maybe no one at UPenn had reason to even suspect he wasn't in his assigned box." I pointed at the laid-out photographs. "But why the hell was Dover bringing him on a sightseeing trip?"

"Always use the buddy system when traveling."

I considered a plastic bin of wall mounts to the side of the table before suggesting, "I don't think he was prepping these for a show. It looks like he was working on layouts for a book."

"At least it's unique subject matter for a coffee-table display," Quinn said with a shake of her head.

"It might explain why he can afford this place on a teaching salary. A nice advance from a New York publishing house," I explained. "Try checking *Publishers Weekly*. You might find confirmation of a contract and an agent to reach out to for details. Plus, if news like that is public, Rossi could have easily learned about it…." I tapped my chin with my magnifying glass. "He could have come here looking for the skull, thinking Dover still had it after all this time…."

Quinn raised an eyebrow.

"Don't look at me like that," I griped. "You wanted me to do the thing—I'm doing the thing."

"All right. Anything else?"

I straightened my hunched position and winced as my back and shoulder popped. "It might be worth looking into exactly *why* Dover gave up his photojournalism career. Pilfering UPenn of its famous paleontologist head might have put a bad taste in his industry's mouth, you know? It would at least explain—" I stopped abruptly.

"*Explain*?" Quinn prodded.

"*Stuff*," I muttered before hastily squeezing between her and the wall.

"That's real fucking helpful. Thanks." Quinn turned to follow my line of motion. "What're you doing?"

I pushed in a workbench and walked to the far, heavily shelved wall opposite us. Right there, dead center, staring at me with empty and dark orbital sockets—

Edward Drinker Cope.

Chapter Fourteen

"ARE YOU sure it's a *real* skull?" Neil's voice asked over speakerphone.

"No, Neil," I snapped. "I can't tell the difference between human bone and polyresin."

"Millett," Quinn warned. "If you get him started on the history of mourning masks or some shit, I will find you." She had her eyes on the road while driving, but still pointed emphatically at my phone while speaking.

I sat shotgun, holding the head portion of Cope in one hand and his mandible in the other. "A special stationery was necessary to use for those in mourning during the Victorian era," I replied. "The envelope and notepaper were lined in black, and a gradient was used to signify—"

Quinn and Neil both moaned simultaneously.

"You know," I started, motioning at Quinn with the jaw, "one day I won't be around anymore, and then where will you be? Bored as hell."

"With significantly more headspace available," Neil said from the phone resting on my thigh.

Quinn glanced sideways. "Stop waving that at me."

"Oh. Sorry." I lowered the bone. "Neil, if you're going to admit that I'm smart, believe me when I tell you this skull is the real deal." I dug out my magnifying glass again, brought the head closer, and studied inside the socket. "There's a serial number etched into the bone."

"UPenn would be able to confirm it's theirs," Neil muttered.

I stuck the handle of the magnifying glass between my teeth and ran my fingertip around the smooth bone of the eye socket. "*Eeeil*?"

"What?" he asked.

"*Id oou et—*"

"Oh my God. Sebastian, whatever is in your mouth, spit it out," he murmured with an overwhelming sense of restrained tension.

I dropped the magnifying glass onto my lap. "Did you ever get the ME's report for the body parts?"

"In which instance?"

"Erm… mine. The decapitated head, in particular."

"It came back today, actually. But I don't have access to it. Why do you ask?"

"I think we've overlooked a glaringly obvious clue to who the Collector is."

"I thought it was Rossi," Neil said.

"It *is*," I replied. "But proof of that will get you both reinstated. You do want your job back, right?"

Neil grumbled.

"The orbital socket is smooth on a regular skull," I said. "Not perfectly round, but no jagged edges. Mine had one of the eyes removed, remember? That takes skill and practice and training to do without leaving a mark. Rossi isn't a doctor. He'll have left identifying cuts all over the bone."

"That's damn right," Quinn said, loud enough for Neil to hear. "Millett, what about trace evidence? Tell me you got something before being slapped on the wrist with a suspension."

"Sure, I got it. It's in my email, which I've been locked out of. Apparently I'm lucky to have not been arrested for obstruction of justice," he said sarcastically.

"What did you do to Wainwright this morning to piss him off so much?" I asked.

"I bet he decked him, right, Millett? You've got plenty of suppressed frustration under those fancy suits," Quinn remarked with a chuckle.

Neil declined to comment further on that topic. "I might have a work-around. How far are you from the ME's office?"

"Leaving Greenwich Village now," she answered.

"Good. Head over there. I'm going to cash in one of my favors on Dr. Asquith."

"Who's that?" I asked as Quinn made an eastbound turn at the end of the block.

"An ME I've worked with on a few cases. You should remember her from the dumpster-diver kid back in May," Neil explained.

"Oh. Right. Vaguely," I said. *Really* vaguely. Quinn had been hauling my ass into the Emporium so I wouldn't snoop on her conversation with Calvin.

"Anyway, she's still new enough to not have had the hopes and dreams beaten out of her. I'll tell her to expect you, Quinn."

MEDICAL EXAMINERS are weird.

And not weird like me. I meant, weird like they were in their own fucking stratosphere. But having a unique sense of humor probably made their jobs easier, considering they dealt with the very intimate remains of humans who once experienced love and loss and every emotion in between. I couldn't imagine doing that day in and day out. I didn't think I'd be able to professionally distance myself from the person they once were, to the corpse on the table now. I cared too deeply about stories to *not* care what they did with their time on Earth, and why they were moved to do so.

I guess that's why I collected antiques. Their stories were easier on the heart and the mind.

Less stinky too.

Anyway, whatever favor Neil had pulled from his magic hat worked. Quinn, well acquainted with the staff at the Manhattan office of the Chief Medical Examiner, greeted folks as if it was a usual day. Her presence was unquestioned. I was told to sign in and was given a visitor's badge to wear before taking the elevators downstairs. I'd left Cope in my messenger bag, safely stowed in the trunk of Quinn's car. The last thing I needed was to get stopped by security on our way out of the ME's office and they think I was trying to smuggle old bones out.

"I can't believe the morgue is in the basement," I said.

"That upsets you?"

"It's banal."

Quinn laughed a little. She put her hands in her pockets as the elevator pinged and the doors slid open.

Waiting against the far wall was a petite woman with a huge grin on her face. She seemed about my age but Quinn's height, with long light-colored hair pulled into two braids. She clapped her hands together, bounced on her toes, then ran straight at me as we stepped into the hall.

"Mr. Sebastian Snow!" she exclaimed, bypassing Quinn entirely. She grabbed my hand and shook it enthusiastically. "Detective Millett mentioned your name on the phone. I'm real happy to finally meet you!"

I winced, sure she'd about dislocated my already-bruised shoulder. "Ah—hi. Pleasure to meet you," I said through gritted teeth.

Quinn watched the animated doctor with that telltale eyebrow raised. "Dr. Asquith, right?"

"That's me," she said without breaking eye contact. "Mr. Sebastian, you have *very* soft hands. Has anyone ever told you that?"

"Uh… my fiancé. Sometimes. Usually to remind me that I'm not cut out for manual labor."

She snickered and finally released me from a Guinness Record–breaking handshake. "He's a smart man. And handsome. All that red hair." She grabbed her chic pigtail braids and gave them a tug. "I wish I had red hair. I was thinking of dying it, but knowing my luck, it'd come out blood-colored, which around this place?" Her eyes grew, and she laughed like we'd missed the punch line of a really good joke. Also, I don't think she'd taken a single breath since the elevator doors opened.

"You know my fiancé?" I asked curiously.

"Oh, sure. It's hard to miss a guy who's this tall," Asquith answered as she raised her hand over her head, then jumped for good measure. "Did you know that *I* was the ME on your case at Snow's Antique Emporium? In May. The dead boy in the dumpster. I love the name of your shop. It's so… romantic. *Sensational*."

I was hardly one to judge, considering most folks thought I was nuts to varying degrees, but umm…? The darling doc needed to see sunlight more often.

"We're on a deadline," Quinn said. "I believe Detective Millett informed you I was here for an in-person look at the wound patterns of Monday's victim?"

"Sure, sure," Asquith replied. She grabbed my arm, wound her own through it, and dragged me down the hall. "Although Mr. Sebastian isn't *really* here to identify a body as suggested by the front desk, is he?" She looked up at me with another wide smile. "But I know when to be quiet." She winked and made a button motion over her lips.

I craned my neck to look at Quinn, who was following with a very disgruntled, back-seat-driver-who'd-been-told-to-can-it expression.

"You're not squeamish, are you?" Asquith asked me as we neared an open door at the end of the hall. She then playfully slapped my chest and answered her own question. "No, of course you aren't."

She led me, and by extension, Quinn, into a sparsely furnished room that had harsh overhead lighting and a nauseating chemical cleaner smell lingering in the air. She ushered me toward a bank of freezers, told me to stay, then snapped on a pair of latex gloves pulled from the pocket of her lab coat.

Asquith opened the locker marked 17, pulled out the retractable gurney, unzipped the bag, and displayed the skull from inside as if it were a trophy. "Ta-da!"

"Where's his face?" I asked, acknowledging how *wrong* that sounded.

"We had to strip the flesh. It was decomposing. Plus it's the only way to inspect the bone for additional trauma." She picked up an evidence baggie. "And here are the teeth that were collected from the Emporium yesterday—the central and lateral incisors, as well as one canine."

Quinn approached the gurney. "So what kind of weapon was it that dug out the eye? Butter knife? Pocketknife? Machete?"

Asquith stared at Quinn for a long, borderline uncomfortable moment. Then she imitated a loud buzzer sound. "Wrong, wrong, and wrong. Would you like to phone a friend, Detective Lancaster?"

Quinn put her hands on her hips, I think purposefully showing off the shoulder holster as her unbuttoned coat opened with the motion. "Just tell us what the damn weapon was."

I took out my phone and checked the newly adjusted timer app. Seven hours left.

Yes, please.

Asquith set the bag of teeth aside and then tossed me a pair of latex gloves. "If you don't mind, Mr. Sebastian."

"We don't have time for games, doc," Quinn said firmly.

"Oh, *pffft*," Asquith declared. "Destress your chest, Detective."

"Excuse me?" Quinn said in a dangerous voice, her face discoloring with what I figured was a pinkish red I'd been told was similar to and yet so different from a blush.

I hastily put the gloves on and grabbed what remained of poor Daniel the Intern. The kid had seen better days, that much was certain. "Walk it off, Quinn," I said, knowing I'd be getting my own ass-kicking from her later.

Asquith leaned over the table to put her finger on the brow of the skull. "What do you see?"

"Not a whole hell of a lot in this lighting," I replied.

"That's right," she said, almost cooing. "You have achromatopsia." Asquith pattered across the room and flipped two of the three light switches. "How's that, Mr. Sebastian?"

"Er—better, thanks." I gave her a wary look as she returned to my side. "Sorry. *How* do you know about my vision condition?"

"People talk, you know." She again tapped the skull. "Take a look."

I felt unduly cautious in that moment. I couldn't pinpoint what exactly caused the hairs on my neck to stand up. A lot of folks knew about my issue with lights. Whether or not they understood the particulars of achromatopsia or any of the symptoms beyond light sensitivity, many seemed to at least be aware that I was not like most people. I had limitations, with sometimes curious workarounds, but I wasn't particularly anxious these days about people knowing. People staring. In fact, the more who understood achromatopsia, the better. Maybe that way there'd be a cure before I died an old man, having never experienced the fiery red of Calvin's hair.

Asquith smiled, pointed at my eyes, then at the skull. "My bones are down here," she teased.

I hesitantly gave the skull my undivided attention. Daniel looked like Cope. And with the exception of Cope's discoloration due to age and storage, bones were bones were bones. Frankly, it had a way of humbling a man.

"I don't see any sort of damage," I said to Asquith. I put a finger in either socket and felt along the edges for where an untrained hand would have gouged into bone while severing an eyeball. But I couldn't find any cuts or nicks. I stopped manhandling the skull and put it on the gurney. "Is this a trick question?"

Asquith laughed. "Yeah. There are zero cuts to the bone," she said before giving Quinn a leveled look.

"What's that mean, then?" Quinn asked quickly.

"It means, I suspect whoever did the cutting had a very sharp instrument and knew how to use it," Asquith said.

I FELT like I'd been kicked in the chest.

It was hard to breathe—impossible to speak.

All of my sleuthing, researching, interviewing… in the blink of an eye, none of it mattered anymore. Because I couldn't argue with scientific evidence. It was like telling Neil the fingerprint he lifted wasn't actually a fingerprint. It didn't work that way.

Life in a modern, industrialized, urban environment didn't *work that way*.

Dr. Asquith had shown me forensic proof that the hand responsible for removing Daniel's eye and teeth had gone to medical school. She explained, while showing us original photographs taken by Neil, that even the severing of the neck was precise and professional.

"*They knew exactly what they were doing*," she'd said.

Which would mean the same for all the other body parts strewn across New York City.

And that… Rossi was not our guy and Dr. Gould was not his assistant.

I was left with a long-lost skull, no way in which to deliver it to the Collector, no suspect to punch in the fucking face, and a fiancé who, because of me, wasn't going to see the sun rise tomorrow. I felt absolutely dead and rotting inside.

Crouching, I grabbed the handle on the woven metal gate of the Emporium and lifted it up and over my head. I took out my keys, unlocked the front door, and leaned inside to tap in the security code. I turned and stared at Quinn, who was standing a step back from the storefront.

"I'll call Wainwright," she said. "Tell him how much time is left…. Have him expedite information from Telecom on that burner number."

I nodded.

"I'll try the courier angle one more time," Quinn continued. "No one was ever able to describe the courier beyond it being a woman… there were no receipts… but there's still shady, cheap companies operating like that. Collector probably sought them out specifically."

Again, I nodded. Had I not stopped nodding after acknowledging her first comment?

"It's not over yet, Sebastian," she said.

Yes, it was.

"Sure," I said thickly.

Quinn pointed at the shop. "Stay here. I'll call you soon." She walked back to her car, parked on the side of the road.

I stepped into the shop, gently closing the door behind me. My dark, silent cave was a microcosm of serenity among a world of chaos. Maybe if I never left, if I isolated myself from all of humanity inside this time capsule, I'd survive. Heartbroken, lonely, devastated, and a shell of the man I'd become… but I'd survive.

I trudged through the congested aisles toward the counter.

But what sort of life was that?

What was the sense of existence without… *existing*?

It's not that I couldn't live without Calvin.

I could.

I *had*. For thirty-three years.

It was only… after he fit into that odd shape missing from my heart… I didn't *want* to live without him.

I set my bag on the counter and methodically removed the contents: glasses case, laptop, keys, magnifying glass, extra sweater, skull. I emptied my pockets next. Phone and wallet. I stared at the items while absently unbuttoning my coat. I waited for something to jump out as a tool MacGyver would have used to save the day.

But nothing happened. I had lost every goddamn spoon to my name. I frowned and checked the bag's front pocket. Ah. The rapidly written note of details from my call with Calvin.

God…. *Calvin.*

I brought the note closer and studied my shitty penmanship.

Machinery.

Five to seven stories.

Exposed brick and broken wooden floors.

Humming.

Bumpy road.

"Bumpy," I murmured.

And like that, the most inconsequential clue flipped a switch in the deepest recesses of my brain.

If Calvin had been hauled from Midtown to north Brooklyn, he absolutely would have been incapacitated. Otherwise, whoever had tried to abduct him would be dead. Because good luck to anyone who single-handedly tried to take Calvin down in a physical fight. But what did that mean? Logically, whatever drug had Calvin so out of it on the phone probably would have been administered pretty quickly in the vehicle. And yet, the road had been bumpy enough that Calvin was able to acknowledge *and* retain that fact when he said he could remember nothing else.

So a really bad road? Like… potholes?

Or cobblestone.

"Son of a bitch!" I shouted. I grabbed my phone off the counter and dialed Neil. "He's in Vinegar Hill," I said before he had a chance to fully answer the call.

"What? How do you know?"

"Calvin said the road had been bumpy and he could hear humming. *Neil.* Vinegar Hill is a declared Historical District. The surviving roads are made out of Belgian block."

"But humming?" Neil asked, wary but on high alert.

"ConEd's power plant," I answered.

He swore. "Where are you?"

"The Emporium."

"I'll be there soon," he said, abruptly hanging up.

I shoved a few things into my pockets, grabbed Cope, and jumped off the steps. I ran along the aisles toward the door, only skidding to a stop when I saw the signed mystery novel Beth had brought me yesterday, left on a table. I set the skull on a nearby display case and picked up the Miss Butterwith title. The old gal always got the bad guy in the end, with the help of her feline companion, Mr. Pinkerton, as well as Inspector Appleby.

I felt a smile tug the corner of my mouth as I considered me, Neil, and Quinn to be a similar band of musketeers. If a geriatric sleuth could save the day, then one with bad eyesight and a quicksilver tongue should be capable too, right? Of course, Miss Butterwith was fictional and I was real, but still.

I opened the book and stared at the signature. It wasn't worth what Beth's account balance was, not by a long shot. But I knew I'd let it slide. Because Christopher Holmes's signature was priceless to me, even when comparing it to the original editions of Max Brödel's medical illustrations Beth had snagged from my shelves a few weeks ago.

I looked at Cope and dropped the mystery book back on the table. "Medical illustrations."

Unsurprisingly, the skull did not respond.

I grabbed Cope. "What happens when you combine medical knowledge, Victorian America, Calvin, and *me*?" I asked him.

Cope didn't appear to have the answer.

"*Sensationalism*, that's what!" I ran out the front door, nearly slipped on the first step, caught myself, then remembered to lock the door before starting toward Good Books.

"Sebastian!"

I paused midstep and looked toward the road. Marc Winter was climbing out of a cab and walking toward me. "I don't have the time," I said.

"You need to make—is that—what is *that*?" Marc pointed at my skull as he stepped over the slush accumulating on the edge of the road.

I looked at Cope and then held him up to provide a better view. "Edward Drinker Cope, once famous paleontologist, now a museum artifact."

Marc was bristly as he joined me on the sidewalk. His eyes darted to Cope a few times, sort of like he had just seen a car wreck and couldn't quite pull himself away from the horror. "I had an extremely unpleasant meeting with a Detective Wainwright this morning," he managed at length.

"My condolences." I tucked Cope carefully into the fold of my arm.

"Wainwright was asking about my whereabouts the last few days. About my *baby sister's* whereabouts."

"Wow," I said, mildly surprised. Wainwright not only listened to my harebrained ramblings yesterday but pursued the possibility in an official capacity. No doubt he was now comfortable in writing the Winters off as harmless, as I had been, but still. After suspending Quinn and Neil, the last thing I'd expected was Wainwright entertaining a word I'd said.

"He says Calvin has been abducted." Marc took another step forward to loom over me.

"That's correct," I said calmly. Perhaps too much so. Or maybe it wasn't calmness at all. Maybe I was simply adrift in a hazy space of sleep deprivation and a fuck-it-all attitude.

"I know you're behind this," Marc said accusingly.

"Behind the abduction? No. Behind the questioning? Yes. I did tell Wainwright to look into you both."

"Ellen lives *and* works in Philly," Marc declared.

"But do you understand why I even had to consider it?"

"Because you're shit nuts?" Marc retaliated.

I sighed inwardly. "Sometimes. But mostly it was because I didn't believe you had a sincere bone in your body regarding Calvin."

"He's my *brother*," Marc said, his mouth a thin line. "You want to hear me say it? Fine. I screwed up." The muscles in his jaw jumped much like Calvin's did under stress. "I didn't understand Calvin, and I didn't want to try. And to be honest, I still don't understand him. Or why the *hell* he'd want to marry a smartass like you."

"Thank you," I said dryly.

"But…." Marc struggled for a moment. A long moment at that. "Calvin was never happy growing up. *Never*. He didn't have a good relationship with our father, and God knows I didn't do much to ease the tension…." Marc stared at the road as a few taxis drove past, splashing dirty snow and slush on the sidewalk. "When he spoke your name last Christmas… all I could think was, his own family never made him smile like that."

Marc cautiously put his hand out. I looked between his face and the offering several times, not rising to the bait.

"I can live with the two of us never being friends. And I'm sure you can too. But whatever it is you're doing right now," Marc whispered, words catching a bit, "bring my brother home."

I waited, but the punch line never came. So I took Marc's hand and shook it. "I will."

Chapter Fifteen

"BETH!" I shouted, throwing the door open to her shop and stepping inside.

She jumped from where she stood hunched over the counter. Beth put her bejeweled glasses on and frowned at me. "You about gave me a heart attack, Sebby. And this is a bookstore! Keep your damn voice down," she chastised at an equally loud volume.

I walked inside, letting the door fall shut as I approached the counter.

Beth's eyebrows went up. "Are you—taking a human skull for a walk?"

I looked at Cope and set him on top of Beth's crossword puzzle. "Max Brödel."

"That's *not* Max Brödel," she said, pushing Cope away with the end of her pen.

"No, I mean Brödel of the medical illustration books I sold you. I want to take a look at them."

"I've already sold one," she said while walking around the counter to stand in front of me. "Sebby, what's going on? Is Calvin still missing? No one's told me anything."

I held a hand up to stop her. "Which one did you sell?"

"Which Brödel book? *Operative Gynecology*," Beth replied, perplexed.

"I want to see *The Vermiform Appendix and Its Diseases*." I sidestepped Beth and went to her large glass case of rare and antique collectables. For a brief moment, a copy of Edgar Allan Poe's *Tamerlane* had resided here last Christmas. That really did seem like ages ago. I moved around to the back side, opened the sliding door, and gently removed the big hardcover reference book.

"Hey. What are you, an amateur?" Beth tossed me a pair of cloth gloves.

I missed, picked them up from the case top, and tugged the gloves on before opening the book. I carefully flipped through the pages as Beth joined me. "Calvin was kidnapped by someone who has a fairly intimate understanding of both Victorian America and medicine."

I could feel Beth staring at me. Gauging what to say—what was *okay* to say. "How do you know?" she inquired, voice uncharacteristically gentle.

"On each message I got, there were drawings of human body parts. And from the very start of all this, I was bothered by how… *clinical* they were. Not romanticism art of the time period, but medical art. Hand-drawn with a purposeful, antiquated appearance." I kept flipping until I came upon an intense, lifelike drawing of a woman's torso, complete with muscular structures and indicators for doctors on how to make incisions. I tapped the page. "Purposeful because the Collector was copying the work of Max Brödel, a pioneer in his field at Johns Hopkins University at the turn of the century, who would be a history lesson for the medical students of today!"

I shut the book and declared loudly, like a real-life game of Clue, "I accuse Dr. Asquith in Vinegar Hill with a benzodiazepine!"

I THANKED Pop, said goodbye, and hung up. Neil was driving over the Manhattan Bridge, the early-setting sun already dipping over the horizon with the promise of another cold, wintry night on its way. He reached with one hand to change the whispering radio station from metal to jazz. A concession to me without an argument.

"I hope your father got more information to work with than I did," Neil remarked. "Dr. Asquith wasn't at the ME's office when I called. She never returned from her lunch break."

"My dad had a meeting with an administrator at NYU," I answered. "She's an old friend of, and occasionally something more to, Benjamin Dover. She's actually the one who filed a missing person report on him."

I looked at Neil briefly. He had one hand draped casually over the wheel. The BMW—I'd been told—handled night and day compared to the CSU van he occasionally drove to scenes throughout the five boroughs. Whatever that meant. But anyway. Neil looked pretty cool in that seat, exuding a gentle, authentic confidence I'd never quite seen before. Dirty distortion cast by the overhead lights of the bridge reshaped his face as we passed under them.

Neil glanced sideways. "I'm listening."

"While attempting to make a name for himself and get noticed by magazines like *National Geographic*, Dover apparently discovered the ideal subject for a project in a museum in Pennsylvania."

"UPenn."

"Bingo. This administrator claims the story goes: He checked out the skull, like a library book. And went on an adventure around the world, taking photos of Cope among modern paleontologists, at museum exhibits, dig sites—you get the idea."

"Hmm."

"Apparently a few better-known journalists thought it was a tacky project—called him out on it. Dover never returned Cope to UPenn, maybe out of fear they'd report his indiscretion to the cops or something. But I don't think they even noticed its absence until AMNH requested the artifact."

"*How* could they not?"

"It could have been overlooked during a catalog overhaul of manual to electronic. This was in like '94—'95?"

"Even if they had caught on to Dover never having returned the artifact, the Art Crime Team didn't exist with the FBI yet," Neil continued thoughtfully.

"And local police tend to have better things to look into," I concluded. "Anyway. I guess he figured enough time had passed that no one would remember the events that chased him out of his budding photojournalism career. So he signed what his sometimes bed-friend described as a 'high-six-fucking-figure' contract."

"For pictures of a skull?" Neil asked, looking at me in disbelief.

"And the story. It's a good story," I admitted. "Plus, when Quinn and I—er—were in his apartment, I saw some of the photos. They're impressive. He had a real eye, at least back then."

Neil made a turn as we got off the bridge and entered Brooklyn. "How does Dr. Asquith tie into this? You're really certain it's not Rossi?"

"Unfortunately, yes," I agreed. "I'm not sure how Dr. Asquith learned about the Cope skull. She doesn't appear to have any sort of connection to either museum. But I don't think *how* is important to our case. I'd jump right to the *why*."

"If the skull is worth whatever someone is willing to pay," Neil said, "that might be good incentive for someone saddled with medical school student loans."

"Could be."

"But she's five foot nothing," he continued. "How does someone like her take down a tank like Calvin?"

"Feigned innocence. A true psychopath." I looked at Neil again as we came to a red light. "He knows her. Has no reason not to trust her. Hell, he'd have willingly jumped into an ME's van if she asked for assistance. One shot of something like diazepam to a major artery, and he'd be down, maybe unconscious, in under a minute. As long as she can keep him drugged enough not to escape but also not die, I'm at her mercy and this game of hers continues."

Neil hit the accelerator again. "All this because the drawings were too anatomically correct?"

"She said 'sensational.'"

"What?"

"At the ME's office. She said she was so happy to finally meet me. And that the Emporium's name was *sensational*." I took in a slow, steady breath. "The Collector said that on the phone this morning… like… asking if I failed, would I promise to battle them until the very end and make it sensational."

Neil snorted. "A modern war between intellectuals."

"Marsh and Cope all over again, losing everything in an effort to destroy each other," I said quietly.

Neil reached and turned the radio off.

The clock read 5:00 p.m.…. We barely had three hours left.

The transition to Vinegar Hill was understated, but the tiny little neighborhood made its historical mark known through the architecture of the homes and streets.

"A whole other sort of war was waged in Vinegar Hill," I murmured, staring out the passenger window at the passing high-rises and converted warehouses.

"What's that, Sherlock?"

I smiled absently. Neil had always refused to call me Sherlock when we were an item. It was nice to hear him say that now. A subtle apology between us.

"The Whiskey Wars. After the Civil War, a large population of Irish immigrants in this area became infamous for their moonshining business and what became the IRS battling them over not paying taxes on the alcohol."

Neil didn't say anything, but I heard the quietest chuckle escape his lips.

We'd turned onto Bridge Street, and out of the darkness, an all-brick—count them—seven-story warehouse appeared. It was nearly the expanse of the entire block in length, and the boarded-up doors on the ground floor suggested it was still sitting empty and unused, despite being prime real estate in the next "big neighborhood" to turn into apartments or a rooftop bar or even an art gallery.

"Stop! Neil!"

He slammed on the brakes. "What?"

"This is it." I turned my head and pointed. "Look there—the power plant. You can hear the humming from here."

Neil shut the engine off and quickly climbed out from behind the wheel.

I followed suit, still clutching Cope in one hand and moving around to the trunk of the BMW as Neil opened it. I watched him grab a pair of bolt cutters and shut the top. "*Really*?"

"I'm CSU," he said with a wide, easy smile. "We're prepared for anything."

We quickly moved from the side of the cobblestone road and toward the nearest door, which had a heavy chain wrapped around the handles. Neil put the cutters on it and managed to slice through the hefty links after a few attempts. He grabbed the broken chain, pulled it free, and threw it into the dead grass. He silently handed me the tool, removed his weapon and a small pocket flashlight, then took the lead up the dark, crumbling set of stairs inside.

"This place ought to be condemned," he whispered in between each creak and groan.

"Historically—"

"Yeah, yeah."

Neil stopped at the landing of each floor and opened the door to the main work room. They all mirrored one another—a massive expanse with nothing but occasional support beams to break up the shadows and give any sense of depth to the room. The walls on the right side were entirely bare brick, and the left were massive, probably antique glass windows that in the daytime would at least make this place not so spooky.

The floors were a mess that hadn't survived the test of time as well as the walls had. The second and third levels were okay. But the fourth was littered with broken floorboards and swatches of dark on dark, suggesting areas had simply begun rotting away.

Neil opened the door to the fifth-level floor and flashed his beam inside. I hiked up the next several steps in order to get a better vantage point over his shoulder. In the silence between us echoed a snap, a crack—

"Seb!"

I lunged forward, throwing myself up the stairs, which was not an easy task, just as a portion of the wall and roof over the stairwell literally caved in on itself, effectively separating the two of us.

"*Jesus*," I whispered, trying to suppress a cough from the hundred years of dust now in the air.

"Seb?" Neil called again, voice muffled through the collapsed brick.

"Shh. I'm okay," I said in a low voice.

A portion of his face appeared through the debris. "Don't move. I'm going back downstairs. There's doors on the other side of each room—it's probably a matching stairwell. I'll come around to meet you."

"What if the boogeyman gets me?"

"Don't move," he replied with a touch of exasperation.

Neil's steps receded until I was alone between the fifth and sixth floors. Stay here. *Like hell.* I held up Cope in my hand, only to realize his jaw was… somewhere in the wreckage behind me. I'd lost it in my juggle to save the bolt cutters.

"Shit."

I hesitated for about a nanosecond before continuing up the remaining steps without the mandible. I reached the landing for the sixth floor and, with one hand feeling along the wall, found the threshold for the main work area. The door was slightly ajar, which, considering all the floors before had been securely closed, was warning enough for me. Gripping Cope and bolt cutters big enough to kill a man, I slipped inside.

This level was above the rooftops of surrounding buildings. Sickly city glimmerings and fragile moonlight mixed together and filtered in through the bay windows. The floor was illuminated enough to make out the odd machine here and there. Textile tools probably. Definitely from a lifetime ago.

And there, second support beam deep, closest to the windows, was the crumpled figure of a man.

My man.

I was so close. I wanted to run toward Calvin with open arms and save him from this hellhole. But the floor was likely to be as dangerous as the others. So I carefully, silently, slid along the wall behind me, reached the corner, and then moved the same way along the windows. In passing each plate of glass, I blocked out the light enough to silhouette my figure on the dusty floor. Eerie, with the cutters and Cope in either hand.

My teeth chattered from the cold, and my breath came out in shaky puffs. But I reached Calvin. Tears ran down my face as I dropped my belongings to the floor and bent down beside him.

"Calvin?" I whispered. It took considerable strength to hoist up a completely limp brick wall. "Cal? Honey?" I hefted him around enough in order to rest his back against the pillar. I put my numb fingers to his neck and checked for a pulse.

Alive. I could barely feel it. But he was alive.

I moved my hand to his cheek, stroking the cold, pallid, bristly skin. "Calvin?" I tried again, a bit louder.

I watched his face carefully. One eye twitched. Then both. In a droopy, drugged-out manner, they slowly opened. He didn't seem to register at first that I was me or that I was even a person crouched in front of him. But then he jerked suddenly, tried to bring his arms up to fight, before I realized they were tied around the back side of the beam.

"Calvin." I took his face into both hands, holding him firmly. "It's *me*."

Calvin stilled. His breath was shallow. "Baby…."

I smiled as if it were the very first time I'd heard that nickname. "Hey. How are you?" I whispered.

Calvin let out the saddest attempt at a laugh. "*Tired*."

"You know," I said, quickly wiping my cheeks with the sleeve of my coat and grasping for a playful tone, "if you didn't want an extravagant wedding, you could have said so. This is a little extreme."

Calvin smiled, even as his eyes fell shut. "Get… me home. Please."

I leaned forward and kissed his chilled, chapped lips. "Copy you, Major." I got up, knees cracking as I collected the bolt cutters, and moved behind the beam. I snipped the zip ties off Calvin's wrists, and his arms fell to his sides.

There was no way I could carry him out like this. *Maybe* with Neil's help, but not in the sort of condition Calvin was in. He was dehydrated, overdosed, and in shock from the cold.

I don't know how in hell Asquith managed to drag him inside. Unless she'd quite literally… *dragged him*. In which case, God only knew how many bumps, bruises, or possible breaks he may have had.

I got down beside Calvin again as I pulled out my cell phone to call Neil. The light on Calvin's face shifted, as if someone had stepped past the windows from farther behind me. Jesus, Neil had been fast.

I lowered my phone. "Neil. I found him!"

"Mr. Sebastian!"

The shudder that rippled through my body was as if someone had just taken a step over my grave. Even Calvin cracked open an eye and turned his head toward the voice.

Asquith stepped out from the shadows along the brick wall. Had she been here the entire time? Hiding in perfect darkness and watching everything I'd done?

She leaned over, her hands on her knees. "I believe you have something for me."

I didn't take my eyes off her, instead reached behind me and blindly felt around until I'd touched Cope. I stuck my fingers into his eye sockets and held out the skull. "Here. Edward Drinker Cope's skull. Game is played; mystery is solved."

She whistled and quickly snatched the skull. "Wowie. This is pretty incredible. I have a collection he's going into. Now, I *know* what you're thinking, 'You're a medical examiner, of course you have some super creepy display of human body parts!'" She chuckled, snapped on a flashlight in her hand, and examined Cope. "I have a fragment of Lincoln's skull—it was removed when doctors attempted to treat his wound. A brain section of Albert Einstein—"

"Those are in a museum," I retorted.

"*Yeah*," she chuckled. "And they're missing one."

Asquith raised the light directly at me. I winced and blocked the beam with my hand.

"I don't *own* it, sadly, but I did travel to St. Petersburg to see Rasputin's penis. It's pretty neat. Still has hair on the sac."

She lowered the light. Spots danced in my line of vision, and I hastily blinked them away.

Asquith straightened her posture. "But Cope. I've wanted to meet him my entire life. He donated his brain and skull to science, as a bet." She held Cope as if he were Yorick. "To prove even in death that he was superior to Marsh. He wanted their brains weighed and measured." She looked at the two of us and explained, "He was super racist. A true congenital prick. Marsh never did take him up on that bet. So Cope was sitting on a shelf in UPenn for a hundred years. And then some selfish *motherfucker* took him so I never had the opportunity to visit him in medical school. I have been searching for Cope ever since."

I got to my feet but froze when Asquith shifted the flashlight and skull to one hand and removed a small compact pistol from her coat pocket. I slowly raised my hands. "Please let me get Calvin out of here. He needs medical attention."

Asquith grinned widely. "Did you like the puzzle?"

I heard Calvin slump to the floor behind me, but I didn't dare take my eyes off Asquith. "If you tracked down Dover on your own, you must have seen the skull in his apartment. It was sitting right out in the open."

She nodded solemnly. "I did. I could have taken it then and there. But these museums, so chock-full of useless administrators and self-centered curators, were more concerned over passing the blame for who lost Cope instead of *finding* him. They needed to reevaluate their priorities."

"So you started with Frank."

"Sure!" Asquith agreed. "I read about the visiting exhibit. That's how I figured out UPenn was *finally* in a frenzy over Cope. And Frank Newell should have gotten the puzzle immediately. The clues were so obvious, and he was a paleontologist, for Christ's sake! He should have *known* the story of Cope's skull. If he'd actually cared at all, he'd have gone to visit UPenn like me, to find it not available in their artifacts catalog!"

Calvin was dragging himself along the floor. It pained me not to look, not to check on him.

Asquith didn't seem concerned about his movements. "Frank was a loser. And that intern. He wanted a doctorate, right? He should have *known*."

I swallowed hard. "He was a kid in love."

"He should have been in love with learning," Asquith chastised. She showed me those pearly whites in another huge unnerving grin. "Like *you*, Mr. Sebastian. Owner of the popular one-stop shop for Victorian gizmos and gadgets. Smart, sassy, *sexy*, if some people are to be believed." She added the third comment as if it were a scandalous secret between us. "And after that Moving Image case—seeing the things you could do. The dangers you would face. Oh, I knew. I *knew* you cared."

"I cared for Calvin."

She shrugged and cocked the hammer on her gun. "Whatever. You still played. Do you feel smarter? Did your ego get sufficiently stroked?"

I opened my mouth. To say what, I didn't know. I was trying to accept the fact that I was about to be shot again. And with a cheap, dangerous gun like that, I wouldn't live.

But at least I'd seen Calvin one more—

A shot rang through the room, just about piercing my eardrum. A half a second later, or before—it was hard to gauge—Asquith screamed. The Cope skull in her hand shattered as a bullet went through it, and half her hand was blown completely off. She dropped her weapon and grasped the profusely bleeding appendage to her chest.

I turned to see Calvin had dragged himself to a discarded pile of boxes under the nearest window, where his weapon and badge had been resting the entire time. He lowered his hand, dropped the SIG to the floor, and appeared to fall unconscious.

"Fucking ginger bastard!" Asquith cried. She bent down and grabbed for her pistol with her good hand.

I picked up the bolt cutters from the floor and charged at her, the floor cracking and shattering beneath my feet.

Chapter Sixteen

I'D KNOCKED Asquith upside the head with the cutters and promptly fell through the disintegrating floor. Clawing frantically on my way down, I'd caught hold of a support beam on the fifth floor, slowed the descent, then toppled the remaining six or so feet like a rag doll. It was enough to render me unconscious after whacking my head. When I came to, I was strapped to a stretcher and being rolled toward an ambulance. The block was lit up like a party—lights strobing, people calling, radios blaring. I hated parties. I hated people. I wanted to go home.

I remembered asking about Calvin. Remembered harassing the confused EMTs about my fiancé and whether he was safe and that I didn't need a damn ambulance and to let me go. Neil had been there. At some point he'd simply… appeared. He'd taken my hand and given it a firm squeeze before I was lifted into the bus, swearing that Calvin was okay. I'd faded out after that. Although I briefly recalled waking in the hospital. Not opening my eyes—it was always too bright—but hearing my father's gentle voice as he spoke with a doctor.

It seemed another concussion had been the worst of my aches and pains. I'd been kept under observation overnight because of my history of being conked on the head. But I was okay the next day. No worse than how my mysteries usually played out. I'd discharged myself the first chance I had, dressed in clean clothes Pop brought for me, and gone to visit Calvin's room. It was flanked by uniformed officers standing guard, but upon seeing me, I was let inside without question.

Calvin was propped up in bed. He was awake—a sort of exhausted alertness about his features. He startled when the door opened, turned his head abruptly, but then the rigidness of his posture eased. Calvin cracked a weary smile. "Hey, beautiful," he whispered.

I sat down in the chair beside the bed. "Hey, handsome."

Calvin reached his hand out. I took it and held on. His familiar warmth and grip all but undid every frayed and worn thread I had left keeping me together.

"Please don't cry," he murmured.

I shook my head, sniffed loudly, and brought his fist up to kiss his knuckles. "I'm not."

Calvin brushed a bit of hair from my eyes with a finger. "Thanks for being a busybody." His voice was still rough. Worn out.

But he was *alive*.

I took a deep breath and smiled. "Sure, anytime. You won't get rid of me that easily."

"I *did* put a ring on it," Calvin said thoughtfully.

I laughed. "Yeah, you did." I sandwiched his hand between mine. "I like you," I murmured.

"I like you too."

I'd been right about Asquith. The obsession with Victorian medical history led to a body part collection. Quite impressive, Neil and Quinn later informed me, after having been reinstated and finishing the case where I'd left it abandoned like a car on fire. It sounded as if Asquith, even after having found Edward Drinker Cope herself, still grew as easily bored as I did and was never satisfied for long.

The only difference was, I didn't kill people to quench the thirst for adventure.

The fact she was destined to rot in a jail cell forever was of little solace to the families of Dover, Newell, and Howard. But at least I'd stopped her. If that meant anything.

I WOKE up to the gentle murmur of Bing Crosby's "I'll Be Home for Christmas" on the record player downstairs. I cracked open an eye, glanced at Calvin's vacant pillow, and reached out to touch it. Cold. After sitting up, I swung my legs over the side of the bed and stood. I tugged my arms through the sleeves of a sweater, put my glasses on, and stumbled half-awake down the stairs.

"Hey. Mom and Dad said we had to wait until at least seven o'clock before opening presents," I teased.

Calvin sat on the floor of our living room in front of the Christmas tree. The supposedly rainbow lights wrapped around it cast snowflake-like shapes across his face as the illumination filtered through the boughs of the tree.

Calvin rubbed Dillon's stomach as he looked up at me. "I didn't want to toss and turn you awake."

"I promised the doctor you would rest," I told him, moving around the lazy dog and sitting on Calvin's right.

"I'm fine, Seb." He set his coffee mug down in front of him and touched my face. "I'll *be* fine," he corrected. "Really."

"You're not lying?"

"I don't lie to you."

I smiled and rolled my eyes playfully. "Yeah, I know. Your heart is too pure." I stared at the humble number of wrapped packages under the tree. "Well, when in Rome." I grabbed one and offered it.

"Second Christmas in a row we didn't do so well on the gift-giving front."

"Third time's the charm." I watched Calvin take the small box with a knowing expression on his face. "That's from me," I added.

"I'd certainly hope it's from you."

"There were nurses fighting over who got to take your temperature at the hospital," I stated as Calvin tore the Emporium gift wrap from the jewelry box.

"Stop," he said with a chuckle.

"I had to sleep with one eye open at your side. I thought for sure they were going to take me out in order to be your future plus-one."

Calvin snapped open the box and stared at the contents.

I glanced between him and the ring. "Is something wrong with it?"

"What?" He looked at me, distracted.

"I told the jeweler you wanted matte like mine." I held my hand up against the box. "I warned him I couldn't see color."

"No," Calvin quickly answered. "This is perfect." His Adam's apple jumped a little as he tugged the wedding band free and put it on.

I shifted sideways to stare head-on at Calvin. "We have to be at the City Clerk's Office tomorrow at 10:00 a.m."

"I didn't want to say anything negative about the wedding," Calvin replied, looking at me with the sweetest, most easygoing smile I'd seen all month. "Because you were trying so hard. But I'm really glad we're skipping the ceremony."

"You and me both. I think our sort of romance runs in a different vein," I replied.

He raised an eyebrow. "Yeah? How's that?"

I leaned back on my hands. "Crimes, clues, my hunky husband telling me to stop, but secretly, he kind of enjoys my sleuthing…. It's romantic."

Calvin snorted and laughed. "That's *not* romantic, baby."

"No?"

"Absolutely not."

"Correct me if I'm wrong."

Calvin reached out, tugged my sweater to pull me back in, and kissed my mouth. "*This* is romantic," Calvin whispered. "Us. Here. Merry Christmas, Sebastian."

"Merry Christmas, Calvin."

C.S. POE is a Lambda Literary and two-time EPIC award finalist, and a FAPA award-winning author of gay mystery, romance, and paranormal books.

She is a reluctant mover and has called many places home in her lifetime. C.S. has lived in New York City, Key West, and Ibaraki, Japan, to name a few. She misses the cleanliness, convenience, and limited-edition *gachapon* of Japan, but she was never very good at riding bikes to get around.

She has an affinity for all things cute and colorful and a major weakness for toys. C.S. is an avid fan of coffee, reading, and cats. She's rescued two cats—Milo and Kasper do their best on a daily basis to distract her from work.

C.S. is a member of the International Thriller Writers organization.

Website: cspoe.com

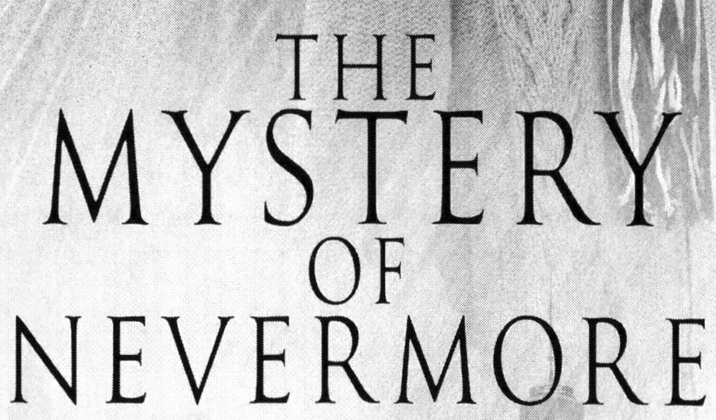
THE
MYSTERY
OF
NEVERMORE
SNOW & WINTER: BOOK ONE
C.S. POE

Snow & Winter: Book One

It's Christmas, and all antique dealer Sebastian Snow wants is for his business to make money and to save his floundering relationship with closeted CSU detective Neil Millett. When Snow's Antique Emporium is broken into and a heart is found under the floorboards, Sebastian can't let the mystery rest.

He soon finds himself caught up in murder investigations that echo the macabre stories of Edgar Allan Poe. To make matters worse, Sebastian's sleuthing is causing his relationship with Neil to crumble, while at the same time he's falling hard for the lead detective on the case, Calvin Winter. Sebastian and Calvin must work together to unravel the mystery behind the killings, despite the mounting danger and sexual tension, before Sebastian becomes the next victim.

In the end, Sebastian only wants to get out of this mess alive and live happily ever after with Calvin.

THE MYSTERY OF THE CURIOSITIES

SNOW & WINTER: BOOK TWO

C.S. POE

Snow & Winter: Book Two

Life has been pretty great for Sebastian Snow. The Emporium is thriving and his relationship with NYPD homicide detective, Calvin Winter, is everything he's ever wanted. With Valentine's Day around the corner, Sebastian's only cause for concern is whether Calvin should be taken on a romantic date. It's only when an unknown assailant smashes the Emporium's window and leaves a peculiar note behind that all plans get pushed aside in favor of another mystery.

Sebastian is quickly swept up in a series of grisly yet seemingly unrelated murders. The only connection tying the deaths together are curiosities from the lost museum of P.T. Barnum. Despite Calvin's attempts to keep Sebastian out of the investigation, someone is forcing his hand, and it becomes apparent that the entire charade exists for Sebastian to solve. With each clue that brings him closer to the killer, he's led deeper into Calvin's official cases.

It's more than just Sebastian's livelihood and relationship on the line—it's his very life.

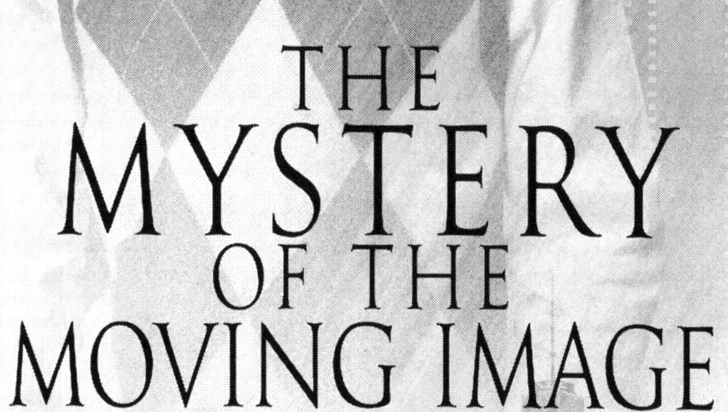
THE
MYSTERY
OF THE
MOVING IMAGE
SNOW & WINTER: BOOK THREE
C.S. POE

Snow & Winter: Book Three

It's summer in New York City, and antique shop owner Sebastian Snow is taking the next big step in his relationship with NYPD homicide detective, Calvin Winter: they're moving in together. What should have been a wonderful week of playing house and celebrating Calvin's birthday comes to an abrupt end when a mysterious package arrives at the Emporium.

Inside is a Thomas Edison Kinetoscope, a movie viewer from the nineteenth century, invented by the grandfather of modern cinema, W. K. L. Dickson. And along with it, footage of a murder that took place over a hundred years ago.

Sebastian resists the urge to start sleuthing, even if the culprit *is* long dead and there's no apparent danger. But break-ins at the Emporium, a robbery, and dead bodies aren't as easy to ignore, and Sebastian soon realizes that the century-old murder will lead him to a modern-day killer.

However, even with Sebastian's vast knowledge of Victorian America and his unrelenting perseverance in the face of danger, this may be the one mystery he won't survive.

SOUTHERNMOST MURDER

C.S. POE

Aubrey Grant lives in the tropical paradise of Old Town, Key West, has a cute cottage, a sweet moped, and a great job managing the historical property of a former sea captain. With his soon-to-be-boyfriend, hotshot FBI agent Jun Tanaka, visiting for a little R&R, not even Aubrey's narcolepsy can put a damper on their vacation plans.

But a skeleton in a closet of the Smith Family Historical Home throws a wrench into the works. Despite Aubrey and Jun's attempts to enjoy some time together, the skeleton's identity drags them into a mystery with origins over a century in the past. They uncover a tale of long-lost treasure, the pirate king it belonged to, and a modern-day murderer who will stop at nothing to find the hidden riches. If a killer on the loose isn't enough to keep Aubrey out of the mess, it seems even the restless spirit of Captain Smith is warning him away.

The unlikely partnership of a special agent and historian may be exactly what it takes to crack this mystery wide-open and finally put an old Key West tragedy to rest. But while Aubrey tracks down the X that marks the spot, one wrong move could be his last.

www.dsppublications.com

For more
great fiction
from